"This book is an excellent depiction of life at sea on a warship. You will enjoy reading about the crew of *Kraken* as they join together to overcome adversity."

**—Captain Richard Arnold, Former Commodore,
Destroyer Squadron 7, USN (Retired)**

"In these times of unrest in the Middle East, a band of fellow naval officers pursue their dreams of starting a cruise ship adventure. Little do they know that others have a different concept. Intrigue, adventure and surprises compound their voyage to either a success or failure. A must-read for seafaring adventurers."

—Rear Admiral Frank X. Johnston, USMS (Retired)

Privateers
by Robert M. Saunders

ISBN 978-1-64663-308-1

This is a work of fiction. The characters are both actual and fictitious. With the exception of verified historical events and persons, all incidents, descriptions, dialogue and opinions expressed are the products of the author's imagination and are not to be construed as real.

Published by

 köehlerbooks™

3705 Shore Drive
Virginia Beach, VA 23455
800-435-4811
www.koehlerbooks.com

PRIVATEERS

A Novel

ROBERT M. SAUNDERS

VIRGINIA BEACH
CAPE CHARLES

To my wife, Sandy, and my children, who pushed me to tell stories.
To the sailors, chief petty officers, and officers who sailed with me.

Anchors Aweigh!

CHAPTER 1

She was truly magnificent. Like an artist's model—graceful, with beautiful curves. Adam Decker couldn't help but stare at her as she moved past him.

The lyrics from an old AC/DC song ran through his mind. *She was a fast machine. She kept her motor clean. She was the best damn woman that I'd ever seen.* Just watching her made him feel young again.

Adam had always loved ships and this one—this particular and specific one—a US Navy destroyer . . . Well, he was in love again. Adam followed her lines from the knife-edged bow to the stern. He scanned the ship's decks and marveled at the weapons systems, the radar antennas, and even the lifeboat canisters. He gazed appreciatively at the sailors in their crisp, white uniforms as they stood attentively at the rails.

Adam's eyes shifted up to the ship's superstructure, toward the conning tower where a sailor on the starboard bridgewing was shooting bearings to identify the ship's exact position and help predict the point for their next maneuver. A cool breeze momentarily broke the still summer air, and Adam smiled slightly as he inhaled the saltiness of the sea.

He sighed and slowly shifted his gaze as he spied movement in the harbor just aft of the ship—a young couple on jet skis racing up the starboard side of the ship and moving fast. Adam heard them laugh as they sped over the small wake of a sailboat slowly moving in the opposite direction toward the Coronado Bridge.

"Boats," he whispered with a hint of a frown, "hazards to navigation."

"Adam!" A voice snapped him out of his daze. "Hello!"

He turned and smiled. "Sorry," he said to his three friends.

Scott Foster, Paula Cook, and George Bannister were spread around the pub table with their beers. The four former Navy officers had just spent the last two days attending the crew reunion of their old ship, USS *Boxer* (LHD-4).

"I was just thinking about all of the times I stood on the ship's bridge as we transited the San Diego harbor." Adam sipped his beer and gestured toward the harbor. "Do you remember all those boats that would speed alongside and then cross in front of the bow, like those idiots?"

Scott and Paula nodded in unison.

"Can't say that I did," grumbled George. "I never got to sit in those comfy seats on the bridge. My time was always spent belowdecks— usually in Engineering Main Control." George took a long swig of his beer. He set down the glass, leaned forward, and leered at Adam. "As any respectable engineer would," he growled.

"They had chairs in Main Control too," Adam teased. "Nice, big, fat comfy chairs," he added.

"And throw pillows, and cocktails, and nice warm quilts," Scott joined in.

"And," Adam added with a smirk, "none of the stress created by idiots in sailboats."

"Don't be a smart-ass." George eyed Adam.

Adam laughed and looked to Paula, who said nothing. She wasn't going to antagonize the salty old engineer.

Adam raised his glass. "To the USS *Boxer*," he toasted. "And to you—my friends. Thanks for the weekend." All four tipped their glasses and drank.

Paula smiled warmly. "I'm glad that you decided to come out here and join us for the reunion, Adam." She set her drink on the table and placed her hands in her lap. Leaning slightly forward, she started to speak, hesitated, and continued. "I can't begin to tell you how sorry I was to hear about Chrissy. She was way too young."

Adam bit his lip but smiled. His wife of twenty-five years had died of cancer the previous November. "Yeah. She was truly the best and deserved much better than me," he whispered. His smile faded.

Paula reached around Adam's shoulder and grasped his neck. She squeezed slightly. "You two complemented each other. And she was a good friend—to all of us."

Adam's smile slowly reappeared and he nodded in agreement. "Yeah, she was amazing."

Adam was third-generation Navy. He never met his grandfather but knew that he had served during World War II. Adam's father had also been a sailor. He had completed a four-year active-duty tour and served in two ships from 1958 to 1962.

Adam was the first member of his family to make the Navy a career, and the first to earn an officer's commission. He completed thirty years on active duty with service on five warships and a variety of shore duty stations, serving half of his career as an enlisted man. He advanced through the ranks and ultimately wore the anchors of a chief petty officer. At that point his hard work and positive attitude were noticed by senior leaders and the Bureau of Naval Personnel, who approved Adam's application to commission as a limited duty officer.

His last ship tour, in the *Boxer*, he reported aboard as a lieutenant commander.

It was on this ship where he qualified as an underway officer of the deck, which put him in charge of the bridge and the ship's operations while at sea. As officer of the deck, Adam became adept at maneuvering the ship—especially during times of crisis. He spent as much time on the bridge as possible and became an expert in managing and directing all ship functions from the bridge.

But that life ended six years ago. Since then, he had discovered loss and loneliness.

The death of his wife only compounded the emptiness he felt since retiring from the Navy and removing his uniform for the last time. That uniform had defined him. Everything that he had achieved in a thirty-year career was worn on his collar and above the left breast pocket of his uniform blouse. He missed the camaraderie of the ship's crew and the adventure of being at sea, but most of all he missed his wife.

Adam was ready to head home to Colorado when the reunion ended. He invited Scott, George, and Paula to lunch before catching his flight that evening. All four were now working on their fourth round of beers and beginning to feel the effects of the alcohol.

"I do miss being at sea," Adam remarked as he glanced again at the harbor. "I would give anything to again command the deck as we transit the harbor."

Scott's eyes were bloodshot and drooped from lack of sleep. He lowered his head and raised his glass.

"Hear hear," he toasted. "I'd give anything . . . to have . . . another liberty port with you . . . fine folks," he stammered.

George eyed Scott and frowned. "Rookies," he said. "Can't hold their liquor." George shifted his attention to Adam. "Have you ever thought about joining the merchant navy?"

Adam shook his head. "And do what? Be an administrative officer on some freighter? I don't have the qualifications or the licenses to get on the bridge. The merchant fleet really doesn't sound like my cup of tea anyway."

"How about working on a cruise ship? I hear that they're hiring experienced naval officers," Paula remarked.

"Sure," Adam laughed. "I could sail with Captain Stubing on the Love Boat. Mix drinks with Isaac the bartender. No thanks."

All heads turned at the sound of a tray of glasses being dropped. Adam felt sorry for the red-faced young waitress, who quickly scooped up the larger pieces of broken glass.

"I know!" Scott chimed in. "Why don't we buy an old retired and mothballed Navy ship and turn it into a . . . cruise ship? Then we could sail around, and we would be in charge."

The table fell silent as Adam, George, and Paula stared at Scott before bursting out laughing. George picked up Scott's beer and sniffed at it.

"What did you put in this thing?" he asked as he handed the drink back to his intoxicated friend. He lowered his head and raised his eyes in a condescending fashion. "Are you suggesting that we somehow find an old ship, pull our funds together, get her ready to sail, and then take a bunch of civilians off the coast of California for gunnery exercises? You're definitely cut off—no more beers for you, sunshine."

"No, no, no." Scott slowly shook his head. "It would just be cool to take an old Navy destroyer or frigate or maybe . . . a cruiser . . . No, they're too big. But something out to sea and maybe make a few bucks while doing it." Scott paused. "It'd be fun! Right?"

George threw back his head and laughed again. "So you believe that there are people who would pay good money to sail around on a small, old, rusty ship? Did you ever serve on one of those boats?" He held up a finger. "First of all, where would people sleep? In the ship's berthing areas? Those spaces are nasty and have no privacy."

George sipped his beer. "Second, where would they eat? What would they do while we're underway? There's no swimming pool or shuffleboard games on deck." George harrumphed and gulped down more of his drink.

"I don't know." Scott shrugged and continued to slur his argument. "Maybe there are people who just want to experience life at sea like a Navy sailor."

"I changed my mind." George motioned the waitress to the table. "Another round please. And a shot of Cuervo for my delusional friend."

"Wait a minute." It was Adam's turn. "Why couldn't you buy an old mothballed ship and turn it into a cruise ship? I'll bet Scotty is right. I'll wager that there are people out there who would be interested in cruising for a few days on an old destroyer. After all, people lined up in droves to ride the ships during our family tiger cruises!"

Adam locked eyes with George. "We wouldn't put weapons on board, but that doesn't mean that we couldn't turn the old weapons platforms into museum-type pieces for show."

He paused. "Maybe we could even hold some sort of training. We could conduct firefighting drills and show our riders other things like how to navigate by using a sextant."

"Are you saying," George interrupted, "that you know how to use a sextant?"

"No." Adam smiled. "But I know a lot of ex-sailors who do." Adam leaned back in his chair. "I wonder if this type of thing is possible?"

Paula looked at her wristwatch. "Yikes, I've got to head to the airport. Sorry, George, can't share the last round with you. What do I owe?" She opened her purse.

"I've got this." Adam stood and wrapped his arms around Paula's shoulders. "Thank you for talking me into coming with you. You were right, I needed this."

Paula squeezed him back. "I'll give you a call later this week. Be safe getting back, guys. See you later." She threw the purse strap over her shoulder, blew a kiss, and walked outside to hail a cab.

Adam, George, and Scott spent the next hour arguing about the possibilities and potentials of turning a warship into a cruise ship. At 2:30 Adam paid the tab, and then he and Scott shared a taxi to the airport. George decided to walk the beach for a while before he headed back to his house in Pacific Beach.

Discussions and thoughts of purchasing ships and recruiting crews were forgotten . . . for now.

CHAPTER 2

The two Iranian fast boats cut through the dark waters of the Arabian Gulf in predatory silence. At five knots they provided enough speed to maintain steerage and avoid colliding with each other. Unlit, they appeared only as shadows in the water, the faint green beam of the surface-search radar repeater on the bridge offering the solitary glimpse of light.

On the hot and muggy bridge, the lead boat's captain slid a dirty uniform sleeve across his forehead to catch a few beads of sweat. Squinting at the radar repeater, he followed the yellow blip of their target as it moved slowly from the western side of the screen toward the radar's circular center. The blip finally approached the point where it was ten nautical miles away. Both boats simultaneously revved up their engines and changed course to intercept.

The lead boat's captain again squinted as he peered through the bridge window and spotted the target's running lights on the horizon. The *Point Barbara*, a merchant ship heading toward the shipping port of Shuwaikh in Kuwait, cruised forward at twenty-two knots.

The boats picked up speed and flew toward the targeted ship, the boat crews poised and ready at their battle-station assignments. Once they were within two miles of the *Point Barbara*, the lead boat illuminated every available light, including the high-beam searchlights, with the second boat quickly following suit. The captain wanted their target to see and fear them.

He glanced at the foc'sle, or forecastle, where the .50-caliber gunner stood at his weapon, his knees bending each time the boat plunged into a wave's trough.

The *Point Barbara* continued plowing through the waves toward them.

As the Iranian boats neared 700 meters, they split up and took individual courses down opposite sides of the merchant vessel. The *Point Barbara* continued forward with no sign of slowing. Long, steady blasts from the ship's whistle indicated that the captain was aware of their presence and wanted to avoid a collision at sea.

The lead boat's captain smiled and continued down the *Point Barbara*'s starboard side. The boats cleared the ship's length in unison and maintained their path for another 500 meters.

At the lead boat's signal, both boats swung around and began a path back toward the *Point Barbara*. This time, instead of splitting up, both boats lined up behind each other and cruised up the ship's starboard side. The lead boat's captain signaled the foc'sle gunner, who began firing rounds forward and away from the large ship.

The *Point Barbara*'s captain appeared unfazed by these actions, continuing to speed forward as he refused to alter course. A smile momentarily reappeared on the fast-boat captain's thin face. He admired his target's bravado.

The boats passed the ship and again swung around approximately 500 meters ahead of the ship. Back in line, the two boats began another run down the *Point Barbara*'s starboard side. As the boats neared the ship, the lead boat's gunner again fired his weapon in quick bursts, joined by the gunner on the second boat. Tracer fire surged into the dark night as both gunners fired at the water, intentionally missing the ship.

Suddenly, the lead boat's gunner was knocked back from his weapon and thrown to the deck. The merchant ship's crew was firing water cannons. Bursts of water smashed into the two gunboats, successfully pushing them away from the ship.

The lead boat's captain narrowed his eyes and gritted his teeth. He shifted his gaze toward his attackers and then back to the forward gunner. He snatched the mic to the ship's sound-powered phones and ordered the gunner to fire at the merchant ship. The gunner swung his weapon around, pointed it at the midship water cannon, and began firing.

Sparks flashed as bullets penetrated and ricocheted off the *Point Barbara*'s hull. The ship's crewmembers abandoned the water cannons and dove to areas of cover. *Point Barbara*'s captain shouted orders, and the ship began to turn to the left.

The boats sped by the ship once more, turned, and began another run up the ship's starboard side, machine guns blasting. The big ship continued swinging around to avoid the confrontation. When the *Point Barbara* was turned 180 degrees and sailing away from its original course, the gunner quit firing. The boats then stopped in the water and set up a small blockade.

They waited until the ship was out of sight before they sped back toward their home port.

CHAPTER 3

Adam stared at the window of his dark bedroom.

The sound of a car driving past his house broke the dead silence. He looked at his alarm clock and realized that he'd been awake since 3:30 a.m.—over two hours.

He rolled onto his back and placed both hands behind his head as he gazed into the dark room, thinking about the reunion. It was great to see Scott, George, and Paula again. In the morning he would order a bouquet of red carnations and send them to Paula—thanking her again for dragging him along.

He smiled as he remembered Scott and George arguing about buying a warship and turning it into a cruise liner. *Drunk talk*, Adam thought.

He furrowed his brow and chewed on his lower lip. *I wonder if it's even possible for an individual to buy an old warship*, he thought. Adam pulled his laptop out of the docking station at the base of the lamp by his bed, sat up, and placed the open laptop on his thighs, typing *purchase US navy warship* into the search bar of his browser. The screen listed several news articles that discussed the US Navy mothballed fleet and the ultimate destination of these once great ships. Some were sold to foreign countries, some were used as target practice, and some were sunk to begin the formation of reefs on sea beds.

Adam finally ran across an article that discussed the possibilities of purchasing a decommissioned US Navy warship. It not only confirmed that an individual could—it also identified how to begin that process. The US General Services Administration, or GSA, held online auctions where a variety of government equipment, real estate, vehicles, and sailing vessels could be purchased.

Adam pored through the sites, searching for a decommissioned ship that was scheduled for dismantling and scrapping. He reviewed fishing boats, power barges, and survey boats, but none of these vessels met his criteria. After several pages (and thirty minutes) he found a potential hit—the USS *Ingraham* (FFG-61).

Adam quickly pulled up Wikipedia to learn the history of the *Ingraham*. This was an Oliver Hazard Perry–class frigate that had been commissioned in 1989 and ultimately decommissioned in 2014. The twenty-five-year-old warship was berthed at the Naval Sea Systems Command in Bremerton, Washington, and scheduled to be dismantled and scrapped but still looked to be in pretty good condition.

He closed the laptop and turned off the light. In the morning he would call his friends and let them know what he had learned.

Adam woke again at 7 a.m. on the dot. He showered, dressed, and threw his dirty clothes into the laundry hamper. He made up the bed and placed the two red decorative pillows against the headboard.

When they were first married, Chrissy had scolded Adam for plopping his head onto one of those pillows while watching TV in bed.

"What are they there for then?" he asked as Chrissy pulled the pillow from under his head.

"Decoration!" she quickly replied. "And don't let me catch you using these again!"

From that point on Adam would tease his wife by allowing her to catch him as he placed his feet, legs, and even a beer on top of the pillows. Each time he was caught, he feigned the most innocent look and claimed forgetfulness. It never worked. He and Chrissy had made that bed together every morning for twenty-five years. With a sad smile he wished that he hadn't given her so much trouble about those pillows.

Following a breakfast of coffee and cold pizza from last night's dinner, Adam called Scott Foster. Scott's wife, Briget, answered Scott's cell phone. "Hi, Adam. Heard you had a great time in San Diego. How are you doing?"

"Hi, Brige, doing good. Is Scott around?"

"He is," she laughed, "and stop calling me Brige. You know that I hate that."

Adam heard a door open and close, and then Scott's voice was on the line. "Hey, man, how ya doing?"

"Good!" Adam hated small talk. "Scott, do you remember when we were sitting at the bar talking about buying a mothballed Navy warship?"

"Yes, I remember. I wasn't that drunk," Scott replied sarcastically. "I also remember you laughing at me and the unsavory remarks regarding my idea."

"Well," Adam began, "I've been thinking, and I believe that you may have actually come up with a pretty darn good idea."

"Go on." Scott waited. Adam described the GSA website and the opportunities available.

"We could actually do this," remarked Adam. "We could buy a small ship like a frigate or destroyer, fix it up, and recruit a crew of former sailors—you know, guys like us who still want to go to sea." Adam shifted the phone to his right ear. "Once we have all of that in place, we could start running short cruises up and down the West Coast for people who want the experience of sailing in a real warship. What do you think?"

"Are you asking me if this is plausible or if I'm interested in being part of it?" Scott asked.

"Both," Adam cried. "You were . . . *are* an amazing surface warfare officer and a natural ship driver." He paused. "We've both been through a major ship's overhaul yard period, and we understand the planning and maintenance associated with refurbishing a warship."

Adam continued, "I would like to have you, George, and Paula help me research this and, who knows, possibly buy our own ship. Then we could actually be in charge—as you mentioned back in San Diego."

Scott was silent for a moment. "This sounds really interesting . . . and fun," he finally responded, "but, number one, how do you expect us to finance this project? Number two, how much do you think a ship would cost? Three, how do you determine the costs of refurbishment, even if you do get funded, and four, where would we get the maintenance for the overhaul, and who could we hire?"

Adam took a deep breath. "I don't know yet. But I do know that this would be a huge project and I wouldn't be able to do it alone. Like I said, I would need you guys as partners in this business." Adam chewed his bottom lip. "George is an amazing engineer and he's been through at least seven major ship overhauls. He knows every shipyard worker and manager up and down the coast of California and, even more impressively, is owed favors from most of them."

He continued, "Paula's logistics experience and commercial contacts as a Supply Corps officer will prove invaluable when ordering and managing equipment, materials, and other resources. And she has an MBA! And you!" Adam beamed. "Not only are you one of the best drivers, you are notorious for your abilities in commandeering the rarest equipment, materials, and other . . . well . . . desirables."

"Hey!" Scott quickly interrupted. He cupped his hands around the phone and whispered, "We agreed never to speak of that incident— especially within earshot of my wife! Besides I hadn't even met Briget yet, and, and . . . *and* there was never any proof that I had anything to do with that."

Amazingly, Scott had managed to not only find strippers and Bacardi in Muscat, Oman, he also convinced them to sneak on board the ship so that they could hold a performance for a select group of officers. Two days after the incident, the *Boxer*'s executive officer began an investigation after he overheard a conversation about strippers performing in the officers' wardroom. Nobody was talking, and there was absolutely no proof of any wrongdoing—though there was a rumor of a photograph of two shapely and barely dressed women posing with the ship's chaplain.

Scott always managed to make things happen. His out-of-the-box thought process made him the most resourceful individual in the fleet. "This does sound like fun, Adam," he said, "but how can I really be part of this? I've got a wife and two young kids in school. What about my job? I can't just walk away from my life."

Adam had expected this response. "I know." His voice dropped a bit. "But you were the one who thought of this idea, and I can't think of anyone else I'd rather be in business with."

Both men were silent.

"Tell you what," Adam suggested. "Talk with Briget and get her take. Tell her that we'd love to include her in on the project and the business. Didn't she receive her project manager professional certification? We could use someone with those credentials and skills."

"OK," Scott agreed. "I'll talk with her. But before I do, I will need a lot more info—especially regarding the financing."

Although Adam agreed and told Scott he would email within the next few days, in truth he had no idea how to finance such a project. He thought that he would begin by calling his own bank and talking with a business financial loan officer.

Fortunately, the phone calls with George and Paula went more smoothly than the discussion with Scott. George began the call with a few colorful expletives, as was customary with the old engineer. He was another old-school sailor who, like Adam, began his Navy career as an enlisted man. He had served aboard eight ships and three shore-maintenance commands during his thirty-five-year career before retiring as a limited duty officer commander. At that time, he had developed a reputation as the most knowledgeable engineer on the West Coast.

George stood five foot seven, weighed 210 pounds, and had a ring of white hair on his otherwise bald head. He could appear gruff and unapproachable to those who didn't know him, but Adam, Scott, and Paula knew him better.

George was a prankster with a great sense of humor. He also had a soft side; he loved kids. Every Christmas he would contact a local children's hospital in San Diego and find out how many children were hospitalized as in-patients. He would then buy toys for each child, dress as Santa, and visit the kids on Christmas Eve to pass out the toys. George believed his Santa operation was a secret, but Adam, Scott, and Paula all knew, and they loved him all the more for it.

Adam piqued George's interest as he identified the potential ship as an Oliver Hazard Perry–class frigate.

"I love those ships," George said excitedly. "They aren't the old-school steamships that I grew up with. The engineering plant in these babies are powered by LM2500 gas turbine engines, similar to the kind of engines used on DC10 airplanes—really powerful!

"And their variable pitch propeller not only helps absorb the engine power, but it can be adjusted for emergency crash back procedures. On those old steamships, you would need to stop and lock the ship's shaft and then begin turning the shaft in the opposite direction in order to move in reverse, which took an incredibly long period of time. Time, by the way, is extremely valuable when you're in a crisis situation at sea."

Adam hated being patronized. "I'm aware of variable pitch, George."

"Well," George continued, unfazed, "I do love these ships. They are sleek, fast, maneuverable, and just look like old-school warships." He finally paused. "Okay," he said simply. "I'm in."

During his career, Adam had met and served with many Supply Corps officers. He had a great respect for "pork chops" (their unofficial title) and admired not only their business savvy and customer service skills, but also that they were a very tight group—often referred to as the "pork chop mafia."

Paula was a superb pork chop and officer.

During her high school senior year, a representative from the University of Dubuque traveled to Belgium and lured twelve students of her class to the small school in Iowa. Paula loved the Dubuque campus and the classes and ultimately earned her undergraduate degree in business administration. Following graduation, she applied for and was selected for a commission as a Navy Supply Corps officer. Her first assignment was to the *Boxer*, where she met Adam, George, and Scott.

Paula was tall, blonde, and athletically built. Within thirty minutes of reporting aboard the ship, she was already being scoped out and flirted with by all single male officers in the wardroom. She thwarted all advances with courtesy and charm, which endeared her with those she shot down. Adam, George, and Scott took an immediate liking to her. She was a good leader and stood her ground when fighting for a cause.

When Adam called, Paula told him that she fell in love with the idea of turning a Navy warship into a cruise ship when Scott had first mentioned it. Adam was relieved. He fell quiet for a moment. "Paula?" he finally began. "I hate to ask a favor, but you know that I'm not the best businessman . . . and I really don't think—"

She interrupted, "Adam, you're rambling. What do you need?"

Adam sighed. "Would you mind traveling to Denver and helping me develop a business plan?"

Paula giggled. She knew that it killed Adam to ask favors. Adam was grateful that she couldn't see him blush.

"Let me tie up a few loose ends," Paula responded, "and I'll fly out this weekend."

"Thank you," Adam said. "Please plan on staying at my place. Just let me know when you're scheduled to arrive, and I'll pick you up."

"Adam, I'm OK with staying in a hotel," Paula replied. "You don't need the neighbors talking."

"It'll be OK," he said. "Hopefully we won't be in Colorado for long."

After researching and narrowing down a number of investment firms in San Diego, Adam called the business-loan department at the firm that seemed like the best fit.

When he talked with the loan manager, Adam explained his plans to purchase a decommissioned Navy warship, hire a crew of former Navy sailors, conduct a complete shipboard restoration project, and turn the vessel into a cruise ship for a unique clientele. He mentioned his three other partners and that they were developing a business plan that would be completed within the next two weeks. The loan manager was intrigued by the project and told Adam that he would be very interested to hear more—but he needed to see a business plan.

Paula landed at the Denver International Airport on Sunday morning. Adam pulled up to the passenger pick-up area where Paula sat, her three bags next to her on a metal bench.

"Are you still driving this piece of crap?" she asked as he greeted her with a hug.

Adam pulled back and narrowed his eyes. "A 1981 El Camino with a 350-cubic-inch engine, automatic transmission, gloss-black paint, and a black leather interior is not a piece of crap. It is true Americana." He beamed with pride while Paula rolled her eyes. "It's a classic!"

As they drove toward Adam's house, he excitedly relayed his research and his progress with the bank. Paula smiled as she listened. She hadn't seen Adam this animated and excited in some time.

It was a beautiful, sunny, and cloud-free day. Paula sighed at the sight of the Rocky Mountains as they drove west on Interstate 70. The morning sunshine made the mountain range seem close.

"I love the trees and rock formations on the mountains," she said as she looked wistfully out the window. "Why haven't I looked for work in Denver?"

"Beats me," Adam replied. "It would be great to have you here."

They reached Adam's house twenty minutes later. Paula caught the scent of cinnamon the moment she entered the living room. She scanned the room and identified two cinnamon candles on the end tables and was impressed to see that Adam's house was just as neat and orderly as when Chrissy was alive.

After lunch Adam and Paula began organizing the documents and discussing the project. They spent the next ten hours working feverishly on the business plan. The plan would be conducted in four phases:

Phase 1: Purchase the ship, recruit and hire a crew, and schedule an overhaul shipyard.

Phase 2: Contract a long-haul tug company to move the ship to the shipyard for overhaul.

Phase 3: Conduct the maintenance overhaul, schedule and execute sea trials with the crew and contracted shipyard employees, work with the US Coast Guard to train and license the crew in all required maritime certifications, select and contract a harbor for home port, and develop the cruise program and marketing plan.

Phase 4: Upon completion of testing and maintenance certifications, move the ship to the new homeport harbor and begin reserving and selling cruise spots.

Once a home port was approved and contracted, Paula would begin negotiations with needed vendors for insurance, fuel, consumables, and other logistics.

Adam contacted his loan representative and scheduled a meeting with the loan committee in San Diego for a presentation. Adam and Paula flew to San Diego and stayed with George. After unpacking, they sat down and fine-tuned the business plan. George thoroughly reviewed and tailored the engineering and overhaul plans to ensure that no stone was left unturned.

On the day of the meeting Adam dressed in a gray suit with a dark-blue tie while Paula wore a navy-blue business jacket and skirt. As they prepared the leave the house, George inspected his two friends and nodded with approval.

"I didn't know that you could look so pretty," he remarked.

"Well, thank you, George," Paula replied dryly.

"I was talking to Adam," George said and smiled.

As they drove to the bank corporate headquarters, Adam's knee bounced repeatedly.

"Nervous?" George asked him.

"I feel like I'm going to puke," Adam replied.

"You'll do fine," George assured him. "But if you do feel like you're going to be sick, try to aim for the trash can and not on the bank guys—I believe that would be considered a really bad first impression."

They arrived at the firm headquarters and were met in the lobby by the four members of the loan committee, who led them to a large conference room with glass walls and the longest conference table Adam had ever seen. The group sat down, and Paula plugged her laptop into the television system so that the committee could view their charts. As the title page appeared on the large screen monitor, Adam announced the inception of their new company—Warship Tours, Inc.

At the conclusion of the meeting, all members of the loan committee were excitedly speaking of the business plan and future possibilities. The bank would hold a separate meeting with its senior leadership, and they would have a decision for Adam and Paula within a week.

As they left the firm, Adam and Paula were elated. The loan committee's positive attitude and discussion on future prospects left them fully believing that the entire project would be approved. They both decided to stay in San Diego until they received the call. In the meantime, they researched office space and office equipment rentals while also looking for a reputable business attorney.

The call came four days later—the project and the business were approved for complete funding. Adam called Scott and told him the good news. Scott congratulated them and promised to talk with Briget that evening. Adam and Paula met George later that evening and celebrated over pizza and beer.

Three days later Adam, Paula, and George met with their investors to discuss a twenty-year plan, sign loan documents, and determine account information. Next, the team hired a business attorney, Nathaniel Williams, who helped them iron out the details with the loan management team.

Now they just needed to win the GSA auction.

Luckily, the former USS *Ingraham* was still on the auction block. Adam and Paula entered all required information on the site. When requested to enter a bid for the ship, Adam began with one million dollars. A red disclaimer appeared, declaring that the reserve price had not been met. Their bid was too low.

Adam entered two million. Again, too low.

Better to begin low and be disapproved, he thought, *than to overbid*. After four more attempts, he entered $6.5 million and the bid was accepted. If approved, a representative from the General Services Administration would be in contact via telephone.

Two days later, the GSA informed Adam that Warship Tours, Inc., had won the auction.

Adam, Paula, George, and Nathaniel arrived at the GSA offices the next day to review and sign the contracts and all other documents required to purchase the ship. They were led into a room where they met Barry Simpson and Mark Waters, both from the office of the General Services Administration, and Agent Maria Wilson from the Department of Homeland Security.

As the group sat down and Nathaniel pulled files from his briefcase, Agent Wilson turned to Adam. "I understand that you have recently established a company and now want to purchase a military warship. May I ask why?" she asked.

Adam described the entire business project from inception to funding. Agent Wilson took notes and kept her eyes focused on the paper as she continued to ask questions. "And so you're saying that this ship will only travel through and around US sea lanes? You will not be traveling to foreign countries?"

"That's correct," answered Adam. "At this time we have no intention of traveling to foreign countries. However, we will contact Homeland Security and any other required agencies if we consider expanding our tour route."

Agent Wilson continued writing. "Do you plan on carrying weapons of any type? If not, what do you plan on doing with the ship's current weapon systems?"

"Weapons? Are you kidding?" George interjected.

"George!" Adam twisted his head toward George and gestured for him to calm down and stay quiet.

Adam then turned to Agent Wilson. "There will be no weapons on this ship—personal or otherwise. We plan on keeping the weapons platforms on board, but they will be made inoperative. We would like to keep them as museum-like pieces and show them as part of the tours."

Agent Wilson raised her head and looked at George. "What position will you hold in this company, Mr. Bannister?" she asked.

George leaned forward on the table and was about to provide an unsavory comment when Adam grabbed his arm. George slowly sat back in his seat.

"George is a partner in the business," Adam responded. "He is also our chief engineer."

Agent Wilson looked from George to Adam and back to the notebook. She continued jotting notes as she peered at Adam and asked, "Would you allow unscheduled inspections of your ship by representatives from the Department of Homeland Security?"

Adam leaned back in his chair and placed his folded hands in his lap. "We welcome your representatives on board our ship at any time and hope to see you scheduling time to sail with us. My partners and I are all former US Navy officers. We were proud to serve our country with honor and distinction and truly loved our time at sea. Now we have the opportunity to share the experience of sailing on a warship with people who didn't serve. I understand your presence here at this meeting, and I also understand your line of questioning. I don't consider you an adversary, and I hope you feel the same about my team and me."

Agent Wilson closed her notebook, thanked the team, and left the meeting.

"She was nice," George said sarcastically with his hands interlocked behind his head.

The rest of the meeting was spent discussing account information and scheduling dates to transfer the ship from her berth in Washington.

Adam and his team left the GSA offices and high-fived each other as they walked to their cars.

"Great meeting. I'll call you tomorrow morning," Nathanial said as he sped off.

Adam turned to Paula. "Any luck finding office space?"

"It was going to be a surprise," replied Paula, "but I found a place close to the shipyards."

"Let's go take a look," Adam said, opening the car door, "but first let's call Scott."

Across the parking lot sat a nondescript white Chevrolet sedan. The driver, wearing a black suit, white shirt, and black tie, calmly ran his fingers over the brim of a stylish black fedora that sat in the passenger seat. He leaned back in the sedan's seat and appeared to be listening to the radio. A small smile rose on his face as he peered through the car's windshield to get a good view of the new business owners.

CHAPTER 4

The call with Scott did not go as well as Adam had hoped. As Scott expected, Briget was totally opposed to him quitting a good job and relocating their family based on this crazy idea of a business.

Briget reminded Scott of the countless hours he'd spent working his way up to managing her father's bank. They owned a home. They were established in a neighborhood. The kids were involved in Little League and gymnastics. "Why would we just uproot our lives and move back to California just so you can hang around with your old Navy buddies?" Briget challenged.

Scott couldn't argue with her. Briget had been a terrific Navy officer's wife. She attended and even hosted numerous wardroom spouse events; helped make and mail care packages when the ship deployed; and assisted the ombudsman in communicating messages to families. Briget did her time.

Certainly, there were things about the Navy that she enjoyed. She missed the lifestyle associated with being an officer's wife and the camaraderie shared by the officers and even the spouses. Most of all, she loved when Scott wore his white uniform—especially his choker whites. Ever since she saw Richard Gere wear that uniform in the film *An Officer and a Gentleman*, Briget would melt at the sight of it. Scott kidded her that he was going to sew Velcro at the seams so that she could just tear it off him.

But those days were now in the past. Briget expected Scott to grow up and to become a responsible family man. As he exchanged his choker uniform for a business jacket and tie, Scott felt like he lost his swagger. It broke his heart to say no to Adam, but Scott loved his wife and kids. And dammit, he knew his priorities.

The office suite that Paula found was perfect. It contained three small offices, a medium-sized conference room, a lobby, and a small kitchen area with a sink and microwave. The best part of the location was that the offices all faced the harbor, which allowed the occupants to watch the ships moving in and out.

Adam and Paula signed the lease and began filling the space with desks, furniture, and computers. Paula worked feverishly to activate electricity, phone, and computer connections. She then called a local temp agency and contracted a secretary/receptionist to work in the office lobby.

George and Paula negotiated with Redmund Maritime, a towing company, to move the 4,100-ton vessel from Bremerton, Washington, to the NASSCO shipyard in San Diego. Traveling at nine knots, the 1,200-nautical-mile trip would take six days to complete.

George then contacted several of his higher-level contacts at the NASSCO shipyard to schedule a maintenance berth. Fortunately, a berth was available, but only for six months. Predicting the time to complete the overhaul was a crapshoot, and George knew it. There was no way to determine the condition of the *Ingraham* without inspecting the ship. This issue nagged at George and Adam constantly.

While Paula and Nathaniel worked the towing and shipyard contractual and logistical issues, Adam reviewed the staffing and crew requirements. He needed officers and a crew who had experience operating and maintaining warships, but he also needed a customer-friendly and polished team. More importantly, he needed sailors he could trust.

That evening Adam met with George and Paula to begin creating a list of individuals to recruit.

His list was comprised of the operations officer, the deck officer, and the navigator. The three candidates who immediately made the list were Terry Forrester, a retired Navy surface warfare commander and former aircraft carrier operations officer; Danny Stiles, a former surface warfare lieutenant commander and big deck department head; and Victor Wallace, a retired surface warfare chief warrant officer and former ship's navigator.

Terry and Adam had served together when Adam was still a chief petty officer. Terry was a Naval Academy graduate who believed himself to be Navy royalty. Adam considered Terry to be arrogant and a social moron. He stood five foot five, was rail thin, and walked so straight that you'd think that someone had jammed a steel rod up his ass. If you wanted to know just how good Terry was, you just had to ask Terry!

But personality quirks aside, there was no one better at managing and directing the surrounding air and sea traffic while the ship was at sea. Terry could not only monitor and manage the extremely busy three-dimensional box (surface, air, and subsurface) that surrounded the ship, he was also adept at using real-time data to predict potential risks and dangers to the ship.

Additionally, Terry was an exceptional project manager who could expertly multitask a number of projects. Two months after returning from a six-month deployment, the ship that Terry served in was sent to Long Beach, California, for a one-year overhaul. As maintenance manager, he meticulously scheduled and executed every segment of the overhaul and successfully met maintenance deadlines while keeping all costs within budget.

Terry was respected for his rank and expertise, but due to his condescending and patronizing behavior, the enlisted men hated him. Regrettably for Terry, this attitude was noticed by senior leadership. He alienated everyone around him, which negatively affected him as he was being considered for command at sea. To be brutally honest, Terry simply pissed off the people in charge and was ultimately denied promotion and command at sea.

Following retirement from the Navy, Terry opened a small plant nursery in Wyoming.

When Terry answered Adam's call, he lapsed into the haughty and overly confident behavior that Adam had known and deplored him for. Adam explained the business and challenges associated with the overhaul and asked Terry if he would be interested in hiring on as a contractor for six months to help George oversee the project. Upon successful completion of the overhaul, Terry would be offered the position as ship's operations officer if he was interested.

Terry wasn't sure that he could break away from the nurseries. "My business is performing well," declared Terry, "but I'm not sure if my staff could survive that long of a period without me."

In truth Terry rarely visited his nurseries. His staff and his accountant ran all aspects of the business.

Adam knew that the only way to influence this prima donna was to stroke his ego.

"I understand," Adam declared. "That's why you were the only individual I knew could accomplish the herculean task of overhauling this type of ship. After all," Adam continued, "there is only one Terry Forrester."

"What type of salary and benefits come with the position?" Terry asked. Adam smiled. He had him!

Danny Stiles was the polar opposite of Terry. A strong leader who loved his sailors, he was a solid man at six foot two and 210 pounds. Danny was selected for a commission in the US Navy following graduation from college. His last shipboard assignment was with Adam in *Boxer*, but Danny transferred to the US Naval Academy nine months after Adam reported aboard, so Adam didn't get the opportunity to know him better.

While at the Naval Academy, Danny was asked to host a group of Fortune 300 senior business leaders during a weeklong conference and tour at the academy. Danny's leadership style, professional demeanor, and the speed at which he could think on his feet impressed one of them so much that by the end of the week, Danny was offered a job as a national sales director.

Adam knew that it would be tough to drag Danny away from his job, but he called anyway. Danny answered the phone and greeted Adam like an old friend. They laughed about shipboard memories and caught each other up on current events.

Adam described Warship Tours, Inc., and brought Danny up to speed on the purchase of the *Ingraham*. He paused and considered all of the reasons why Danny would not want to leave his posh job. Finally, he asked the question: "We would love to have you as part of this once-in-a-lifetime venture. Would you be interested in joining us as our deck department head?"

Danny was silent for a moment, and Adam braced himself for bad news. Danny finally said, "You know, Adam, I've accomplished just about every sales goal that I set for myself, and, quite honestly, they weren't that challenging to begin with. I never really wanted to be in sales, and I'm actually tired of the lifestyle. I do miss leading sailors and the crisis management at sea."

Adam was stunned. Danny then asked, "When do you need me?"

Adam decided to wait to contact Victor. After all, the ship didn't need a navigator just yet.

Paula arrived at the offices early the next morning and was surprised to find both Adam and George already looking over charts.

"Good morning." Adam raised his head and smiled at Paula. "I got a call from Redmund last night. They'll begin towing the ship tomorrow, so we have five days to finish recruiting our team."

He grabbed his coffee cup, took a sip, and grimaced. "Ugh. Cold." He placed the cup back on the table. "I've locked in our operations and deck officers, so now we need to find some key components to our crew." Since Scott could not participate, they needed an executive officer, and, ultimately, they would need a ship's doctor.

Paula planned on calling Lonnie Taylor, a former enlisted supply sailor, to see if he was interested and available to serve as assistant supply officer. Additionally, she needed a galley staff of four cooks and two clerks to manage stores and supplies, two employees to operate the ship's gift store, and two more for barber/hair-care services as they moved closer to sailing with customers.

All in all, Paula announced that the supply team would staff eleven employees.

All eyes turned to George, who adjusted his reading glasses and focused on the engineering list. "I will need an assistant engineer, a damage-control assistant, two junior engineer officers, a senior ship's electrician, six gas-turbine machinists, one apprentice electrician, one marine welder, and one ship's plumber."

George removed his glasses. "I will also need six general-engineering apprentice mechanics. Total engineering staffing will be twenty-one. In the meantime," George continued, "I've worked with Doug Jones, the NASSCO maintenance manager, and we anticipate contracting a workforce of fifty employees."

CHAPTER 5

Hearing the door to the outer office open, Adam looked up from his desk to see a professional-looking woman standing in the lobby and staring directly at him.

The woman appeared to be in her mid-sixties and wore a long gray skirt and matching jacket with a white blouse. Her white hair was pulled back and tied tightly in a bun. She wore gold wire-rim glasses on her narrow nose and clutched a small purse with both hands at her waist.

Adam stood. "May I help you?"

"I'm Mrs. Eleanor Paisley," the woman answered. "I have been sent here from the Anytime temporary-office-help agency to perform duties as your secretary."

Adam moved to the lobby. "Hello, Mrs. Paisley." They shook hands. For an older woman, Eleanor had a surprisingly strong grip. "I'm Adam Decker, president of Warship Tours, Inc. Please." He motioned her to his office. "Have a seat. Can I offer you a cup of coffee or maybe some hot tea?"

"No thank you," Eleanor answered curtly. She sat straight in the chair with her hands crossed over the purse on her lap.

"Please give me a moment while I grab my associate, Paula Cook."

Adam leaned into Paula's office.

"Our secretary is here," he said and then whispered, "They must be short of executive secretaries. She's a little long in the tooth."

As Adam and Paula returned, Eleanor stood and offered her hand to Paula while Adam sat at his desk. "I'm Eleanor Paisley. I'm from the Anytime temporary-services agency for the secretarial position."

"Hello, Eleanor." Paula rubbed her hand as she was released from Eleanor's grip. "I'm Paula Cook. Tell me a little about yourself and your experience in administration."

Eleanor's resume was impressive. She had spent thirty-six years in various administrative and secretarial positions and retired a few years earlier to care for her ailing husband.

"Don passed two years ago," Eleanor added. She then glanced at Adam, and without any emotion she remarked, "I'm sure that you'll find my skills more than adequate, Mr. Decker. My experience, health, and hearing are excellent regardless of me being long in the tooth."

Paula blushed and Adam burst out laughing. "Eleanor," he said, "you are exactly what we're looking for. I apologize for anything insensitive I said." Still smiling, he wiped a tear from his cheek. "Welcome aboard, and please, call me Adam!"

Lonnie Taylor called Paula after she sent him a message on Facebook. He could barely hide his excitement when he learned of the project. "I'm flattered that you would think of me, Paula. Yes, I would love to be your assistant," he said. "Can I give my boss a week's notice?"

"Absolutely," Paula agreed.

Adam needed an executive officer. He had whittled down the list of potential candidates to two names. His first call went to Bill Stiles, who was an excellent officer and leader. Unfortunately, Bill was now working as a consultant for Shell Oil and living in Brazil.

Adam had the same luck with his second candidate, Carl Bowers. Carl was locked into a contract that had him out of the country for the next three years.

George poked his head into Adam's office as Adam ended the call with Carl. Adam had run out of top candidates and asked George if he had any ideas.

"How about Matt Phillips?" George offered. "He's a damn good ship driver and leader."

Adam had considered Matt but hadn't added him to the list. It was true that Matt was great on the bridge and a solid leader, but Matt and Adam had never really "clicked" socially.

Adam looked at George. "Didn't Matt go into ministry work after he resigned from the Navy?"

"Not sure about that." George scratched his head. "But he may be worth calling."

Adam paused and stared at the phone. Matt was just a little too straitlaced for Adam. His strong religious convictions didn't bother Adam; in fact, Adam shared many of Matt's beliefs. But Matt never wanted to socialize or hang out during port calls, never attended wardroom functions if they included alcoholic beverages, and never swapped stories or jokes with the rest of the officers. He was a loner who probably wouldn't have eaten dinner in the wardroom with the other officers if the commanding officer hadn't made it mandatory.

Adam finally dialed the number. It rang twice before Matt answered. After exchanging pleasantries, Adam asked what Matt had been doing since he left the Navy.

Matt confirmed that he had indeed become an ordained Christian minister. After he was ordained, he searched for a church in need of a senior pastor. Unfortunately, at that time there were no open positions anywhere, so he took a position as the youth pastor in a large church.

Adam told him about the new company and the newly purchased ship, then explained that the ship needed an XO. Adam asked Matt if he might be interested in the job.

There was a long, silent pause, and Adam was about to ask if Matt was still on the line when Matt finally spoke and shared that the lead pastor at his church was extremely beloved and trusted, so the congregation and the church elders did not want the junior pastors to preach sermons. Additionally, the senior pastor was very controlling and did not involve or invite his junior staff to participate in any of the church business functions. Matt just needed more.

"Yes, Adam," Matt said with great enthusiasm, "I'd love to accept the position." He told Adam that he would be in San Diego in four days.

The next morning, Paula, Nathaniel, and George met with Doug Jones at the NASSCO offices.

"This quote is higher than we discussed," Paula remarked.

Doug shrugged. "You wanted the best technicians and need to have this job completed within six months. Based on what we know about the ship, this job will require three shifts working around the clock." Doug lightly tapped the proposal. "I would be happy to adjust the numbers to a more reasonable cost, but it will affect the quality and time in the shipyard."

Paula looked at George and back to Doug. "No," she said begrudgingly. "We agree to these costs and conditions." They signed the contract.

George and Paula returned to the offices and reported the cost increases to Adam.

Adam frowned and slowly shook his head. He held several documents in his hands. "We are quickly burning through our resources," he declared. "I hope the ship is in good condition when we receive it. Any major repairs could put us in serious trouble."

George jumped from his chair as he heard a man shriek. The sound came from the lobby.

Adam quickly moved past Paula and George and saw Eleanor standing in front of his office door, wielding a twelve-inch metal ruler in her hand.

"Eleanor, what's going on?" Adam asked.

Standing in front of Eleanor was Terry Forrester rubbing his left hand and staring at the secretary with a shocked and angry expression.

"This woman," Terry shouted as he eyed Eleanor from top to bottom, "has assaulted and injured me."

Paula and George moved in behind Adam to witness the spectacle. Adam turned toward Eleanor, who maintained that expressionless look on her face.

"Eleanor, what happened?" Adam repeated.

"This gentleman entered the lobby and began walking toward your office." Her eyes never left Terry. She tapped the ruler in the palm of her empty hand. "I stood and greeted him, then asked if I may help him." Eleanor's eyes shifted to Adam, then back to Terry. "The gentleman ignored me, so I positioned myself to deny him access."

Terry, wide-eyed, was still rubbing his hand. Eleanor continued, "The gentleman attempted to move me to the side, so I slapped his hand with my ruler. That's when you joined us, Mr. Decker."

Paula slid into her office and clapped a hand over her mouth to keep from laughing out loud. George didn't move. He would have enjoyed a lawn chair and a bowl of popcorn to watch this entertaining episode.

Adam thanked Eleanor and told her that he would take care of the gentleman. He invited Terry into the office and closed the door.

Terry raised his chin with typical Terry arrogance and pointed a bouncing finger toward the closed door. "You need to fire her, Chief. I will not be treated this way by a common office worker."

Adam was now standing behind his desk. He sighed deeply, leaned forward, and placed both hands on his desk. "Terry," he began evenly, "this is not the way I expected to meet you." Adam shifted his weight from his right to his left leg. "You need to understand something, Terry; this is not the Navy."

Adam paused while carefully deciding his next wording. "As I told you on the phone, I greatly admire your skills and abilities. I truly do. And I also have a huge respect for your experiences and past achievements. But you will never treat my staff discourteously or rudely again."

Adam pointed toward Terry's chest. "You, sir, will walk into the next room, introduce yourself to Eleanor, and apologize to her for your rudeness."

Terry pumped up his chest and was about to retort, but Adam held up a hand. "One more thing, Terry. Don't ever refer to me as 'Chief' again. I was a chief petty officer at one time and very proud to wear the rank, but as you already know, I continued to promote. I would appreciate it if you call me Adam."

Adam cocked his head slightly. "However, if you prefer something more formal, as I am the president of our new company you may refer to me as *sir* or *Mr. Decker*. Once we begin to sail and I take charge of all aspects of the ship, my title will change to captain."

Terry looked deflated. Adam sat.

"But seriously, Terry, I would much rather be called Adam."

Danny arrived in San Diego and showed up in the office lobby the next day.

Adam poured two cups of coffee. "Danny, have you determined what you need for a deck crew, and have you started contacting anyone?"

Danny opened his briefcase and pulled out a sheet of paper. "I've done some calculating and believe that we can operate with this staffing scheme." Danny turned the sheet toward Adam and pressed his finger to the first line on the list. "I'd like an assistant deck officer and will need twenty-four deck hands. I'm looking to hire former US Navy sailors who have had experience on frigates and destroyers. That should keep the learning curve to a minimum."

Adam led Danny out of his office and introduced him to Eleanor. Terry entered the office as the three were discussing where Danny would be working for the next few days.

"Good morning." Terry nodded to the group, then added a quick nod to Eleanor.

"Morning, Terry." Adam had his hand on Danny's shoulder. "This is Danny Stiles. He's going to be our deck officer."

Danny and Terry shook hands.

"Gentlemen." Adam pointed to the conference room. "We have telephones and laptops set up for you in our conference room. I apologize that we don't have more office space, but I'm hoping that we won't be here for long. Please work with Eleanor if you need some private space, and she will schedule time for you in one of the other offices."

Eleanor gave an impassioned look to Terry and Danny.

"OK." Adam clapped his hands. "Let's get to work."

The following morning Warship Tours, Inc., held their very first staff tag-up. Adam stood at the head of the conference table and beamed. He began the meeting by asking attendees to introduce themselves and to provide a quick brief on their background. When each member finished, Adam reminded the group that the ship was scheduled to arrive at 4 p.m. the next day. He announced the hiring of their new XO, Matt Phillips, and that Matt was expected to arrive tomorrow as well. He motioned to Paula to continue with the briefing.

Paula displayed the company's financial charts. "As you can see"—she pointed at a cost chart on the screen—"I've highlighted our recent costs as well as anticipated expenditures. The recent shipyard cost increase has eliminated most of our budget's excess funding."

She turned to face the group. "Please watch your spending very closely because money is going to be tight.

George was next. "My only news," he began, "is that we'll be berthed at pier Charlie." He began to sit. "Oh, I almost forgot, I've hired a former colleague, Gail Stewart, as our damage-control assistant." George then pointed to Terry. "Your turn!"

Before Terry could begin, Paula raised her hand. "I'm sorry," she began. "I forgot to add that I have our assistant supply officer, Lonnie Taylor, who will be here in three days. I've also hired our cooking and baking staff as well as our logisticians and stores crew. Sorry for the interruption, Terry."

Terry smiled and appeared unfazed. "I've found a former colleague who has agreed to join us as the assistant operations officer. Kyle Lewis served with me on the *John F. Kennedy*. He is expected here in about four days."

Terry twisted his thin neck to acknowledge Danny, who sat in the next seat.

"My turn?" Danny looked at Adam. "I haven't had much luck finding an assistant deck officer, but I did reach out to one of my former boatswain senior chiefs, Bobby Hardesty, to take the job as ship's bosun. There's no better deck supervisor and manager than Bobby. He's served on both coasts and I believe has more time at sea than all of us combined." Danny looked at George. "Even you, George!"

George harrumphed.

Matt Phillips was waiting in the parking lot when Adam arrived at the office the next morning. Adam brought Matt into the building, and both men sat down in Adam's office. Adam updated him on the schedule and then escorted him to Paula's office. "Hey, Paula, I want to introduce you to Matt Phillips, our new XO."

Paula smiled, stood, and shook Matt's hand. "Really good to meet you, Matt. I've heard great things about you."

Paula spent ninety minutes discussing contracts and funding. She closed the project binder and concluded with "We've spent a good portion of our budget but should be OK as long as we can avoid any major hits."

The team gathered in the offices and traveled to NASSCO at three to watch the ship arrive. Eleanor stayed back at her desk to hold down the fort.

Adam could hardly control his excitement as they waited. Finally, he saw the tall stacks and the superstructure of the frigate come into view. It seemed to take forever for the tugs to maneuver the frigate toward the pier. The tugs positioned themselves outboard of the ship and inched closer and closer until the ship was finally pushed against the pier bumpers. The men on the frigate's deck tossed six mooring lines to the pier where the shipyard workers looped them around bollards.

George smiled at Adam. "Moored! Shift colors," he said, using the phrase that was passed across a ship's 1MC intercom system when a Navy warship arrived at a port.

Adam stared at the ship from top to bottom and fore and aft. He looked past the surface rust and boarded-up bridge windows and instead saw the sleek lines, the tall stacks, and the massive superstructure of this great ship.

"She's beautiful," Adam whispered.

A crane moved slowly up the pier, carrying the brow that would attach the ship to the pier. Adam waited impatiently as the crane finally pulled up next to the ship and lowered the platform into place. Once convinced that the mooring lines and brow were secure, the shipyard pier supervisor released the tugs and opened the brow for pedestrian traffic. Doug, Adam, and the rest of the team crossed the brow to the ship.

Before Adam stepped onto the ship's deck, he paused, glanced aft, and out of habit he faced the fantail. The ceremony was always the same. Face aft and salute the US flag, turn to face the quarterdeck, and salute the officer of the deck before stepping aboard. The first thing he planned to do was to erect the flag staff on the fantail and have the flag raised each morning and retired at sunset each night.

Adam took it all in. He had come home.

The team walked the main deck surrounding the superstructure while the shipyard team placed *Caution* and *Do Not Enter* signs on hatches and watertight doors. Entrance to all doors and hatches was prohibited until gas-free engineers could certified that spaces to be entered were not oxygen depleted and were free of explosive or toxic gases.

As his team toured the main decks, Adam noticed several issues requiring immediate attention. The decks and bulkheads were covered with rust that would need to be ground down and repainted; the lifeline cables that kept sailors from falling overboard were all missing; and one of the watertight doors on the superstructure was hanging off its hinges. The aft capstan was also dented and sitting at an angle. He wondered what problems they would encounter inside the skin of the ship.

That evening the senior leaders of Warship Tours, Inc., crossed the Coronado Bridge and got together for dinner at one of George's favorite restaurants—the Coronado Brewing Company. A variety of separate discussions soon began within the group, growing louder as alcohol was introduced.

George entertained Paula and Danny by telling an off-color story of his enlisted days. Paula feigned shock at the story's climax while Danny laughed.

"Hard to believe that you were once that young and stupid, George," Adam said.

Paula turned to Adam. "You never talk about your early days, Adam. What were you like when you first entered the Navy?"

Adam smiled. "I was naïve and stupid. I was also a mama's boy." He pinched his chin as he stared into the distance. "I remember the day that I went off to boot camp. I was scared to death. The recruiter was supposed to be at the house early to pick me up and take me to the processing center to get sworn in. My mom and I were sitting in our living room. We were just waiting and talking."

Adam paused as the memory came flooding back. "I'll never forgot the three things that my mom made me promise." He chuckled as if at an inside joke. "Number one, I had to promise not to marry a foreign woman. Number two, never get a tattoo. And three, never go near the water."

A puzzled look crossed his face. "I still don't understand that third one."

The table erupted in laughter.

Located at the table directly next to the group sat a nondescript man in a black suit. Had anyone given this man a second glance, they would have only thought it odd to see anyone in Coronado wearing such formal attire. The man enjoyed his dinner and smiled as he listened to the conversations at the next table.

CHAPTER 6

I t had been four weeks since Warship Tours, Inc., gained physical custody of the *Ingraham*.

The shipyard inspection team worked quickly with the ship's engineers. Divers inspected the hull below the waterline and reported that the ship's screw or propeller looked like it had struck something during the voyage from Bremerton. Another repair and another unexpected cost.

The engineering main spaces were in fairly good shape. Fuel, lube oil, and water tanks were cleaned and resealed, while firefighting systems and piping for other liquids were flushed and cleaned. Fuel for the ship's engines was then transferred to the ship.

George worked with the shipyard team to determine the condition of the engines and respective systems. After thoroughly reviewing the fuel and high-pressure air components, the teams managed to start up and run the port engine for two hours. The starboard engine, however, overheated after only eight minutes of operation. The temperature gauge reached 800 degrees Fahrenheit, forcing George to immediately shut it down.

After a complete inspection, George determined that the main reduction gear had gone bad. *This is definitely not good*, he thought as he wiped grease from his hands.

Gail Stewart, the ship's damage-control assistant, was in Damage Control Central, reviewing the firefighting system charts for the ship. She was responsible for the proper maintenance of damage-control equipment as well as ensuring that all crewmembers were trained in firefighting.

Numerous leaks had been discovered throughout the firefighting system, and Gail painstakingly reviewed charts to locate each valve. She had been staring at the charts for three hours, and her eyes burned. She yawned and rubbed her eyes. This was going to be a monstrous undertaking due to the number of faulty valves. She hoped that she had the people and money to repair the system quickly and accurately.

Terry entered Combat Information Center, otherwise known as CIC, and took a moment to view the entire space. His team worked feverishly to resurrect the long-dead electronic systems. While powering up and inspecting the radars, they discovered that the air-search radar antenna was frozen in place and unable to rotate. Terry's disappointment grew when he learned that they couldn't ping the sonar while the ship was pier-side, but all tests indicated that the ship's sonar system was in good working order.

Danny and Bobby spent the morning inspecting the deck equipment, anchors, chains, and capstans.

"We're going to be chipping and grinding this shit for weeks." Bobby shook his head as he kicked at a patch of rust that covered the ship's deck.

Danny noted that the ship's mooring lines were old and frayed and would need replacing. The anchors and chains were tested and approved for sea, but the aft capstan looked like someone had hit it with a forklift.

Leaving Bobby to supervise the deck-grinding operation, Danny entered the superstructure and climbed a ladder to the bridge. As he toured the space, Danny was happy to see that the ship's command center was clean and that all systems were functional. He walked out to the port bridgewing and peered down at the main deck, where his crew worked on the huge rusted area. Danny's smile disappeared as he wondered how long it would take to get the ship underway.

Paula calculated that the project was dangerously close to hitting the funding ceiling as she and Lonnie balanced the new costs against the forecasted budget.

"We've completely underestimated the costs of furbishing a completely empty ship," Paula commented. "We never even considered bedding, small tools and equipment, and consumables needed for maintenance and upkeep."

Tired of crunching numbers, she leaned back in her chair, laced her hands across her forehead, and took a deep breath. "My eyes are bleeding. Let's go see how the galley is coming along." She motioned Lonnie to follow her as she rose from the desk.

The engineering team had already conducted a thorough inspection of the wardroom and galley water and steam lines, so now hot water was being supplied from shore services on the pier. Meanwhile, the galley team was busy cleaning and stocking the mess decks, galley, and storerooms.

Paula directed the galley team to focus on the crew's mess and wait for a later date to begin work in the officers' wardroom. All members of the crew, junior and senior alike, would eat in the crew's mess until the wardroom was completed.

Only a few of the heads had operational toilets, sinks, and showers, and just two crew berthing spaces had been cleaned and were fit for habitation. The men's berthing space contained seventy-two racks for sleeping, and the women's berthing space contained thirty-five racks.

The senior-personnel staterooms were another matter. Fifteen staterooms were assigned to the ship's captain, executive officer, department heads, and assistant department heads.

Adam and George were sitting in the wardroom when Terry burst through the door. "Are you aware," Terry seethed, "that we are being directed to clean and prepare our own living quarters? I mean sanitize a space just like a common worker." Adam and George glanced at each other, then back to Terry. "I am much too busy with preparing the operations suite to be burdened with such menial tasks."

"You mean you're much too important, right, Your Highness?" George winked.

"I will not be ridiculed." Terry shook a bony finger at the engineer. "Why isn't the supply staff taking care of these responsibilities?"

Adam sighed. "Paula's team is busy with more important tasks." He raised his chin. "You don't need to clean your stateroom, but I will not assign anyone to do it for you."

Terry glared at Adam, turned, and fumed out of the wardroom while Adam and George rolled their eyes.

"About a foot higher," Adam shouted. The two men standing on the scaffolding raised the frame and centered it three feet below the fantail lifelines. "Perfect!" Adam yelled.

The men positioned the frame against the ship's hull and began spray-painting the letters that would spell out the ship's name. One by one the letters were painted white over the haze-gray hull.

The men finished the job, sat down on the scaffold, dangled their legs over the water, and lit cigarettes. They leaned against the hull and smoked while the paint dried.

Adam was about to return to the ship when someone tapped his shoulder. He turned to see Matt standing next to a thin young man.

The young man thrust his hand toward Adam. "Hello, sir," he began. "My name is Hasif." Both men shook hands.

Matt eyed Hasif. "He wants a job."

Adam shrugged and spread his hands. "We really aren't looking for anyone right now. What do you do?"

Hasif bounced his attention from Matt to Adam. "I can do anything. Honestly!"

Adam inspected the man's worn clothing and skinny appearance.

"Sir," Hasif continued, "I don't have any experience on ships, but I'm a quick learner and a very hard worker."

Adam frowned and began to turn away.

"Sir!" Hasif pleaded. "I've heard that you need someone in the kitchens to clean dishes and mop floors. I would be happy to do that. I have been trying to get a job for months, but I'm always told 'You don't have any experience.' How can I get experience if no one will give me a chance?"

Adam managed a small smile. "You need to learn your ship's terminology, kid. It's not a kitchen—it's a galley. And we don't mop floors; we swab decks."

Hasif pulled a small notebook from his back trouser pocket and scribbled down notes.

This small act of notetaking did not escape Adam's attention. He considered the request for several moments and then turned to Matt. "XO, would you mind escorting Hasif to Paula? She needs to decide if we can use him."

Matt nodded and walked a grinning Hasif to meet Paula.

"Thank you, Captain!" Hasif waved as he walked to the brow.

"Captain," Adam whispered to himself. He wasn't accustomed to that title. But he liked it.

Adam turned back to inspect the ship's stern. The two men had finished their cigarettes and were removing the frame. Adam watched as the name of the ship appeared: *Kraken*.

Adam had wanted to keep *Ingraham* as the ship's name, but federal regulations prohibited any US civilian or commercial sailing vessel from using terminology that could in any way falsely identify it as a military vessel. So Adam and his senior leaders held a contest where each department head submitted an idea for a ship's name. The rules of the contest were simple: number one, the name couldn't have ever been used on a US Navy ship; and two, the name needed to be something warrior-like.

Once all names had been submitted, a vote was held. Adam, of course, maintained 51 percent of the vote in case of a tie. The winner would be awarded fifty dollars and provided the honor of breaking the champagne bottle over the hull when the ship was officially named.

Several good names, including *Warrior* and *Sea Serpent*, were nominated, but Danny's submission, *Kraken*, won in a landslide. George entered the name *Rusty* and pretended to be annoyed when his idea lost.

Before tag-up the next day, George and Terry sat in the conference room drinking coffee and waiting for the others to arrive. Every so often, George would sip his coffee, then quickly turn to look at the door in the lobby as if he could see someone entering the offices. Terry, ever neurotic, always took the bait and would also turn to look at the door. While Terry's head was turned, George quickly sprinkled salt into Terry's coffee cup.

Adam entered the lobby with Matt and Paula in tow.

"Can you join us for the tag-up?" he asked Eleanor. The secretary removed her telephone headset and rose from her chair.

Adam, Matt, Paula, and Eleanor joined George and Terry in the conference room. They all found seats. "Danny will be a few minutes late," Adam began. "But let's go ahead and get started."

Terry sipped from his cup and immediately spit coffee across the table. His throat spasmed and he coughed violently, tears streaming down his cheeks. As his coughing subsided, Terry looked into his coffee cup. "Who put salt in the coffee?" he asked.

Adam turned and gave George a knowing look. "I wonder."

George leaned back in his chair and smiled.

The door to the lobby opened again and Danny sprinted into the room and to his chair. "Miss anything?" he asked.

Adam shook his head, then looked around the room "I've got some pretty bad news. We have discovered two significant equipment problems—one in Engineering and the other in Ops. The antenna to the air-search radar is frozen and requires a complete rebuild. Terry has talked with NASSCO and has determined that it will take about two months to get the materials and another ten days to repair the antenna. Anticipated cost for this job is 125,000 dollars."

Adam chewed his upper lip, then continued. "Worse news comes from Engineering. The starboard-engine main reduction gear is completely shot and needs replacement. Because this is an unscheduled project and because US Navy ship repairs take priority, the time to repair the MRG can take up to six months with a cost of over a half million dollars."

Adam's brow furrowed. "Additionally, funding that was scheduled to be used for fuel was used to repair the anchor windlass. And we still need to purchase tools, equipment, and consumables for all departments."

Adam paused to allow this information to sink in.

"I need each of you take a hard look at your equipment and material lists and try your hardest to reduce spending. In the meantime, Paula is going to call our investors and request additional funding."

Adam looked sick.

"If we can't get funding, we will be in serious trouble." The room was quiet.

Later that day, Adam, Paula, and Nathaniel met with the bank loan committee. They itemized the materials and equipment needed to complete all jobs and requested an additional $2.5 million. The committee members slowly glanced at each other.

The loan manager, Roger Blane, thanked Adam and his team for this information and indicated that the loan committee would get back to them with a decision.

Adam, Paula, and Nathaniel were silent as they walked to their cars. Adam finally spoke. "I have a horrible sinking feeling about this."

They shook hands with Nathaniel and promised a call when they learned the news.

The next morning Adam was in his office reviewing fire-system diagrams when Eleanor buzzed his telephone. Roger from the bank was on the phone. Paula quickly entered Adam's office, closed the door, and sat down.

"I heard Eleanor buzz you," she said.

Adam pressed the speaker button on the telephone so that Paula could hear the conversation.

"This is Adam."

"Hi, Adam, it's Roger Blane."

"Roger! It's good to hear from you. Hope you have good news for us."

"Well," began Roger, "the committee discussed your situation."

He explained that the committee was not concerned that the loan would be repaid; the concern was that if the company became successful, future expansions would be hindered by current financial obligations.

Roger then offered, "We believe that we can help you, but regrettably the loan committee cannot approve the amount that you have requested."

Adam felt like his heart was going to beat through his chest. "Well, what amount can you help us with?" he asked.

"The committee has agreed to approve a loan increase of 300,000 dollars."

Adam's shoulders drooped. He looked at Paula, shaking his head. Paula quickly pressed mute on the telephone.

"Are they kidding?" Adam asked Paula. "There's no way that we can even come close with that amount of money. That won't even touch the engine repairs."

"Adam?" Roger asked.

Paula unmuted the phone. "Hi, Roger, Paula here. Adam and I are crunching some numbers. Can you give us a second?"

"Absolutely," answered Roger. "Take your time."

"Thanks, Roger." Paula again pressed mute.

Adam lowered his head and stared at his desk. "What can we do? Should we try to get another group of investors?"

Paula again unmuted the phone. "Roger, is there any way to negotiate this? We have worked all angles of these repairs and have brought these costs to the most reasonable solution possible."

"I'm sorry, Paula," Roger concluded, "but the committee isn't interested in further negotiations. I'm afraid that their decision is final."

"Roger," Adam jumped in, "does the committee understand that we can't become operational without this additional funding? There is absolutely no way . . . I mean to say that we can't continue."

Adam knew that he was becoming angry and might possibly say something that he would regret if he didn't get off the telephone. "Roger, let me call you tomorrow. Okay?"

Roger agreed and ended the call.

"Paula there's got to be something that we can do. Can you rearrange funding? I'm happy to sit down with you to discuss our priorities and crunch our numbers even further."

Paula looked defeated. "OK, Adam. Let's pull all of the data together and see what we can do. Who knows, maybe I missed something."

Adam, Paula, Matt, and Lonnie retrieved all financial documents and began a whiteboard session. After six hours of reviewing and restructuring their costs, the team only managed to reduce spending by $22,000.

Completely exhausted, they decided to quit for the night.

Adam hugged Paula and thanked her for all of her help. He then watched as she left.

Once he knew that she was gone Adam turned off the light to his office and sat in the darkness. There was nothing that could be done to help this issue. They were going to fail before the company even had a chance to get off the ground. Adam would call Roger tomorrow morning and report his team's findings and conclusions. He would beg for more money and hope that the loan committee would be more approachable, but he knew deep in his heart that it wouldn't matter.

Adam felt helpless and hopeless, which only compounded his headache.

It was 11:15 p.m. when Adam left the offices. Walking through the parking lot, he noticed a newer-model, all-white Chevrolet sedan parked next to George's car. A man was sitting behind the wheel and listening to music with the car window rolled down. Adam was surprised when he turned his head toward Adam and spoke.

"Good evening."

Adam tried to discern the man's features, but it was just too dark.

"Evening." Adam squinted to get a better look. "Are you OK? Need anything?"

The man opened the door and stepped out of the car. "Just a moment of your time, Mr. Decker."

"Do I know you?"

The man was dressed in a black suit with a white shirt and black tie. He stood about five foot ten with a slender build. An old-style fedora hat sat atop the man's head, and Adam saw short-cropped brown hair. Adam's initial impression was that this man belonged on a movie poster from the film *Men in Black*.

"My name is Oliver Pratt." He reached over the car and handed a business card to Adam. "I know that it's late, but I have some information that I believe would be beneficial to you and to your company, Mr. Decker."

Adam took the card. It read *Oliver Pratt—Regional Director—Worldwide Services, Inc.*

"Worldwide Services, Inc?" Adam asked. "Look, it's late and I'm really tired. What can I do for you, Mr. Pratt?"

Oliver's grin widened as he extended his hand. "I believe that you will be keenly interested in what I can offer, Mr. Decker. First, please call me Oliver."

"OK, Oliver." Adam accepted the handshake. "Call me Adam. Let's talk in my office."

CHAPTER 7

Adam reopened the offices and walked toward the kitchen. "Care for a cup of coffee, Oliver?"

"I'd love one," Oliver replied. "Thank you."

Adam filled the pot with water and new grounds. "How did you get into the shipyard at this hour? Security here is pretty tight at night."

Oliver removed his hat and smiled. He had a pleasant-looking face, and his hair was indeed cropped short. There was nothing about Oliver that made Adam uneasy.

"I do quite a bit of work in this shipyard and have the appropriate access credentials."

"I see." Adam glanced at the half-filled coffee pot. "Are you part of the NASSCO leadership team?"

"No, I'm not associated with the shipyard." Oliver continued to smile. "But I am interested in ships. Your ship is of particular interest, Adam."

The coffee was finished, and Adam poured two cups. "Cream or sugar?" Adam asked.

"Oh, I prefer it black, please." Oliver took the cup.

Adam escorted Oliver to his office and both men sat across from each other.

"OK." Adam spread his hands apart. "What's this about? Why are you interested in my ship?"

Oliver sipped his coffee. "This is good. Thank you." He set the cup on Adam's desk and sat back in the chair. "Warship Tours, Inc., is an interesting and unique company, Adam. I greatly admire your imagination and energy in coordinating such a venture. I am especially impressed with the way that you sought out and purchased a retired ship of war. Truly brilliant!"

Oliver took another sip. "Your idea to turn this ship into a cruise liner and then staff it with former US Navy sailors is honestly a rare and ambitious undertaking."

Adam chuckled. "Oliver, I really appreciate your kinds words, but I still don't understand what I can do for you."

Oliver leaned slightly forward in his chair and maintained the smile. "I understand that you have recently encountered maintenance and equipment challenges that will cause you scheduling and financial hardships."

Adam's eyes widened. He started to speak, but Oliver raised both hands gently in front of him. "I also understand that you need an additional two-point-five million dollars and an extension in the shipyard so that you may complete these maintenance challenges." Oliver sat back and placed his hands in his lap. "Adam, I can help you."

It was Adam's turn to lean forward. "Who are you, Oliver?"

Oliver's perpetual grin widened. "I knew that I would like you, Adam. Do you know why?"

Adam slowly shook his head and shrugged.

"Because you are a get-to-the-point kind of guy." Oliver pointed at Adam while he spoke. "Do you keep up with the news? I'm talking international news as well as local?"

"Sure," Adam answered.

"Of course you do." Oliver locked his fingers together and continued, "Have you been keeping up with the situation around the Kuwaiti coastline?"

Adam glanced toward the ceiling and then back to Oliver. "Isn't there something going on between Kuwait and Iran? Some sort of diplomatic issue?"

Oliver nodded. "Yes. Good. The governments of Kuwait and Iran have been conducting a war of words over the past four months. The situation began when the Iranian government started complaining about ships transiting through the Strait of Hormuz. Their argument was that shipping was causing congestion in the strait, which interfered with Iranian merchant vessel traffic.

"The Iranians then began demanding tariffs from merchant shipping vessels, specifically those from Kuwait. The Iranians were, of course, astute enough to recognize that any attempt to impose these costs on a military vessel could result in unwanted military action. That was not their goal. They merely wanted to flex their muscle and squeeze some extra cash from Kuwait.

"The Kuwaiti government protested this action and argued the legality of forcing vessels to pay these costs since the area of concern is considered an open sea lane in international waters. Basically, this is piracy at the most grievous level. As you can imagine, Kuwait refused to pay these tariffs and continued moving maritime vessels through the strait.

"Not appreciating this slight, the Iranians have increased their military presence in the gulf and are stopping merchant traffic under the guise of international safety inspections. And if that isn't bad enough, they are now patrolling fast boats to harass merchant shipping bound for Kuwaiti ports."

Oliver drank the last of his coffee and set the empty cup on the desk. "Adam, this harassment has disrupted all shipping in the gulf. Merchant shipping companies, afraid that their vessels will be targeted, are refusing contracts to sail through the Strait of Hormuz. Shipments carrying everything from food products to medical supplies have been reduced and often stopped completely. This is now creating huge and negative repercussions to the Kuwaiti economy."

"Okay," Adam finally replied, "what does this have to do with me?"

Oliver leaned back and laced his fingers across his chest. "Adam, would you be interested in getting rid of all of your company debt while keeping your fine ship?"

Adam bit his lower lip. He wasn't sure what Oliver wanted, but that last question definitely piqued his interest. "What do you have in mind, Oliver?"

Oliver pulled a folded document from his inner jacket pocket. "I am authorized to pay for the entire debt incurred by Warship Tours, Inc. I am further authorized to fund all maintenance and equipment fees in order to get the ship in operational order. This includes the salaries and benefits for a crew of your choice—if you will perform a short-term task for the Kuwaiti government."

Oliver placed the document in front of Adam. The proposed contract included payment of nine million dollars to Warship Tours, Inc.

"Adam," Oliver continued, "my company represents the government of Kuwait. Ever since we caught wind of your proposal to purchase the ship, we have been closely monitoring your business and crew. Again, we are deeply impressed with your initiative and progress. I am here to offer you and your crew an opportunity to assist my clients in removing the Iranian fast boats and reopening the Kuwaiti sea lanes."

Adam stuttered, "You want us to go out and destroy Iranian ships?"

Oliver slowly shook his head. "Not at all. We just want them removed. Consider this, Adam. We can't ask the US Navy to intervene. They won't get between two Middle Eastern countries involved in a regional dispute. But the Iranians don't know that your ship is not an actual US warship. Your presence alone will most likely frighten them back to their home ports. We wouldn't send you in unarmed, either. You would have conventional weaponry that would help you defend the ship if you were attacked."

Oliver's smile softened. "Adam, I understand if you don't want to get involved with this task. There would be risks and some deceptions as you travel to your destination. But," Oliver continued, "if you are interested, I will coordinate the transfer of the ship to a private shipyard; provide a team of experts to repair and restore all equipment; work with your logistics team to obtain all necessary materials for your crew and the ship; and install shipboard weaponry that you deem necessary. Of course, as I mentioned, we will settle all debts and negotiate a healthy compensation package for your officers and crew." Oliver sat back and allowed Adam to digest all of this new information.

After a few moments, Adam questioned, "And we would get to keep the ship at the successful completion of this operation?"

Oliver's smile widened again. "All ownership documents would transfer to Warship Tours, Inc., as paid in full." Oliver's face became serious. "Of course, we will remove the weapons when you return."

Adam paused to absorb all of this information. "This is an intriguing and generous proposition, Oliver, but it could be dangerous, and I'm not sure that all of my crew will be interested. I would like to discuss this in detail with my senior staff. Would you be available to meet with my team tomorrow?"

Oliver stood and offered his hand to Adam. "What time would you like me here?"

Adam arrived at the office the next morning at ten o'clock, greeted Eleanor, and poked his head through Paula's doorway.

Paula looked up from her desk. "Well, well." She smiled. "Running a little late today? Thought you might be taking a holiday."

Adam closed the door, and pulled up a chair. "I have some interesting news."

Adam replayed the events from last night's meeting with Oliver Pratt.

Paula's mouth hung open.

"Are you kidding?" she said as Adam finished his story. "Are you sure that this guy is for real?"

Adam uttered a small laugh. "Really didn't have much time to look into his credentials, but I did ask him to meet with us today at eleven o'clock. What do you think?"

Paula stared off for a few seconds and then began, "Adam, I don't know. Is it legal for us to perform as a military combatant? Kind of sounds like we're being asked to be a seagoing mercenary unit."

Adam felt like he'd been punched. "I don't believe that at all," he began. "I realize that we'll be armed, but I don't see this as a mercenary action. And we'd only be armed to defend ourselves." He paused. "Kind of like carrying a can of mace when you're walking the streets."

Paula raised her eyebrows, but Adam ignored it.

He flashed his most innocent smile. "C'mon, I'm a lot of things, but I am not a mercenary. And we won't be." The smile faded. "We are merely being asked to help keep a bully away from a friend. I thought about this all night. I think that we can use nonlethal strategies and tactics to motivate the Iranians away from Kuwaiti waters."

Paula considered his words. "It does sound fun, but really scary. I wouldn't mind getting involved in this, but, like you, I don't want to hurt anyone. I'd like to hear what Mr. Pratt has to say."

A half hour later, George, Paula, Terry, Danny, and Nathaniel were in the conference room waiting for Adam to arrive. The mood was as festive as a funeral service. They had all heard that an outside visitor was going to be attending today's tag-up, and everyone except Paula believed that their investors were going to close down the project and sell off the assets.

George was depressed. He wasn't even in the mood to screw with Terry.

Danny looked at his watch, then back to George. "Any idea who we're expecting to join us today?"

George shook his head. "Nope. All I know is that we're meeting someone to discuss our future."

Terry looked at George. "Our future? Do you mean the future of the company or the future for each of us?"

George turned to Terry. "Both!" he snarled.

Adam was nervously pacing the lobby floor when Oliver arrived precisely at eleven o'clock. They shook hands, and Adam gestured Oliver toward the conference room. As they passed the receptionist desk, Oliver smiled and nodded at Eleanor.

"Good morning," Adam greeted the group as he led Oliver into the conference room. Adam put his hand on Oliver's shoulder. "I'd like to introduce Oliver Pratt. He is the regional manager for Worldwide Services Incorporated."

Oliver smiled at the group. "Actually, I'm the regional director."

Adam surveyed the room. "I know that you are all painfully aware of our financial situation. Oliver's company, Worldwide Services, is proposing an offer that may help us with our current and future fiscal issues. Oliver, would you like to describe your proposal?"

"Thank you, Adam." Oliver turned toward the others. "As Adam has indicated, Worldwide Services is interested in your company, your staff, and your business."

As he did with Adam, Oliver lauded the team on their unique business operation and plan, then described the events occurring in the Arabian Gulf, especially those surrounding the country of Kuwait.

Oliver paused and asked if there were any questions to this point. After no hands were raised, he repeated the proposal he had offered to Adam just hours earlier.

"Worldwide Services, Incorporated, and the country of Kuwait would like to engage your ship and your services in an effort to remove the Iranian fast boats and reopen the Kuwaiti sea lanes. I do need to mention"—Oliver glanced at each member of the group—"that due to the magnitude of this project, my organization has already thoroughly reviewed the status of the ship as well as the backgrounds of each crew member."

Oliver finished with "Our contractual agreement will result in a complete ship overhaul and upgrade, while the successful project completion will provide debt-free ownership of the ship. Of course, this will also include a very attractive compensation package for the officers and crew. Are there any questions?"

Everyone remained quiet until George turned to Adam. "This guy works for the CIA."

Adam looked at George, glanced at Oliver, and then back to George. "George, Oliver does not work for the CIA. As he indicated, he is merely representing Kuwait for this venture."

George shook his head slightly. "Got it. He's a spook who works for the CIA. How do you think that he was able to review our records like he did? How do you think that he got on the shipyard last night? Why do you think a private company wants to help a foreign government? Adam, he's CIA."

Adam now glared at George. "Look, I don't care if he's the pope. We are being provided a get-out-of-jail-free card. What do you think of the proposal?"

George turned to Oliver. "Where would you take the ship for maintenance and repair?"

Oliver smiled warmly at George. "We operate a small island just west of Long Beach, California. The ship and crew would be transferred there. We have ample off-ship quarters and a dining facility for your people, and a team of experts who will work with you to get the ship in operational order. We anticipate that this process will take two months."

Oliver glanced from one member to the next. "Once completed, we will schedule and assist you during your shakedown and sea-trial cruises."

Adam took a deep breath. "Does anyone else have questions, or does anyone oppose this idea? I will be happy to discuss any opposition now or in private."

Danny raised his hand. "We're going to need a weapons officer if we do this."

Adam nodded. "You're right, Danny, and I already have someone in mind."

Adam told Oliver that he would call within twenty-four hours with a decision as he walked him to the door.

Adam then focused on his team. "OK, here's my two cents. We have capped out on our budget, and we've already been told that we're not going to get much more from our investors. Number one, we still need quite a bit of repair work; two, we have limited shipyard time left at NASSCO; and three, we still need to obtain consumables, tools, and equipment. This group needs our services and is willing to pay top dollar for it.

"I don't necessarily like the operation they want us to perform, but I believe that we can complete it without harming anyone, including ourselves. The best part is that we will own the ship free and clear when this is over."

Adam scanned the worried faces of his leadership team and sighed. "I feel that my back is against the wall, and I don't see any other option than to accept closure and bankruptcy. So, I vote to accept Oliver's proposal. What do you guys think? George?" Adam pointed at George.

George, deep in thought, stood from his chair and nodded. "You know, I really don't have anything better to do right now. I think that we need a solid plan before we move forward, and that includes getting as much information on this guy's company as well as intel with the Iranian navy. But I vote to approve."

George sat back in his chair and crossed his arms. He then leaned forward and pointed back at Adam. "I'm serious, though; this guy is definitely CIA. A special island?"

Adam rolled his eyes and turned to Matt. "What about you, Matt?"

Matt looked troubled and paused before finally speaking. "I'd like a few moments with you in private if you wouldn't mind."

"Sure thing," Adam said as he nodded. "Let's meet right after this."

Adam turned to Terry. "What do you think, Ops?"

Terry sat straight in his chair. "We've all completed tours in the Middle East, and, as you know, intelligence and information is key to the completion of any successful operation. Because of that I would recommend adding someone who has experience with intelligence-gathering in that particular area."

Terry turned to Paula. "I also strongly suggest hiring additional staff for our supply team to take care of our living quarters and other essential personal logistics."

George sneered at Terry. "How about we hire you a butler?"

Everyone except Terry laughed.

Terry glared at George. "You, sir, may be accustomed to living in a pigsty and roaming the passageways in soiled clothing." Terry crossed his arms. "I am not, nor will I ever. I am requesting the same professional courtesies that were provided when we last served aboard ships."

George shook his head and forced a small smile.

"Alright," Adam interrupted. "So I take it that you vote to approve."

"Yes." Terry raised his head slightly. "I vote to approve."

Danny, who was enjoying the banter between George and Terry, turned to Adam. "I vote to approve. I really want to see George and Terry cohabitating as we sail across the globe."

"At a minimum that should prove to be entertaining." Adam turned to his supply officer. "Last but not least: Paula. What are your thoughts?"

Paula smiled, looked at her peers, then back to Adam. "I'm in. Can't let you guys have all that fun without me."

Adam paused. "I almost forgot. Nathaniel, no meeting is complete without a word from our legal expert. What say you, Counselor?"

Nathaniel stood and leaned on the conference table. "I'm troubled by this entire development. Though I'm not an expert in maritime law, I wonder how you will be represented as you sail across the ocean. Will you fly the US flag since your ship is registered in the United States, or will you fly the Kuwaiti national flag since you will be representing that country? What laws will cover you if you become engaged with a foreign combatant?

"I follow the old principle that states if something looks too good to be true, it probably is. But as I said, my expertise is business law, and from a business prospective, I will need to thoroughly review all contracts and proposals." Nathaniel paused. "I'd like to accompany you at any meetings with Worldwide Services, especially during the negotiations."

Adam and Paula both nodded enthusiastically. "Absolutely," agreed Adam. He addressed the entire group. "I will contact Oliver tonight and inform him of our decision. Please get with your teams and inform them of our plan. Work with Nathaniel and Paula if any of them want to resign, but inform them that the salary and benefits negotiations will be held later this week. They may want to consider that information before making a decision.

"Also, remind each of your people that they have signed nondisclosure agreements and that this operation will not be discussed with anyone outside of our organization."

Nathaniel provided a large nod with that.

The meeting ended, and Matt followed Adam to his office and sat in the visitor's chair while Adam grabbed two bottles of water.

Matt looked deeply troubled, and Adam gave him a few moments to collect his thoughts.

"What's going on?" Adam finally asked.

Matt was staring at Adam's desk and slowly raised his head. "Adam, I don't agree with this new business proposal, and because of that I can't join you in this operation." He paused. "One of the reasons that I decided to resign my commission in the Navy was that I am a conscientious objector. My religious beliefs were in constant contradiction with my responsibilities as a warfare officer, and I could not, in good conscience, harm another individual, even in wartime."

Matt took a deep breath and continued, "This new situation is even more troubling because now I could be put into a position where

I might cause harm for mere business reasons." He stared at Adam. "I do appreciate the opportunity to be part of this organization and I would be happy to join you when you start the cruise-line business. But at this time, I don't have a choice but to resign."

Adam considered this new information and stared at Matt while he decided on his next sentence. "I understand your convictions, Matt, but I surely don't want to lose you. I'm really stuck between a rock and a hard place on this. We will go broke and lose everything if we refuse the proposal. If that happens, then I will lose you anyway. Are you sure that there isn't something that we can do to keep you here? Besides, we're not sure that we will be put in a position where someone could be harmed."

Matt smiled weakly. "Unfortunately there's no way to know that. Put yourself in the Iranian navy's shoes, Adam. What would you do if a large warship started pushing you around? Would you back off and let the world know that you're a coward, or would you fight? We both know that our Muslim counterparts can be fierce fighters and will not be labeled as cowards. The chances of you sailing into an altercation are high. I do wish you and the team the best of luck. I will pray that God will keep you safe and show you wisdom and guidance."

Matt stood, shook Adam's hand, and said goodbye.

Adam watched Matt as he left the building. After a few minutes spent staring out of his window, he rose and ambled into Paula's office. Paula was discussing the new proposal with Lonnie, who was excited to participate.

Adam excused himself for the interruption and asked Lonnie if he could have a private moment with Paula. As Lonnie exited, Adam shut the door.

"We just lost Matt."

Adam summarized the meeting and Matt's reasons for resigning.

Paula remained quiet for a few moments and then asked, "What do we do now?"

Adam raised one eyebrow. "I'm going to call Scott."

CHAPTER 8

That evening Adam called Oliver and formally agreed to Worldwide Services' offer to repair and outfit the ship in exchange for services to assist the government of Kuwait.

The next morning Adam, Nathaniel, and the department heads met Oliver in the Warship Tours conference room. As Oliver had indicated, the contract paid all Warship Tours, Inc., debts and assumed responsibility to repair and outfit the ship. The entire cost of this contract would be paid in full upon verification that the Iranian patrol boats surrounding the Kuwaiti territorial waters were absent for a period of two days.

Next, the discussion revolved around officer and crew compensation. Worldwide Services, Inc., proposed $150,000 for the CO and XO, $100,000 for each department head, $85,000 for supervisors and managers, and $70,000 for each crewmember. Additionally, one million dollars in life-insurance coverage would be included for each crew member.

Adam noted that the new mission required the addition of a Weapons Department head and crew.

Oliver jotted down the information.

Adam continued, "We also need one doctor and one senior crew foreman similar to a US Navy command master chief. This individual will be responsible for assisting the executive officer and me in day-to-day administrative tasks as well as supervising the crew."

"Agreed," answered Oliver as he wrote. "Anything else?"

Nathaniel was stunned. He had never participated in a contract that was not contested. "Nothing from me," he responded.

"When can we expect to transfer the ship and crew?" Adam asked.

Oliver closed his laptop. "I will have the contract finalized and delivered to you this afternoon. Once I receive confirmation that you have approved and signed the contract, I will approve the wire transfer for all monetary payments. We will contract air travel for all members of the crew. Expect the ship and crew to be transferred in four days. The aircraft will arrive at the shipyard in time for the crew to travel to and assemble on the pier to help tie up the ship when it arrives. I will contact you when I learn the tug arrival times. Any questions?"

Adam looked around the room. "I don't believe so."

Oliver shook hands with the entire team and quickly left the offices.

"Wow," said Danny when he knew that Oliver was out of earshot.

"That's pretty good money for about two and a half months of work," George commented.

Paula nodded and turned to Adam. "Have you called Scott yet?"

"No," replied Adam. "I'll do that next. Then I need to get cracking on finding a weapons officer."

Scott picked up the phone after the second ring. "Hello, my friend," Adam cheerfully began. "How are you doing?"

Scott frowned. "Are you calling to gloat about your company's success? I can't tell you how jealous I am that I'm not there with you."

Adam's smile grew. "Would you be interested in a second-chance opportunity?"

Scott stopped frowning. "Why? What do you mean?"

Adam described all of the events in the shipyard and how the costs had outweighed the budgeted funds.

He relayed the situation surrounding the first and successive meetings with Oliver Pratt and the proposal from Worldwide Services, Inc. Adam then told Scott that Matt had resigned and that they sorely needed a seasoned executive officer.

"Scott," Adam pleaded, "I need you on the bridge with me during this mission. This job should last six months tops—two months in the yards, and four months at sea. Of course, that includes our shakedown cruises. You will also have the opportunity to stay on as XO after we return. What do you say?"

"You're killing me, Adam." Scott took a deep breath. "Let me talk with Briget again. I'll turn this into a lucrative business opportunity. Who knows, maybe she'll be so tired of hearing me whine that she'll want to get me out of the house for a few months."

Scott told Adam that he'd talk with his wife that night and call back the next morning. Adam crossed his fingers.

Adam knew Cyrus Ko as the weapons department head when they both served in the Spruance-class destroyer *Merrill*. Cy had been an exceptional weapons officer, well known for his ability to target and strike multiple objects simultaneously. Additionally, Cy was extremely knowledgeable of small arms. This reputation made Cy a valuable weaponeer in the US fleet.

A geek who took great pride in learning and becoming intimately familiar with the technical specifics of each weapons platform placed in his charge, Cy was forced to resign his commission under some sort of scandal. Rumors were that he was a little too gun happy.

Adam didn't know what that meant and honestly didn't care. In Adam's opinion, Cy was perfect for this position.

Adam finally found Cy's information on LinkedIn and sent an email asking him to call at the earliest opportunity. After lunch,

Adam asked his department heads to canvass their contacts in an effort to locate an available retired command master chief.

He was looking through his list of contacts when his cell phone rang.

Adam answered and was greeted by Victor Wallace, the former shipmate and retired Navy chief warrant officer Adam wanted as ship's navigator.

"Hey, Vic," Adam responded, "great to hear from you. It's funny, but I was going to call you in a week or two. How are you doing?"

"Adam!" Vic responded. "I'm doing good. Retired a few years ago and I'm now living in Charlotte, North Carolina. I found me a nice gig teaching Junior ROTC at the local high school."

Vic paused. "Matt Phillips called me a few days ago and told me about this new business you're working on. I hear that you've got yourself an old frigate and you're turning it into a cruise liner. Matt also told me you're currently in the market for a navigator and asked if I was interested. Is that position still open?"

Adam grinned. He really liked Vic. "I was planning on calling you next week about the navigator position, but it appears that Matt beat me to it. Yes, the position is still open," Adam confirmed as he laughed. "But I have to tell you, we've had some interesting changes in our mission statement."

Adam described the situation and the new mission.

"You're right," Vic agreed. "That is interesting. Look, Adam, you're aware of my experience and credentials. You're also aware that I'm a heck of a good guy."

Adam laughed again. Vic never took himself seriously, which was another thing that Adam liked about him.

"I like my current job, but it's just too . . . domestic for me right now. The kids are great, but I need a little more excitement. I would take the job if you offered it to me."

"You're hired!" Adam shouted. He was happy to get such a trusted officer and friend in the group.

"Tell me, Adam," Vic continued. "Did you get George Bannister too?"

Adam nodded. "Yes. Got Paula too. Do you remember her? She was on *Boxer* with us."

"Yeah, I remember Paula." Adam heard excitement in Vic's voice. "Thanks, Adam. I really appreciate this. When do you need me?"

Adam calculated the schedule. "We're moving the ship in four days. Can you be here in two weeks? I'll work the logistics in flying you out here."

"Two weeks sounds good," Vic said. "Don't worry about flight arrangements. I'll drive."

They said their goodbyes and Adam hung up.

Three hours later Nathaniel arrived with the contracts. He spent thirty minutes explaining the documents and showing Adam where to sign, then promised to call Adam when the wire transfers had been completed.

That afternoon Adam took a walk around the offices and asked each department head if they had any luck finding a command master chief who would be interested in the crew supervisor position. Every answer they'd received was the same: "Thanks, but no thanks."

While considering alternatives, an idea suddenly popped into Adam's head. He rushed into his office and looked through his book of contacts for Leroy Washington's information.

Adam had met retired US Army sergeant major Leroy Alvis Washington when Adam, as a young Navy first class petty officer, was assigned at the National Defense University at Fort McNair in Washington, DC. A career infantry soldier, Leroy didn't have much good to say about sailors or the Navy as a whole. "Navy squids lack discipline and are too loose on obeying regulations," he believed. But he had been pleasantly surprised by just how much he liked this new sailor placed in his charge.

Adam proved to be a hard worker and extremely disciplined. Leroy took young Adam under his wing and for two years taught him the "rights and wrongs" of leadership. Leroy didn't know it at the time, but a long-term friendship was being forged.

Adam dialed Leroy's number.

A deep voice with a slight Southern drawl answered. "Hello."

"Hello, may I speak to Leroy Washington?" Adam requested.

"Speaking."

Adam smiled. "Hello, Sergeant Major. This is Adam Decker. I served under you during our tour at Fort McNair in Washington, DC. Do you remember me?"

There was a short pause. "Decker? Of course I remember you. How are you doing, sailor?"

"I'm doing great, thanks." Adam could hardly hold back his excitement.

Leroy drawled, "Been a long time, Decker. What can I do for you?"

"Well," Adam began, "I've started a business and I'm looking for a man who is good at leading people. It's a pseudo-military type of job that's going to take us deep into the Middle East. What are you doing these days?"

Leroy sighed, "Oh, I got me a supervisor job at the VA in Washington, DC." He paused. "Tell me about this position."

Adam was now accustomed to explaining the business on the phone. He described the mission and the crew-foreman position that was being offered.

Leroy laughed, "You're offering an old soldier a job on a ship?"

Adam grinned. "I hate to admit that it took a soldier to teach me about leadership. But I need a strong leader and manager for this enterprise. I need someone who has spent time in the trenches and isn't afraid of the stresses associated with war zones. I need a shipboard sergeant major. Are you interested?"

"Tell you what," Leroy said. "Let me think about it. I'll give you a call in a day or two."

Adam hung up the phone and glanced at his watch. It was just after seven. He peered into the lobby and noticed that Eleanor had already gone home.

Adam rose from his desk, stretched his back, and walked around the offices.

Danny and Paula were the only two still at work. He grabbed Danny and quietly pulled him into Paula's office where they both stood across from Paula and said nothing. Paula was so focused on her computer screen that she didn't notice the two large men staring at her.

She finally realized that she wasn't alone and slowly lifted her gaze to see her friends smiling at her.

Paula's eyes darted from Adam to Danny. "What are you two idiots doing?"

Adam placed his forearms on her desk and leaned forward. "That's Captain Idiot to you."

She logged off of her computer. "OK, Captain Idiot. Would you and your manservant like to go out for a bite to eat?"

Adam turned to Danny. "What do you think, manservant?"

Danny laughed and thanked Paula for the invitation but had to decline. His wife, Stacey, had made a special meal and was waiting for him.

Adam and Paula were shutting off the office lights when Adam's cell phone rang. The caller ID in the phone indicated that it was Scott.

Adam answered, "Hey, buddy. How are you doing?" He was surprised to hear a woman's voice.

"Hello, Adam. It's Briget."

"Hi, Brige . . . uh, sorry, Briget," Adam stuttered. "Is everything OK?"

Briget sounded pissed. "Well, Adam, no. Everything is not OK. Why do you continue to badger Scott with this new-business nonsense? You have him so wrapped up in this ship idea that it's all he talks about."

Adam gulped but allowed Briget to continue.

"Tell me what is so important that you continue to call my husband and pull him away from me?"

Adam knew that he needed to be completely honest with Briget.

Any fluff or flattery would be immediately recognized and met with hostility.

"Briget," Adam began, "let me tell you about our situation and why we need Scott."

Again, Adam expertly detailed the history of the company from inception to current date.

Adam talked about Matt resigning and the need for an experienced executive officer.

"Look, Briget," Adam began, "I'm not trying to break your marriage apart, and I think that you know that. You may feel that I'm selfishly trying to grab Scott, but that's not true. I want Scott because, well, honestly, he is the best ship driver that I know. Here's something else—not only will he be paid $150,000 for a four-month job, but he will also be part owner of our ship and this company. This operation will pay off all of the company's debts and provide us with complete ownership of the ship.

"Here's another thing: We expect to expand our fleet after we become more familiar with the cruise-line industry. The revenue earned by this business will allow each senior leader to retire early and continue to earn major annual dividends. Briget, Scott came up with the idea for this company. Your kids, you, and he need to benefit from its success."

Briget was silent.

"Briget, are you there?" Adam asked.

"Shut up, Adam," Briget scolded. "I'm thinking."

Adam knew when to fight and when to be quiet. He quickly determined that it was time to shut the hell up. So he waited.

After what seemed like five minutes, she finally opened up.

"Adam, I know that you have a good heart and that you care for Scott and me. I can also tell that you believe in this company as much as you believe in Scott's ability to help lead this operation."

Again, Briget paused, but Adam was not about to interrupt. "OK, Adam, I tell you what. I'll support Scott's decision and your request.

But we're going to make a deal. We will conduct a trial run on this plan—let's say six months. We will reevaluate Scott's participation in this company when you return from this operation. Will you agree to that, Adam?"

Adam was elated. "Briget, that's more than fair. I will definitely agree to that."

"One more thing, Adam." Briget sounded worried. "You need to promise me that Scott will come home safely."

Adam was taken aback. How could he promise something like that? He didn't know how to respond. What would he say to Briget and Scott's children if something did happen to him?

"Briget," Adam began, "I can't guarantee what will happen to Scott or me or anyone who sails with us. But I can promise that I will do everything in my power to keep all of the crew, including Scott, safe and to bring them home on time. I hope that's enough."

"Thank you, Adam," Briget answered icily. "Scott will call you tomorrow to discuss his plan."

Adam hung up the phone. He should have been the happiest guy on the planet, but for some odd reason he had a lump in his throat and his stomach had soured.

Adam and Paula went out for pizza and beer. They talked about the ship and giggled as they described members of the crew who they considered to be quirky. Adam was glad that they decided to go out. He needed to decompress a bit, but as much as he tried to keep the mood light, he kept remembering Briget's words and the promise that he made.

Adam caught himself staring at the bubbles in his beer as they floated to the top of the glass.

"Paula." He pulled his eyes away from his beer. "What happens if I can't bring our people back home safely?"

Paula took a long drink and set the cup on the table. "Adam, there's no way to predict what will happen while we're gone. You have the rare opportunity to be in charge of a ship at sea. You already know that being a captain has great privileges as well as huge responsibilities. As such, you are expected to take risks and, of course, be accountable for all of your decisions and orders.

"You can't dwell on the unknown future, and you certainly can't begin to second-guess decisions that you haven't made. We can only hope that this operation will be uneventful, but if it isn't, we'll deal with it. Cheers!" Paula raised her glass.

During tag-up the next day, Adam updated the department heads with news on the approved contract and additions to leadership.

George stood and applauded when he heard that Scott had accepted the position as XO.

"When is he going to be here?" he asked.

Adam explained that Scott's scheduling was being worked on and would be communicated as soon as it was confirmed.

Terry raised his hand. "Excuse me. I had hoped that I would be considered for the XO position when it became available. After all, I am a very senior and notable officer. Is there any reason why I was excluded from this selection process?"

"Maybe," George quickly answered, "they couldn't find a butler tall enough to kiss your elevated ass."

Terry snapped his head around. "You, sir, are an uncouth cad."

George smiled and said nothing.

"Alright, guys," Adam interjected. "Terry, as I discussed with you previously, your expertise on this ship is operations. I need you there. There is no one on this ship who has your talent, your expertise—"

"Or your ego," added George.

"Silence!" shouted Terry.

"That's enough, George!" Adam almost laughed.

George maintained his smile and sat back in his chair.

Terry stormed out of the conference room when the meeting ended.

Adam stopped George at the door. "Why do you keep antagonizing him?"

George turned and faced Adam. "I don't know. He just brings out the worst in me."

"Lay off of him for a while, will you, George?" Adam asked.

"I'll do my best." George gave his best innocent smile as he turned and left the room.

Eleanor followed Adam into his office and addressed him as he sat as his desk. "I received a call from our attorney, Mr. Williams. He confirmed the crew's flight information and is going to email that to me later this morning. Additionally, he and I are working with the bank and the insurance companies to create accounts for each crew member."

Adam thanked Eleanor, and she returned to her desk.

A few minutes later, she buzzed Adam's phone. "Mr. Ko is returning your call. He's on line one." Adam picked up the phone from its cradle.

"It's been a long time, Adam. How are you doing?"

Adam wasn't much for small talk, but he enjoyed catching up with Cy and, of course, remembering the good times they spent on the *Merrill*.

It didn't take long for both men to tire of this chatter, so Adam got to the point.

As he did with countless other people, Adam described the business they had created and the ship they had purchased.

"You bought a ship? What kind of ship?" Cy laughed.

Adam proudly and a little smugly informed Cy of their possession of an Oliver Hazard Perry–class frigate. He then talked about Worldwide Services and outlined their short-term business opportunity.

Adam was animated. "This four-month mission will eliminate our debt and give us a solid start for our business. As you know, there are several conventional weapons systems onboard. Of course, they need to be repaired and made operational, but I need someone who is knowledgeable with these systems and the respective fire-control systems. I called you because of your unconventional and out-of-the-box strategies as well as your expertise with shipboard weapons.

"Would you be interested in taking over as weapons officer for the two-month maintenance period and the follow-on assignment? You will have the authority to hire a team of your choosing and to purchase any additional equipment or platform that will help us succeed in this operation."

"That's quite a story, Adam," Cy admitted. "It's also a really interesting and exciting opportunity. I'd like to seriously consider this prospect, but there are a few issues that I need to weigh. First, I already have a job—a good one at Lockheed. The program I was working on ended and I was laid off three weeks ago, but I believe that other programs are coming online shortly. I'm also scheduled to vacation in Scotland and Ireland with my girlfriend during this downtime. We're leaving in ten days."

Cy stopped momentarily. "But that is pretty good money for a short-term job, and I would love to help strategize a plan for an operational unit. Plus, I'd get to shoot big guns again and maybe even blow something up."

Adam smiled as he heard the excitement in Cy's voice.

"Tell you what, Adam. Count me in. This sounds like too much fun, and I'd hate to miss it."

"Great." Adam was relieved. "But what about your trip? Won't you lose money on penalties for rescheduling? And what about your girlfriend?"

Cy chuckled. "I'll talk to Linda. She'll understand. And if she doesn't . . . I'll find another girl. And I won't lose any money on airline penalties or fees. I'm sure that you'll take care of that for me."

Adam laughed. Cy hadn't changed. Still cocky.

"You can count on it. We'll even cover your bar tab. Start contacting anyone you want on your team. I'm leaving that completely to you."

Adam provided contact and address information, and Cy promised to be in the offices in two days.

That afternoon, Adam was reviewing a risk and threat assessment for the Arabian Gulf region when his telephone buzzed.

Eleanor indicated that a gentleman was in the lobby to see Adam.

Adam hung up and opened the door. He spotted a tall, thin black man standing in the lobby, staring out of the office window. The man was wearing khaki pants and a blue polo shirt. He had excellent posture.

Adam grinned. Even as a civilian, Leroy Williams projected confidence and strength.

"Sergeant Major!" Adam walked up to Leroy and extended his hand. "What the hell are you doing in San Diego?"

Leroy turned and flashed that toothy smile that Adam well remembered.

"Please, it's just Leroy. I wanted to see this ship that you're so jazzed about and hear more about the supervisor position, so I booked a flight and decided to spend a couple of days in San Diego." Leroy eyed Adam up and down. "You're looking well, Mr. Decker. Put on a little weight. How is that pretty wife of yours?"

Adam's smile never wavered. "C'mon, let's go into my office and catch up."

Adam introduced Leroy to Eleanor, and both men entered Adam's office.

Leroy's smile and eyes fell as Adam shared the news of his wife's death. "I'm so sorry. She was a wonderful woman."

Adam knew that Leroy's pain was genuine.

He moved to a happier topic. "Tell me what happened after you transferred from DC."

The two men talked about the old days, and Leroy smiled and listened intently as he was updated on Adam's military career.

"You were a diamond in the rough," Leroy commented. "I knew that you would do well . . . for a squid, that is."

Adam laughed. "I have to tell you, Leroy. Of all the leaders I worked for while I was rising through my enlisted ranks, you were the best. You took the time to teach and mentor me. I'm not sure if I appreciated it back then as you stuck your foot up my ass, but I'm happy now that you demanded accountability and responsibility."

Adam crossed his arms, tilted his head back slightly, and grinned. "I also can't tell you enough how it pains me to say that I learned all of those lessons from an Army guy."

Leroy chuckled.

Adam stood and leaned forward on his desk. "I need a man of that caliber to lead my crew. I need a no-nonsense, tough leader who is not afraid to give bad news to his crew or to his captain."

"And you think that's me?" Leroy asked.

Adam nodded and smiled. "I know that's you. But before you begin considering anything, let's take a walk and I'll introduce you to my department heads, and then I'll introduce you to our ship."

Leroy met and talked with all of the senior leaders. Paula and Danny were especially taken by Leroy's charm and Southern personality. Adam and Leroy then jumped in George's car and drove to the ship. Adam explained that all NASSCO work had come to a halt and the shipyard team was now preparing the ship to be transferred to the new location.

He parked the car, and both men quietly stared at the ship.

"Wow," Leroy whistled. "She's a beauty."

Adam just grinned. "Just wait until she's finished."

Adam escorted Leroy on board, and they toured the main decks, with Adam pointing out each weapon and radar system. He opened a watertight door on the superstructure, and they entered the skin of the ship. They climbed the ladders to the bridge and walked aft to CIC. Leroy asked question after question. He looked around every corner and peered into every crevice. He was a sponge absorbing every piece of information that Adam provided.

For two hours they climbed ladders and toured spaces. Adam took great joy in teaching Leroy naval vernacular, and by the end of the tour Leroy was becoming accustomed to using terms such as *head*, *deck*, *hatch*, and *galley*.

When Leroy crossed the brow and stepped back to the pier, he turned and stared at the warship with appreciation. "You know, Adam, this is the first time I've ever stepped foot on a ship."

Adam turned to Leroy and laughed slightly. "Are you serious?"

Leroy met Adam's gaze. "Well, I did spend a little time on that river-cruise boat at Disneyland."

Both men laughed hard.

Leroy turned back to gaze at the ship. "I think that this will be fun."

Adam put a hand on Leroy's shoulder and turned him back toward the car. "C'mon," he said, "let's go back to the office and talk."

Adam had never seen Leroy like this. During the short drive the old soldier talked nonstop and asked questions about the ship's engines, steering systems, weapons platforms, and day-to-day life at sea.

Adam parked the car outside of the office and opened his door. Leroy became quiet and stared forward. He did not move to open the door.

Finally, he turned and looked at Adam. "I would like to be part of this business of yours, Adam. I retired from the Army after it stopped being fun. It just wasn't exciting anymore. I still loved working with the troops, but the training lost its luster, and everything just became so mundane and routine. If I understand you correctly, I can do that again. But on a ship, well, it's a completely different dynamic. This is exciting. What's the chain of command? How do I address you and the other senior leaders like Paula and George?"

Adam burst out laughing. "I'm seriously glad that you're so excited about this operation and the company. We do have a chain of command of sorts, though we won't be as militant as the Army or Navy. We're still working out the details of our organizational system and would gladly accept any guidance and wisdom that you could offer. For all intents and purposes, I am the ship's captain. You can call me *Captain*, or if you prefer, just call me Adam. We'll figure out the rest of the formalities as we move forward."

Adam reached out and shook Leroy's hand. "Welcome aboard, my friend. We're going to do great things together."

CHAPTER 9

Leroy flew back to Atlanta the next morning to resign from his job and find someone to watch his house and car. He promised Adam that he would return in time to fly with the crew. In the meantime, Scott was scheduled to arrive in San Diego that day, and Paula agreed to pick him up at the airport.

Adam and George met with Oliver to discuss the ship's transfer. Oliver greeted them in the office lobby where they saw Nathaniel working with Eleanor on crew pay and insurance documentation. Nathaniel followed the three men into the conference room, sat at the table, and pulled a pen and pad out of his briefcase.

Oliver retrieved four sets of documents from his briefcase, then passed a document to each of the attendees and kept one for himself as he discussed the plan for transferring the ship. Oliver's team and the tug crews would work together to tow the ship to the new port at Brown's Island Shipyard. Adam's crew was not required during this process; however, Oliver requested that George and his group of engineers conduct a thorough walk-through of the ship over the next two days to ensure that all external intakes and inlets were closed and secure.

Two large troop-transport aircraft would fly Adam's people to the Brown's Island airfield. Once on the ground, the crew would help with mooring and pulling shore power cables from the pier to the ship.

Oliver poured a cup of coffee and continued, "When the ship has been completely tied to the pier and all shore cables are in place, a kick-off meeting will be held at the island dining facility to introduce the crew to our maintenance team and to discuss schedules."

Oliver sipped his coffee. "By the way." Oliver returned his cup to the table. "The maintenance schedule will be broken down and listed by days. D-1 will be the day that the ship arrives. D-2 is the following day, and so on."

George pointed at Oliver. "Will we be graced by your presence on the island for the entire maintenance period?"

Oliver turned to George. "I will be on the island for the first three days and then routine visits after that."

Adam glared at George, who just shrugged.

Adam raised a hand. "Our new Weapons Department head may be requesting some additional and possibly unique armament. I would like to schedule time to discuss if these additions are possible."

Oliver nodded. "Of course. I'll set up a meeting in the afternoon."

They spent the rest of the morning discussing the maintenance schedule.

As the meeting concluded, Adam informed Oliver that more crewmember hires were expected. Oliver explained that their transportation process would be the same as the first. New-hire information would be generated by Eleanor, who would then communicate the new information to Nathaniel and Oliver. Oliver would coordinate flight plans and other logistics.

After Oliver and Nathaniel departed the offices, George looked at Adam. "I'm truly convinced that Oliver is a spook. He may not be CIA, but he's with some Secret-Squirrel agency."

That thought had taken up residence in Adam's mind too.

Later that afternoon Adam sat at his desk and looked through his contacts on his computer. He had no idea how to recruit a doctor for the ship. Any doctor worth his salt was either in private practice or working for a reputable medical firm.

He asked his department heads if they knew of a doctor who was looking for a job full of fun and adventure. Each answer was the same: "No."

George had the only logical advice. "Give Oliver a call," he recommended. "He seems to have an answer for everything else."

Adam walked back to his office and called Oliver to explain the trouble he was having. Oliver told Adam that he would make a few calls. Hanging up the phone, Adam leaned over his desk and rubbed his eyes. He sat in that position for the next thirty minutes.

That afternoon, Paula drove to the airport to pick up Scott. During the drive they chatted about the ship and the upcoming move to the new shipyard. Scott confided to Paula that he was concerned about his new position as XO. He was confident in his skills as a ship driver, but he had never held a position of senior leadership like that.

Paula giggled. "Scott, you've got the biggest ego on the planet. I've never known you to second-guess yourself."

Scott worked up a weak smile. "Yeah," he said, "but my ego is just another way to mask my insecurities."

They arrived at the offices and met Adam in the lobby. He excitedly bounced around each of the offices and provided Scott the grand tour, making a point to introduce Scott to each of the department heads and, of course, Eleanor. He then grabbed Scott by the arm and pulled him out of the front door and toward the car.

Adam talked nonstop about the mission as they drove to the ship. He described his meeting with Oliver and how the Brown's Island shipyard was going to upgrade and repair the vessel. They rounded the corner, and the *Kraken* came into view.

"Wow," Scott whispered. "She's amazing!"

Adam grinned. It was nice to have someone else share in his

appreciation of the ship.

At the bridge, Scott jumped up and sat in the starboard-side captain's chair. "Never thought we'd ever be in this position," he said, smiling at Adam.

Adam came alongside his friend and peered out of the forward window. "Scott, we are going to have more fun than ever before."

The following morning George and Scott caught up and drank coffee in the office's conference room. They were laughing and swapping old stories when a tall, thin black man walked into the office.

Scott stood. "May I help you?"

The man smiled. "I'm not sure. What can you do?"

George grinned, while Scott frowned.

"I'm not sure that you're in the right place," Scott replied.

The man glanced at George, half smiled, and turned back to Scott. "Are you suggesting that you're not sure about my decision to be at this location, or do you believe that I may be lost?"

George stood and put his hand on Scott's shoulder. "Scott, this is Leroy Washington. He's our new crew supervisor. That's a politically correct description of the ship's master chief."

Leroy grinned and offered his hand to Scott. "Nice to meet you, Scott. I'm just a wise-ass at heart. Hope you don't mind."

"Yes, he is!" Adam entered the room.

Scott smiled and grabbed Leroy's hand. "Nice to meet you, Leroy. I'm Scott Foster."

"Scott's our new exec," Adam said.

Leroy continued smiling. "Of course he is. That's why I'm messing with him."

Scott twisted his head to Adam. "I'm glad he has a sense of humor." Scott turned back to Leroy. "So, what ships were you on, Leroy?"

Leroy's grin widened, but he said nothing. George snickered while Adam shared Leroy's resume with Scott.

"OK," Scott finished, "it's the perfect leadership team. We've got a captain who has never been in command of a ship, an XO who has never held a seagoing position higher than division officer, and a ship's master chief who was a soldier and who has never been at sea." Scott nodded. "Confidence is just oozing out of my pores."

Leroy looked at Adam. "He's a smart-ass too."

Adam nodded violently.

Eleanor walked in. "Excuse me, gentlemen. Adam, Mr. Pratt is on the telephone."

Adam excused himself and asked Scott to begin the tag-up, then walked to his office to pick up the telephone. Oliver was his usual upbeat self. He told Adam that the Worldwide Services' leadership team was very excited about the upcoming move to the new shipyard.

Adam shared the news about the arrival of Scott and Leroy and that the process of "buttoning up" the ship for transfer was almost finished.

Oliver congratulated Adam on their progress. "I have good news," Oliver announced. "I have found a ship's physician who will meet your needs. Doctor Mark Kelly is a retired US Air Force flight surgeon who is available and interested in becoming a member of your crew."

"That's terrific," Adam said. "When should we expect Doctor Kelly to arrive?"

Oliver explained that he was currently involved in a contractual position with another firm, but negotiations had begun to free the doctor in a few weeks.

Oliver continued, "I expect the good doctor to arrive at Brown's shipyard around the midpoint of the maintenance period. In the interim we have a fully staffed medical team and facility on the island."

Adam again thanked Oliver.

"Oh, one additional item," Oliver added. "I've taken the liberty of talking with your secretary, Mrs. Paisley, and offered her a continuation of employment while the ship is undergoing maintenance. I've asked Mrs. Paisley if she would consider moving to Brown's Island during this period so that we could maintain business and administrative continuity. I'm happy to announce that she has agreed and is very excited to continue being part of your team."

Adam was surprised but happy with the news. He had not considered asking Eleanor if she would be interested in staying with the company.

"Thank you," Adam told Oliver. "It makes sense to keep Eleanor. I appreciate that you thought of this."

Cyrus Ko parked his 1965 Corvair Monza in the parking lot adjacent to the Warship Tours, Inc., corporate offices.

He'd spent the last nine hours driving from his apartment in San Francisco, and he was dead tired. All he wanted was to find a nice place for a meal, a hot shower, and a bed. First, he had to check in with Adam to obtain tomorrow's itinerary.

He shut off the car and pulled the key from the ignition. The key hung from a ring with only one other item attached to it—a shiny .308-caliber rifle bullet. The bullet primer had been removed and a hole had been drilled through the bullet to allow room for the key ring.

Cy stepped out of his car and turned to look at the main entrance to the office as the door opened and a man in his mid-thirties stepped through. He looked over at Cy and walked toward the car.

"Nice ride," Scott said, his eyes dancing over the classic. He switched his gaze to Cy. "Help you with something?"

Cy shut the car door. "I'm looking for Adam Decker. Do you know where I could find him?"

"Yeah, he's right inside." Scott offered his hand. "I'm Scott Foster. Are you with the shipyard?"

Cyrus wasn't in the mood to be interrogated but maintained a civil attitude.

"Actually," he said without accepting Scott's handshake, "Adam called and asked me to visit."

Scott dropped his hand and looked Cyrus over. After a short pause he escorted Cy inside and asked him to wait in the lobby while he found Adam.

Scott opened Adam's office door and slipped inside. "There's a guy here to see you. Not sure who he is, but he seems full of attitude."

Adam rose and walked to the lobby. He lowered his chin to his chest, shook his head, and laughed when he saw Cy.

"Cyrus Ko." Adam walked to Cy and gave him a hug. "It's been a long time."

Scott watched the scene from Adam's office doorway.

"How are you doing?" Adam asked.

Cyrus looked past Adam to Scott, then back to Adam. "Just drove in and feelin' a little tired and cranky."

Adam turned to Scott, who was still standing in the doorway. "Scott, I'd like to introduce you to someone." Scott joined the two men. "This is Cyrus Ko, our new weapons officer. Call him Cy." Adam turned to Cyrus. "Cy, meet Scott Foster, the ship's XO."

Scott and Cyrus shook hands. "Gotta tell you, at first I thought you were some angry guy who was looking for trouble," Scott said.

Cyrus eyed Scott. "I am."

Scott released Cyrus's hand and to Adam said, "I'm heading to the ship to check on the transfer. Mind if we chat when I get back?"

Adam agreed, and Scott left the office. "Kind of a stiff, isn't he?" asked Cyrus.

"Not at all," Adam answered. "In fact, you two are cut from the same type-A-personality asshole cloth."

Cy chuckled.

Adam provided the travel schedule to Cyrus. "Go ahead and get your things in order. Our flight leaves tomorrow at 0800. Transportation to the airfield leaves at 0630 tomorrow, so please be in our parking lot on time."

Cyrus told Adam that he needed to find a storage facility for his car and then get some sleep. He promised to be on time.

Everything was set. George signed the inspection documentation, and then he and Gail drove to the offices to report to Adam, who was finalizing some scheduling details with Scott and Paula. Eleanor was in the lobby talking with Hasif. She had taken a liking to the young steward and often complimented him on his manners and courtesies. Leroy and the rest of the crew had been informed of the travel schedule and been "let go" for the day. Terry departed a few hours earlier to take care of some last-minute personal items, and Adam sent Danny home to spend his last night with his wife and kids. Adam had returned the rest of the furniture to the office lease company for a reduction in the final lease payment.

All they could do now was sit back, relax, and wait for the morning.

CHAPTER 10

Adam, Paula, and George took a taxi the next morning to the office parking lot where Oliver and Eleanor were already looking over the four commercial buses that would transport the crew to the airfield. One by one the crew arrived and checked in with Eleanor before they started their trek.

The two Worldwide Services passenger jets landed at the Brown's Island airfield exactly at 1030. The *Kraken* crew loaded their gear and themselves onto four buses sitting on the edge of the runway.

The *Kraken* appeared on the horizon.

Tugs pushed the ship to the pier and held it in place while the crew tied the mooring lines to the pier-side bollards. Once the ship was firmly secured, the crew reboarded the buses and were driven to the dining facility for lunch.

Oliver led Adam, Scott, and Leroy to a group of offices next to the dining hall. Eleanor was already inside setting up computers and filing cabinets. Adam chose an office for himself, and the four men entered and sat around the desk. Oliver discussed the schedule and the critical path of each segment. He stressed that the key to success in this project was to maintain the schedule while also producing high-quality work. By the end of the discussion everyone understood that there was very little room for schedule slippage.

That afternoon Scott and George walked the pier and watched as the Brown's shipyard workforce prepped the ship for the overhaul. George felt like a kid on Christmas morning. He had never seen such a high-tech shipyard.

"And how do they keep it so clean?" The industrial equipment looked brand new, the cranes looked as though they'd never been used, and all of the workers wore uniform coveralls that were stain free. It was almost like standing inside of a huge science laboratory.

George was scheduled to meet with the supervising technician in charge of repairing the engineering plant. He was curious to see how the shipyard was planning on repairing the starboard engine without removing it from the ship.

Danny and Bobby met with the supervisor responsible for bridge and deck maintenance. The ship's exterior was going to be completely resurfaced. This process involved sandblasting, priming, and then painting. Additionally, all deck equipment was being replaced or repaired.

Bobby had generated a list of tools and materials that he needed for the boatswain's locker. He handed that list to the deck-maintenance supervisor, who quickly reviewed the list and replied, "No problem."

Adam was in his office reviewing maintenance documents when Cy tracked him down. Cy began by informing Adam of a few ideas that he believed would help with the Kuwait situation.

"We need an intelligence analyst," Cy began. "We're going into a hot zone where we will need to be aware of the threat. We will need to define and analyze the risks associated with our mission. An intel analyst would give us an edge."

Cy clasped his hands behind his back and leaned toward Adam. "I know a guy. Frank Johnston worked with me at Lockheed. He's a top-notch analyst who is looking for a career change."

"OK," Adam replied. "What have you got?"

Cy slid a sheet of paper across the desk. Adam read the resume while Cy patiently waited.

Adam finished and looked at Cy. "Why is Frank looking for a career change? What's wrong with him?"

Cy bit his lip. "OK. There is more." He looked embarrassed. "About a year ago Frank went through a nasty divorce, which plunged him into debt. During the divorce he kind of went off the deep end and began drinking and hanging out in casinos."

Adam eyed Cy dubiously.

Cy ignored the accusatory look and continued, "Adam, he really is a great analyst. He just went through some bad times. He lost his wife, his kids, and his house. His poor judgment in lifestyle also cost him his clearance and then his job."

Adam interrupted, "Well, if he has no clearance, how can he be an intel analyst?"

"He's still well connected and can get info and intel from a variety of sources." Cy was almost pleading. "Adam, I guarantee that he will prove his worth."

Adam promised Cy that he would think about it. "What else do you have?"

Cy shifted gears. "I've got an idea on how we can get rid of the Iranian patrol boats without using lethal force." Cy pulled out a cut sheet for the long-range acoustic device, or LRAD. "This is a communication device that can be used as a sonic crowd-control weapon."

Cy pointed to the photo on the cut sheet. "But if the tone is amplified and then targeted, individuals can be subjected to a significant amount of sonic pain. Basically, the targeted individuals just want to get away from the loud noise, so they flee from the scene. The LRAD is currently being used by US police and military forces for crowd control and maritime applications."

Cy recommended purchasing two systems. He walked up to Adam's dry-erase board and grabbed a pen. He drew a top-down view of a ship on the office whiteboard.

"These devices," he began as he drew two circles, one on top of the hangar on the starboard side, and the other on top of the port-side hangar, "would be mounted here." He turned to Adam. "We could target a bad guy in almost any direction."

Adam studied the cut sheet and nodded. "I like it. But what happens if this thing doesn't deter our adversaries, or they become more aggressive? What then?"

Cy locked eyes with Adam and smiled. "Adam, at that point we'll have no choice but to defend ourselves."

Adam promised to talk with Oliver about the LRAD.

"Anything else?" Adam asked, expecting Cy to say no.

Cy considered the question. "Actually, there is," he began. "I understand that you're planning on installing anti-submarine warfare torpedoes."

Adam nodded. "Yep. Those are pretty standard for this type of vessel."

Cy returned the nod. "That's true, but do you really expect a submarine threat with this mission?"

Adam leaned back in his chair. "Probably not. Why?"

Cy crossed his arms. "I'd like to have the torpedoes modified for anti-shipping. We can get them to travel about three feet below the waterline."

Adam nodded. "Whatever you think, Cy. Oh," Adam added, "please make sure to inspect every weapons platform as it's being installed. I want to make sure that we will be ready for anything."

The days flew by quickly as the crews worked around the clock. Adam was extremely pleased with the shipyard's progress. The nasty process of sandblasting the main deck and superstructure was finished. Painters were now busy coating the ship's skin with primer and paint before the salt air could begin rusting the exposed metal.

Scott and the department heads were also happy with the work progress. The surface-search radar was repaired and operational, and Terry was busy scheduling and coordinating operations-related training for his team.

Leroy spent his time learning the spaces and ship's operations while getting to know the crew. Adam rarely saw his crew supervisor, but he heard rumors that Leroy was a no-nonsense leader. Adam knew that Leroy held his people accountable for their actions, and he wasn't surprised to overhear a few complaints about the "hard-ass Army sergeant."

True to his word, Adam gave a lot of thought to hiring Frank Johnston. He weighed the pros and cons of Frank's situation and finally agreed to hire him only because Adam was a sucker for a hard-luck case. He called Cy and shared the news that he was hiring Frank, but on one condition. Adam told Cy that Frank would be assigned to Terry as a member of Operations.

During Oliver's next visit to the island, Adam requested the purchase and installation of the LRAD systems. He noticed Oliver's perpetual smile drop a bit when he provided the cut sheets for the two systems. Oliver scanned the documents, then looked back to Adam—his smile had returned. "Adam, this type of weaponry may not be enough to eradicate the threat."

Adam maintained eye contact. "Oliver, as we discussed previously, I'm looking for a nonlethal solution for this operation. I will use conventional weaponry, but only as a last resort."

"Of course." Oliver considered the new request. "I'll see what I can do."

Frank Johnston landed at Brown's Island on a Worldwide Services corporate jet two days later. A waiting van loaded Frank's gear and took him to the office complex.

Adam watched the van pull into the parking area and went out to greet him.

"Frank." Adam smiled and reached for Frank's hand. "Welcome aboard. It's great to finally meet you." He escorted Frank into the office and sat him down. Adam offered water and coffee, but Frank declined.

"Frank," Adam began, "Cy has told me all about you, and I've really been looking forward to meeting you."

Frank smiled thinly and dropped his eyes to the floor. "Told you all about me?" he asked.

Adam waited for Frank to regain eye contact.

"Look," Adam said. His smile dropped a bit but maintained warmth. "I could tell you that I don't care about your past, but I'd be lying. And I don't plan on starting our relationship by lying to you."

Frank looked uncomfortable.

Adam continued, "Cy tells me that you are a hell of an analyst. He also tells me that you had some really bad luck over the past year and that you made that luck worse by heading down the wrong path. Now, I need a sharp intelligence analyst, and you come highly recommended. But I don't need a head case on my staff. We're about to go somewhere that requires us to be constantly focused. I need to know that you are the right guy for this job."

Frank took a deep breath. "Adam, I appreciate you giving me this opportunity. What you said is true. My wife left me after nine years of marriage and took everything that was important to me." Frank narrowed his eyes and leaned toward Adam. "I'm tired of feeling sorry for myself. I've been sober for over six months now, and I want . . . no, I need to get back to doing what I know how to do. I promise you that I will not let you down."

Adam changed subjects. "Were you in the military, Frank?"

"No," he replied. "I have great respect for our soldiers in the service, but I never thought of myself as the hero type."

Adam smiled again. "I'm not looking for heroes. But I need to warn you that you are joining a group of individuals, most of whom have served in the military at one time or another. Once operational, I expect that they will perform in a regimented and disciplined manner. This is going to be an alien concept to you, and I don't want you to feel like the odd man out." Of course, Adam knew it would be inevitable.

Frank shook his head. "It's no problem. I used to work with a lot of former military guys. I think that I'll be OK."

Adam hoped Frank was right.

Two weeks later the crew celebrated the overhaul halfway point at the dining facility. Adam and Oliver agreed that the crew and shipyard workers deserved a much-needed day off, and treated them to a steak and shrimp dinner. There was no alcohol, but the dining hall cooks served ice cream sundaes with all the toppings. Four of the *Kraken* crew brought out musical instruments and played old rock-and-roll songs. Everyone in the dining facility enjoyed the music whether they liked that genre or not.

Doctor Kelly had arrived the day before. He sat at a table with Danny and George and listened to George's lies and sea stories while he shoved spoonfuls of hot fudge into his mouth.

Doc Kelly was what Adam expected a doctor to look like. He was in his mid to late forties, about six feet tall and 190 pounds, with a thick head of graying hair and a matching bushy, grayish mustache. Adam's first impression was positive. The doc seemed very professional and, at the same time, very personable. Doc Kelly also had a dry sense of humor, and Adam laughed at the stories he told about being an intern and about his time in the military.

Adam joined Paula and Scott, who were eating ice cream and talking about 1980s situation comedies. Scott argued that the show *Married with Children* was by far the funniest of that decade.

"Maybe the raunchiest," argued Paula. "But the funniest show was *Seinfeld*."

Scott shook his head violently. "That was a nineties show. You can't count that."

"No, no, no," Paula calmly countered. "Seinfeld premiered in 1989. So there."

Scott laughed. "You're a dork."

"Now, Scott," Adam playfully reprimanded. "That's not very XO-like."

Paula turned to Adam and with a serious look added, "Nothing Scott does is XO-like."

As their laughter died, Adam commented that the ship was really looking good. He was surprised that the LRAD systems had already been received and mounted. Scott mentioned that training on those systems was scheduled to be held later that week.

"Good," Adam replied. He told Scott that all department heads and division officers needed to attend that training. Scott was nodding when Leroy stepped up behind Adam, leaned over, and whispered in Adam's ear.

Adam looked straight forward and then rose from his seat. "Excuse me, guys," he said and then followed Leroy out of the dining facility.

"What's this about?" Adam asked when they were outside and alone.

Leroy looked around to make sure that nobody was listening. "I received an anonymous tip that one of our crew members in Deck Department is distributing amphetamines for profit."

Adam stared into the distance. "Do we have a name?"

"I've narrowed it down to two individuals," Leroy answered. "Carl Stuckey and Darren Turner."

Adam paused while he considered his next action. He locked eyes with Leroy. "OK, please find Scott, Danny, Bobby, and Oliver and meet me in my office in fifteen minutes."

A few minutes later Adam shared the story with the group. Adam directed Bobby and Leroy to find Carl and Darren and escort them to their quarters. Ten minutes later, both accused were standing in front of their respective quarters.

Adam replayed the story and asked each man if the rumors were true. Both men adamantly denied the accusations. Adam asked each of them to open their lockers for an inspection.

Carl immediately moved to his locker, unlocked the door, and stepped to the side. Adam and Leroy pushed aside clothes and reached inside pockets. They opened the locker drawers and searched through all items where they believed someone could hide drugs.

Adam then asked Carl to turn out his pockets. Carl quickly pulled out his coverall pockets. The only items in his pockets were a wallet and locker keys. Adam thanked Carl for his cooperation and apologized for the inconvenience.

Once Carl had departed, Adam asked Darren to open his locker for inspection.

Darren reminded Adam that they were no longer in the military and that it was unconstitutional for Adam to perform a "search and seizure" without probable cause. Adam turned to Scott, who had raised an eyebrow. Adam turned back and asked Darren if he was refusing to cooperate.

Darren looked at the faces of each man in the room. "I'm not refusing anything," answered Darren. "I just feel like I'm being singled out in a witch hunt, and I don't believe that you can legally search my stuff."

Adam nodded and bit his upper lip.

He turned to Scott. "Please terminate Mr. Turner's employment, effective immediately. Work with Danny to box up Mr. Turner's personal belongings and have them delivered to the airfield. Bobby." Adam turned to the bosun. "Will you please escort Mr. Turner to the airfield?" Adam looked around the room and found Oliver. "Would you please arrange air transport for Mr. Turner? I don't care where the plane lands. Just get him off of this island immediately."

Oliver nodded. "We can fly in ninety minutes."

Adam thanked the group and walked out without acknowledging Darren Turner.

With Leroy in tow, Adam turned to the crew supervisor and pointed at the berthing quarters. "I want that piece of shit out of here, and I want the entire crew to see how quickly we made it happen."

Leroy smiled.

The repainting of the ship's exterior was completed a week later.

Danny stood on the foc'sle and admired the fresh coat of haze gray on the superstructure. He was satisfied with the appearance of all deck equipment, including the two anchors and anchor chains.

While traveling aft on the port side, he glanced at the still-empty life-raft brackets. He had been told that an order foul-up had delayed the shipment but that the rafts should arrive within the next forty-eight hours.

As Danny arrived on the fantail, he walked up to the reconstructed capstan and slid his hand across the freshly oiled equipment.

Almost there, he thought.

Paula's crew had been working alongside their shipyard counterparts to clean up and refurbish the officers' wardroom and chief petty officer galley. All berthing areas, including officer staterooms, were completed and ready to be occupied. Terry vocally lauded Paula and anyone else who would listen for the fine work done with his stateroom. The CHT human waste systems were completely flushed, cleaned, and sealed, which now allowed all crew heads to be open and functional.

The ship's cooks and Hasif, as steward, were setting up shop. They stowed food in the pantries and refrigerated goods in the ship's reefers. Doc Kelly had received a huge shipment of medical supplies. He spent his days in sick bay organizing the space, inventorying and securing the controlled medications, and reviewing the crew medical records. Adam, Scott, and the senior officers began bridge-officer refresher training. The team routinely met on the ship's bridge and simulated maneuvers while directing bridge commands with Engineering and CIC.

Terry created a work space for Frank just behind Radio Central. Frank had been communicating with several of his contacts to gain information and intelligence surrounding the Arabian Gulf and the Strait of Hormuz. He provided weekly briefs to Adam and the department heads at their tag-up each Wednesday.

Leroy was becoming well-known by all members of the crew. He enjoyed walking the spaces of the ship and meeting the individuals responsible for each area. The crew equally enjoyed talking with Leroy. They respected the man who they were learning was a disciplinarian who demanded professionalism and accountability.

The ship's weapon systems had been installed, modified, and made operational. Cy reviewed his list of armament. The Mark 32 torpedo was a standard US Navy weapon for anti-submarine warfare. Cy took pride in the fact that these weapons had been modified for surface attacks.

There were two triple-tube launchers, and Cy had four torpedoes in his arsenal; there was the forward 76 mm naval gun, and four .50-caliber machine guns with 20,000 rounds of ammunition. Finally, there were the two LRAD systems. Though these were typically used for communications, Cy was training his team to use them as nonlethal deterrents. There was also a variety of small arms, including 1911 .45-caliber pistols, AR-15 rifles, and 12-gauge shotguns that could be used by his weapons teams in certain circumstances.

Cy knew that the typical frigate was armed with CIWS (close-in weapons system) anti-air Gatling guns, but he felt confident that their ship was well armed for this particular mission and that they would be able to defend themselves against the Iranian fast boats.

The bridge was in relatively good shape. Vic and Danny worked with the shipyard maintenance team to clean and paint the bridge and ensure that the deck grating on the port and starboard bridgewings was sturdy. The team had also inspected the navigation system, which was operating perfectly. Now Vic concentrated on developing a solid library of navigational charts and ensuring that his bridge team was familiar with his system of navigation.

With three weeks to go before sea trials, the *Kraken*'s crew packed up and moved aboard the ship.

The wardroom, galleys, and messes became operational, and the crew was required to operate as if the ship were at sea. The officers and crew were subjected to intense training and drills that included general-quarters "battle stations" drills, firefighting drills, and maneuvering drills. Each day the scenarios became more and more challenging and extreme. The crew was unexpectedly wakened in the middle of the night to fight and defend the ship against imaginary foes.

Danny was relieved when all of the life rafts were received, inspected, and installed. Each member of the crew was then assigned to a life-raft station and trained to locate that particular station should the order to abandon ship be announced.

Two weeks before sea trials, the engineering plant was inspected one final time and then lit off. George sat in Engineering Main Control and monitored the systems for four hours before he turned over the watch to his main propulsion assistant.

"What an amazing system," he gushed as he reviewed the results of the LM2500 engines' performance. All systems from the electrical switchboards to the diesel generators were operating at 95 percent efficiency. George didn't know where these shipyard technicians and maintenance workers came from, but he was extremely happy to work with them on this project.

The engineering plant was finally shut down after forty-eight straight hours of operation, and George and the shipyard team reviewed the data from the plant output. The plant was scheduled to be relit at the beginning of the final week in port. All system tweaking and adjusting would need to be accomplished by that time.

Oliver scheduled a team of inspectors to observe and review the operations of the ship and crew. Crew performance and ship inspections would cover three solid days and nights and would scrutinize the training of the crew as well as their reaction to a variety of situational drills. Adam and Scott were exhausted but very confident that the inspectors' results would be positive.

In the meantime, the crew continued to be trained and drilled.

CHAPTER 11

The big day arrived for Engineering to light off the plant.

The entire shipyard technical team departed the ship and allowed the *Kraken* crew to operate their own systems.

George and his team assembled in their assigned areas. They checked and rechecked all systems. When the system checkoff list was completed, he gave his approval to light the plant. George didn't think it possible, but all adjustments made over the past week had the plant operating at near-perfect efficiency.

Shore power cables were detached and removed from the ship, and the engineering plant was now generating power for the entire ship.

The ship continued to operate as if it were at sea. Watch standers on the bridge, in CIC, in engineering, and on the foc'sle and fantail vigilantly stood four-hour watch tours. Off-duty personnel either rested or conducted routine maintenance checks. All radar and electronic gear were functioning at peak performance while respective technical operators ran and tested each piece of equipment.

The team of inspectors arrived at 1000.

The crew of the *Kraken* performed exceptionally well over the grueling three-day inspection. Reaction times at night as well as in the day were well within limits. All drills were observed and meticulously graded. The inspection team asked to meet with Adam and his officers following the completion of the last drill.

Adam was nervous as he walked to the wardroom. His crew had performed well, but he had also been through numerous Navy inspections where the grades were always subjective.

Hell, Adam thought, *we could be downgraded because some grouchy inspector hadn't had his morning coffee.*

Scott met Adam in the passageway just outside of the wardroom. Scott was sweating and looked like he wanted to vomit. Adam gave a thumbs-up in an effort to calm the XO down. They entered the wardroom to see the inspection team reviewing documents on the table. The rest of the officers sat on the couch, waiting for the debrief.

The inspection team stopped talking, and their supervisor turned to face Adam. The supervisor indicated that the grades for each drill and inspection had been tallied, and though there were some recommendations for additional training, the overall grade for the crew and ship's operation was "satisfactory."

The inspection team supervisor provided Adam with a one-page list of training recommendations. He and the rest of the team congratulated Adam and his officers, and then quickly departed the ship.

Adam wanted to shout for joy. He toured the room and passed his thanks to each member on his leadership team. He then traveled to the quarterdeck and grabbed the microphone to the ship's 1MC intercom system.

He pressed the transmit button and began his first ship's announcement: "Good afternoon, *Kraken,* this is the captain speaking. I've just received the grades from the inspection team, and I'm happy to announce that we have earned a passing grade. We are now cleared for sea trials in two days. Your hard work and professionalism were key to this great success. Congratulations and thank you. Captain out."

He released the transmit button and returned the mic. Adam was floating on cloud nine.

George and his engineers worked with the shipyard team the next day to completely fill all required tanks with fuel, lubricants, and fresh water. Once the tanks were filled, George received word from the bridge that the ship was listing three degrees to the port side. He worked with Gail to right the ship by shifting liquid ballast from port to starboard tanks. The *Kraken* was ready for sea.

The announcement to prepare the ship for sea was given. All members of the crew traveled to their assigned stations in preparation to get underway. Adam and Danny walked the pier one last time, watching the shipyard team assemble to cast off the mooring lines. The crane was already in place and attaching the cable that would lift the brow.

Adam and Danny crossed the brow and waved to Oliver, who watched the evolution from the pier.

Adam made his way to the bridge. "How are we doing?" he asked Scott, who had just entered from the starboard bridgewing.

Scott read from the checklist he was holding. "All stations report ready for underway. We're ready to single up the mooring lines."

Adam smiled as he scanned the bridge. Sailors, his sailors, were manning the bridge stations. Vic reviewed the projected course at the chart table while Scott peered through binoculars, searching for hazards to navigation on the port side.

"Single up lines," Adam ordered the phone talker, and immediately the doubled-up nylon lines that held the ship to the pier were reduced by one. Sixty seconds later, the phone talker reported all lines singled up.

Adam sat in the starboard bridge captain's chair and turned to Scott, who inspected the checklist one final time and then gave Adam a thumbs-up. Adam ordered all lines hauled in. He marveled at Scott's expertise as he maneuvered the ship away from the pier and to the open sea. Scott was a natural. It was as if he had never been away from the bridge. Scott was no banker—he was a sailor! And it was a crime to force him to do anything else.

"Set a course for the training area," Adam ordered Scott. "What is our projected arrival time?"

Vic looked up from the chart table. "We should be at the staging point in one hour."

Adam hopped out of his seat and left the bridge. He traveled quickly to Main Control and entered the engineering space, where he spied George at the far end of the control panel.

"Everything looking good?" he asked. George glanced at Adam and then back to the controls.

"Couldn't be better. I mean that," George added. "I've never seen a system run so well."

"Good," Adam remarked as he left. "Because we're going to start with a full-speed run."

As he walked back to the bridge, Adam ran into Paula on the crew mess decks. She was pointing at something that Adam couldn't see, but Lonnie was busy writing notes.

"How's my favorite pork chop?" he asked. Paula snapped her head around at the sound of Adam's voice. She nodded to Lonnie, who turned and walked into the galley.

"We're looking good. Lonnie and the cooks are securing everything for sea. Seems we forgot to lock down a few things before we left port."

Adam didn't want to know. He gave a quick nod and continued his walk.

Back on the bridge he sat in his chair and watched as the ship slowed to the staging point. Scott announced that Engineering was ready to begin the first run.

The first day ended successfully. All engineering and navigation drills were run and re-run to test the ship's capabilities. Adam and his team were extremely satisfied with the results.

Sitting in his chair on the bridge, he thought of all the bridge watches he stood during his naval career. *Hours and hours on your feet scanning the horizon to ensure that potential navigational threats were identified before they became an issue.*

George entered the bridge and leaned against the forward window, snapping Adam out of his daydream.

"So, still sitting in comfy chairs on the bridge, huh?"

Adam chuckled. "Still," he confirmed.

"Never sailed on a ship with a plant this strong," George remarked. "She's truly a beauty. Your CIA spook did good."

Adam did wonder who Oliver was and who he really worked for, but at this point, it didn't matter. He told George to go and get something to eat and a good night's rest. Round two was scheduled for tomorrow. Adam wanted George rested and ready.

The ship's senior leaders met on the bridge at 0600 the next morning. Once all reports were received, Adam told the team to get on station—navigation and weapons drills would begin at 0700.

Adam glanced at Leroy. The old soldier looked terrible. He was unshaven, his sunken eyes had dark rings underneath, and he seemed a little green. He asked Leroy to remain on the bridge after the rest of the staff departed.

"Are you feeling OK?" Adam asked.

Leroy nodded and covered his mouth as he belched. "I've felt better. Never been on the ocean before. I'm having a little trouble adjusting to being inside a room that's constantly moving."

Adam widened his eyes and laughed. "You're seasick?" Adam's grin grew. "So much for the easy life of a squid."

Leroy was in no mood to be screwed with. "If you're quite finished," he slurred, "I'm going down to my rack to lie down."

Adam's smile softened. He placed his hand on Leroy's shoulder. "Go down to the crew's galley and get some saltine crackers. They will help soak up the fluid in your stomach. Then go out on deck and get some air."

Leroy eyed Adam dubiously.

"I know it sounds like the opposite of what you want," Adam continued. "But trust me, you'll feel better in a while."

Leroy nodded and left the bridge.

Adam happened to glance at the helmsman, who was grinning. "We've all been there," Adam reminded the sailor.

"Amen, sir." The smiling sailor turned to mind his helm.

Cy and Terry met in CIC to prepare for the weapons-firing exercises. Terry directed his team from the chair mounted in the center of CIC, while Cy sat and faced his console. He pulled the key ring from his pocket and rubbed the .308 bullet between his thumb and forefinger. He closed his eyes and smiled as visions of combat and battle flashed through his mind. The smooth metallic touch of the dead rifle round aroused and excited him.

Terry's order to begin the drills snapped Cy away from his thoughts.

He shoved the key into his pocket and focused on the firing scenarios.

Cy and Terry coordinated the plan to engage, track, and hit every target and hazard that was thrown at them. Throughout the day they off-handedly remarked to each other that their teams must have gained wisdom and experience since their days on active duty because there was much less emotion and a great deal more focus.

Cy lit up the LRADs and ran each system for two hours. He then directed his team to quickly mount and fire each .50-caliber gun. He wanted to be out on deck shooting the guns but begrudgingly remained in CIC to supervise the drill sets. He also wanted to fire the torpedoes but, because of the limited number of torpedoes on board, opted to test-fire them instead.

When the drills ended, Cy leaned back in his chair in CIC. He congratulated himself on a successful performance, secretly hoping that they would soon have the opportunity to use the weapons for real.

The *Kraken* returned to Brown's Island after three days of high-powered and dynamic sea trials. Adam and his team did their best to twist and shake the thirty-year-old ship, but the *Kraken* was as strong and powerful as the day it was first launched.

Though they were moored at the pier, Adam kept the ship running under its own power. He allowed anyone not on duty to go ashore and relax for the brief shore-leave period. Once the brow was secured to the pier, Adam, Scott, and the department heads met with Oliver at the office complex.

Oliver stood from his desk and pumped Adam's hand. "Welcome back," he greeted the team while he flashed his smile. "Did you have any problems? Did everyone survive?"

Adam sat as the team crowded in behind him. "The ship ran great. No problems at all. The only personnel casualty was that Leroy suffered a nasty bout of seasickness."

George snickered. "Seasickness."

Oliver threw back his head and laughed. "Well, I hope that he's recovering."

Adam and his team briefed Oliver on the sea trials, the inspections, and the crew's performance. Oliver praised Adam, the department heads, and the entire crew.

"Now," he continued, "are you confident in the abilities of the ship and crew? Do you believe that they are able to perform and complete the operation?"

Adam turned to his department heads. Paula and Scott nodded while the others remained silent. Adam turned back to Oliver. He raised his chin and confidently stated, "We're ready."

The *Kraken* left port at high tide the next morning.

Adam sat on the starboard bridge captain's chair, watching the sea and anchor evolution while Scott navigated the ship out of the harbor. As the ship sailed into open water, Scott walked to the starboard side and stood next to Adam.

"Some of the crew asked me to talk with you about something," Scott began, peering out of the bridge windows. "We're going to be crossing the equator in a couple weeks, and several of them want to know if you would approve a shellback initiation ceremony."

Adam turned his head toward Scott. "Are you kidding me?"

Scott shook his head. "Nope. Apparently, we have about fifteen members of the crew who have never crossed the equator, and because of that, they are still slimy pollywogs." Scott grinned. "That includes Leroy."

Adam chuckled. "Do we even have the supplies to do that?"

"From what I understand," Scott continued, "the appropriate materials and supplies have been brought on board. We're talking about a good old-fashioned shellback crossing that will include feeding our pollywogs nasty-tasting stuff like *patis*—you know, that Filipino fish sauce? It would do for the truth serum." Scott paused. "One of our saltier crewmembers even brought a Jolly Roger flag on board. The skull and crossbones." Scott again looked at Adam. "What do you think?"

Adam gazed thoughtfully out of the starboard bridge window. He turned to Scott. "I would never think of getting in the way of hundreds of years of maritime tradition. Sure, tell them that we'll have a shellback ceremony." Adam raised a finger. "But you need to also tell them that I expect the decks to be fully cleaned after the ceremony. I don't want the ship smelling like fish sauce."

Scott smiled and headed back to his station.

"One thing, Scott." Adam lowered his finger and pointed at Scott as the XO performed a perfectly executed about-face. A devilish grin appeared on Adam's face. "Leroy is my pollywog on that day."

Scott smiled and snapped a two-finger salute. "Wouldn't have it any other way."

The following morning, Danny and Paula were quietly sipping coffee in the wardroom when the door slammed open. Both jumped and swung around in their seats. Terry, his face beet red, charged into the space, stopped, and quickly snapped his head from left to right as he scanned the wardroom. Paula noticed a highly visible vein protruding from Terry's neck.

"Where is that so-called engineer?" Terry shouted.

"Are you looking for George?" Danny asked as he sipped his coffee.

"Yes! George! Who else would I be talking about?" Terry was extremely agitated. He placed his hands on his hips and leaned toward Danny. "I have suffered enough of his shenanigans. First an ice-cold shower and then the power in my stateroom goes out. I know that he purposely . . . I know that he's behind this."

Danny turned to Paula, smiled, and turned back to Terry. "Haven't seen him," Danny simply replied.

"Haven't seen who?" George ambled into the wardroom. "Morning," he said as he poured a cup of coffee.

Terry matched George's steps and stopped directly behind the engineer.

"I know that you purposely turned the water cold when I got into the shower." Terry's hands remained on his hips. He resembled a tall chicken as he bent forward and looked up at George. "You also turned off the electrical power in my stateroom."

George slowly turned to face Terry. He sipped his coffee, then glanced at Paula and Danny, who were enjoying the moment.

George shrugged. "I'm not sure why you had cold water and no power in your stateroom this morning. C'mon, Ops, think about it. Do you know how difficult it would be to shut off hot water to one person's shower at the exact moment when that person got into it? And do you know how hard it would be to isolate a stateroom's electrical power and, again, shut it off exactly at the moment when that person entered the space? I'd need spies and perfect coordination to perform a feat of that magnitude. You're giving me way too much credit."

George took another sip from his cup.

Terry gritted his teeth. The vein on his neck seemed to pulse.

George pointed his coffee cup toward Terry. "What I can do is take a look at these issues as soon as I get back to Main Control, though."

The color in Terry's cheeks returned to normal. He glanced at George one last time, turned, and stalked out of the space.

George, Paula, and Danny heard a faint "thank you" as Terry disappeared.

George leaned against the wardroom counter and faced Paula and Danny.

He smiled. "Yep, I'd need some serious spies and coordination for a prank of that magnitude," he said as he winked.

Morning tag-up on the bridge was held as usual. No surprises were brought up, and discussions were bland and routine.

Adam did notice that Terry seemed a bit upset about something. He also observed that Leroy was still a little green around the gills. It didn't help that Cy, standing next to Leroy, was purposefully eating smoked sardines from a small tin. Cy would tip back his head, slide a small fish into his mouth, and then suck it down. The noise of the fish being sucked into Cy's mouth was enough to affect the old soldier. Leroy excused himself from the bridge immediately after the conclusion of tag-up.

Adam stopped Cy and asked him what he was doing.

Cy tossed the sardine tin into a small waste can and looked at Adam. "Just having a little fun." Cy licked his fingers. "You know the funny part?" Cy asked as Adam raised his eyes. "I don't even like sardines."

Adam gave a short laugh. "Just be careful. I believe that Leroy could be a formidable and devious opponent."

Cy smirked and started walking away.

"Hey, Cy!" The weapons officer turned back. Adam pointed to the trash can. "Take your fish tin with you. Don't want the bridge smelling like sardines all day."

The port-side door to the bridgewing opened, and Bobby entered with two large young men. Adam recognized them as part of Danny's team of boatswain's mates. They were obviously brothers and probably twins due to the remarkable resemblance to each other.

Bobby led them to Adam.

"Morning, Captain," Bobby began. "I'd like to introduce you to my two nephews, Timmy and Tom Rauske."

Both brothers leaned forward and extended their hands. Adam responded and noticed how his hand fit neatly in those monstrous palms. *These guys are huge!* Adam thought. *Probably farm boys from Nebraska or Oklahoma.*

"I'm going out on a limb here," Adam said as he smiled. "I'm going to bet that you're twins."

Tim and Tom glanced quickly at each other and then back to Adam. They nodded in unison and replied, "Yes sir."

Adam turned to Bobby. "They don't say much, do they?"

Bobby reached up and clapped a hand on the shoulder of each nephew. He grinned. "Only when they have something important to say."

Adam nodded. "Glad to have you on board. We need good men to take care of Bobby when we hit port."

Bobby laughed and escorted his nephews off the bridge. "Back to work," he growled as he shut the door.

That afternoon when Adam met with Scott, George, Paula, and Vic they discussed the need to take on supplies and fuel before heading southeast for the trek to the Middle East. Adam directed Vic to plot a course for Pearl Harbor, Hawaii, then asked Paula to communicate with her logistics contacts to request supplies and fuel. They agreed to provide status at tomorrow's tag-up.

Later that evening, Paula went searching for Adam and found him in CIC reviewing the LRAD systems.

"Do you have a minute?" she asked.

Adam nodded and escorted her to his at-sea cabin located behind the bridge. He sat on his bed and motioned for Paula to pull up the metal chair next to the small desk.

"What's up?" he asked.

"We have a problem." Paula began. "I've contacted just about every logistician and maritime supplier in Pearl Harbor, but we are being denied entry to the port." She brushed aside the hair that had fallen over her right eye. "Apparently, we are being denied access because we and the *Kraken* are considered a mercenary platform, and that type of vessel or organization isn't welcome in a United States port."

Adam stared at her. He couldn't hide the shocked look on his face.

"Unbelievable. Mercenaries? Who is calling us mercenaries?" Adam shut his eyes and sighed.

"There's more," Paula said, and Adam regained eye contact with her. "Do you remember our good friend Agent Maria Wilson from the Department of Homeland Security?"

Adam leaned forward. "Sure. Why?"

Paula continued, "Well, Agent Wilson emailed me. She is in Pearl Harbor and asking to fly out to the ship for an inspection."

"Craaapppp!" was all that Adam could muster. "I completely forgot about her." Adam tilted his head back and considered banging it against the ship's steel bulkhead.

He suddenly sat up.

"Hey, can you contact Oliver from out here?"

"I believe so," she answered.

"Give him a call and tell him what's going on. Ask if he can get involved and if there's anything that he can do for us. You never know, maybe he has another secret island somewhere around Hawaii where we can take on fuel."

Paula quickly left the stateroom.

Why does it always have to be a fight? Adam thought as he closed his eyes.

The next morning Adam began the day by walking the main decks. He ended on the fantail, where he stretched his arms high and took a deep breath of the clean ocean air. He felt wonderful.

As he exhaled, he thought, *This is what heaven must be like.*

He stepped further onto the fantail and noticed what looked like trash scattered on the deck. Upon closer inspection he saw that it was actually flying fish that had been active the previous night, having tried to fly over the fantail but only making it halfway. Adam had seen this many times before, and he thought that it was both sad and funny to see the failed results of what must have seemed to these little fish as a reachable goal.

Looking at the fish, he considered the *Kraken*'s mission and hoped that no such fate awaited him, the ship, and his crew as they set out for their reachable goal.

At tag-up Adam briefed the department heads and Leroy of the situation with the Pearl Harbor refueling request. George laughed when he heard that Agent Wilson wanted to inspect the ship.

"I knew that she was a peach the moment we met," he quipped. "Won't she be surprised to see our cruise liner now?"

Adam ignored George. "Paula has been in contact with Oliver and has briefed him on the situation. We're hoping that he can quickly come up with a solution for supplies and refueling."

Paula raised her hand. "Actually, I just got off the phone with Oliver, and he's asking how comfortable we are with performing an UNREP."

Danny's mouth dropped open. He quickly composed himself and asked, "We're going to do an underway replenishment?"

Adam was expressionless. "No, Danny, Oliver is asking how comfortable we would be with that."

Danny scanned his fellow department heads. He was exasperated. "Adam, we haven't trained for that. The last time I did an UNREP was over eight years ago. I can't be sure of the last time that any of my team did that either."

Adam frowned. "I know. Me too," he admitted. "But I really don't think that we have much of a choice." Adam looked at Paula. "What's Oliver's plan?"

Paula quickly glanced at the group and then turned to Adam.

"We're going to have a replenishment ship alongside us in four days."

Danny shouted, "Four days?!"

Adam looked to Danny and remained calm. "Can we be ready by then?"

Danny shook his head and laughed. He walked to the starboard bridge window and stared into the distance. After a few moments Danny turned and straightened his posture. "We'll be ready. I picked Bobby as our bosun because he's the best. If anyone can have our guys trained and ready—it's him." Danny returned his gaze to the window. "I only hope that we have good weather."

Adam looked at George. "How about it, George?" Adam asked. "Are you up for an UNREP?"

"Sure thing, boss," George answered smugly. "We'll be ready."

Leroy and Scott waited for the rest of the team to leave the bridge.

"What's an UNREP?" Leroy asked.

"It's an acronym for underway replenishment. We're going to refuel at sea with another ship," answered Adam. "It sounds easier than it truly is," he added.

"Basically," Scott interjected, "there's a delivery ship full of fuel. They set the course and speed. We steam up behind it, and once we're alongside, we match the course and speed. Then the delivery ship sends over fueling lines, we connect them, and they pump fuel to us while we both steam forward."

Leroy looked from Scott to Adam. "This sounds like a dangerous operation."

Adam nodded. "It is. We need to constantly stay parallel to the delivery ship while also maintaining the same speed and distance, or our two ships could collide."

All three men were quiet.

Scott broke the silence. "Maintaining a course isn't the biggest problem. The hard part is doing it as both ships negotiate the moving seas. High waves will push you into the other ship if you're not careful."

Leroy looked more green than usual.

Adam, Scott, Danny, and George planned the UNREP and the crew assignments. Scott agreed to take the bridge during the evolution so that Adam could focus on all of the fueling stations.

All that morning, the ship and crew drilled on underway evolutions. Bobby was a tyrant who pushed for deck-performance perfection while breaking some sailors' old habits. Leroy volunteered to help work a fueling rig. He quietly watched Bobby and the other veterans go through the motions of receiving the shot line and hauling in the fueling lines that would ultimately be attached to their ship.

Bobby clapped Leroy's shoulder on the way to the chief's mess after the morning drills. "You did good out there," complimented the old bosun. "You'd have made a fair boatswain's mate."

Leroy smiled.

Training and drills continued for the next two days. After the ninth evolution, Danny told Adam that the crew was as ready as they'd ever be.

Adam and Scott were discussing the next day's evolution when Paula walked on the bridge. She approached Adam and handed her cell phone to him.

"Agent Wilson," she said simply.

Adam took the phone. "Agent Wilson, what a pleasure it is to hear from you."

"Hello, Mr. Decker." Adam heard that flat delivery in Agent Wilson's voice. "I understand that you are not willing to undergo an inspection provided by the Department of Homeland Security."

Adam's mind raced to remember what Oliver had prepped him to say.

"Agent Wilson," Adam began, "that is completely untrue. We experienced difficulty in obtaining permission to refuel in Pearl Harbor, so we were forced to make other arrangements. Regrettably these arrangements take us out of United States territorial waters, where I understand you are unable to perform any type of inspections." Adam smiled. "I believe it has something to do with jurisdictional authority."

Agent Wilson's response was carefully worded and delivered without emotion.

"Mr. Decker, your request for entrance to Pearl Harbor and the subsequent refueling were only refused until your ship had undergone a thorough inspection. I thought that this was completely understood. I request that you turn your vessel toward the United States naval station in Pearl Harbor where you will prepare to be boarded by a Department of Homeland Security team. At that time, you will be inspected for weapons, illegal narcotics, and other types of contraband."

Agent Wilson paused and continued after a few moments. "Once you have been cleared for entry, you and your crew will be allowed to visit the port to purchase supplies and other logistics while allowing your crew time on the island for leisure and relaxation."

It was Adam's turn to pause. "Agent Wilson," Adam replied, "I understand your requirements and request. However, as I previously stated, we have changed course and have made other arrangements for supplies and fuel. Once completed we will then sail into open waters for a three-month shakedown cruise. I will communicate with you as we prepare our return so that we may discuss inspections with your team. I do apologize for any inconvenience and hope to see you soon."

"Mr. Decker," the agent responded dryly, "you obviously have associates who are tied closely with senior organizations in the United States government."

Adam raised his eyebrows through the ensuing silence.

"I have been directed to allow your vessel to pass through US territorial waters without forcibly performing inspections. I have also been directed to allow you passage without pursuit."

Adam could hear the frustration in her cold voice.

"I must tell you, though, that once you return, I will personally ensure that you, your ship, and your cargo are meticulously inspected before any of your crew are allowed entrance back to a United States port. I'm sure that you already know this, but should we find anything in your vessel that ties you to any sort of illicit or illegal activity, your entire crew will be detained and you will be prosecuted to the highest levels that our laws allow."

Adam wondered who Oliver knew to get Agent Wilson so pissed off.

"Wow," he replied. "I guess you and I won't be seeing each other socially, will we?"

Another long pause. "I hope you have a nice day, Mr. Decker," Agent Wilson responded icily. "I'm sure that you and I will be meeting soon."

Adam handed the phone back to Paula. "George was right. She's nice," he said as Paula chuckled and shook her head.

Much to Danny's disappointment, there was heavy cloud cover the next morning as the *Kraken* approached the UNREP rendezvous point.

The delivery ship was flying a United States flag but had no markings or name on the hull.

"Never seen an oiler like this," Scott admitted as they neared the fueling ship.

Chatter over the radio had been constant for the past twenty-five minutes. The bridge officer on the oiler was curt and professional as he directed the speed and course for the evolution.

A true artist, Scott maneuvered the *Kraken* into position and slowly pulled alongside of the huge tanker. The *Kraken* was 150 feet off the port beam when Scott slowed down to match the delivery ship's speed. Once the two ships were cruising in a parallel course, the deck crew from the oiler fired a shot line to the *Kraken*.

The *Kraken* crew hauled in the shot line, which was in turn attached to the phone-and-distance, or P&D, line—a sound-powered telephone cable that, once connected to each ship's bridge, allowed the two ships to communicate with each other.

Two more lines were delivered to the *Kraken*'s refueling stations and attached to larger fueling rigs. While the *Kraken* was being fueled, a highline cable-and-pulley system was strung between the two ships. Crates of food and other consumable supplies were transferred from the oiler to *Kraken*.

The fueling evolution lasted three hours. It would have been a flawless event except that one fueling hose did not initially seat correctly to the *Kraken*'s rig, and forty gallons of fuel sprayed on the warship's deck.

The highlight of the day was Leroy's seamanship during the evolution. He was quickly becoming an experienced sailor. His wisdom, however, was lacking when one of the shot lines was dropped and became loose. Leroy unknowingly reached down and grabbed the fast-moving line before he could be warned. The nylon line ripped through Leroy's hand and burned off two inches of skin from his palm. Leroy was told to go to sick bay, but the old soldier refused to leave until the entire evolution had been completed. He earned great respect from the old bosun and the entire deck team for his toughness and dedication.

Pumping ceased when the ship's fuel tanks were filled.

Scott gave the order to steer slightly left in order to create distance between the two ships.

While the *Kraken* pulled away from the delivery ship, Scott addressed Adam, who was seated in his bridge chair. "Excuse me, Mon Capitan."

Adam turned his attention to the XO.

"Back in the day we would play a breakaway song when we completed an UNREP." Scott smiled. "It just so happens that we have one ready to play . . . with your permission of course."

Adam waved a hand in a gesture of approval.

Scott pointed to the bridge bosun, who keyed the 1MC intercom mic and hit play on his CD player. AC/DC's "Highway to Hell" blared over every 1MC speaker on the ship.

Adam turned quickly and saw Scott smiling. The XO shrugged. "Seemed appropriate."

Adam rose from his chair and laughed. He yelled for the ship's navigator: "Vic, set a course for Papua, New Guinea."

After dinner Adam and George grabbed a cup of coffee and toured the main decks. The sky had cleared, and the temperature was a nice, balmy seventy-five degrees. They worked their way forward to the foc'sle where they quietly sipped their coffee and leaned against the starboard lifelines.

The sun was just beginning to set. The ocean on the horizon appeared to be on fire.

"I've always loved to watch the sun set on the ocean," Adam confessed as he gazed into the distance. "And there's no better way to see it than when you're steaming at sea."

George nodded slowly. "I agree," he said. "Sunrises are beautiful too. Even powerful." He paused as he considered a moment from years past. "Back when I was much younger," he shared, "I was at sea on Easter morning."

He turned to look at Adam. A smile crossed his lips. "I was serving onboard the *Midway* at that time." George slowly glanced back at the horizon. "Our ship's chaplain scheduled a sunrise service in the hangar. I remember that there was a pretty good-sized crowd attending."

He sipped his coffee and continued. "As the chaplain finished his sermon, the elevator to the flight deck opened, and the ship was positioned so that we could observe the morning's sunrise."

George squinted at the memory of the bright light entering the ship's hangar. "I saw the most beautiful sunrise that I have ever seen. The sun was this massive fireball. When it climbed into the sky, I truly believed that the entire ocean was on fire. I'm not sure if it was the sermon or the sunrise"—George locked eyes with Adam—"or the combination of the two. But it was the most religious moment . . . the most powerfully religious moment of my life."

Adam had rarely seen George speak so candidly about his

personal reflections and never heard George speak of religion.

George continued, "I believe that God has a special relationship with the ocean and that every now and then . . ." George smiled and repeated softly, "Every now and then I believe that he allows us mere mortals to witness that beauty and power."

George looked out over the ocean and was silent.

Later that evening, Adam made one last sweep to the bridge before heading to his stateroom for the night.

Danny was standing bridge-officer duty and staring through binoculars out of the port-side window. He turned at the sound of the bridge door opening to see Adam entering.

"I was just going to call you," Danny said. He handed the binoculars to Adam. "We have a contact bearing one hundred and sixty degrees relative. We haven't attempted radio contact yet, but it appears to be a US warship."

Adam took the binoculars and scanned the horizon. He spotted a ship positioned approximately three miles off the port beam and steaming a parallel course with the *Kraken*.

"Looks like a cruiser," Adam said. "Wonder what she's doing out here?" He handed the binoculars back to Danny. "Keep an eye on her and let me know if she tries to contact us."

CHAPTER 12

Hasif set the plate of scrambled eggs, sausage, and toast on the wardroom table directly in front of Adam. "What would you like to drink?" he asked his captain.

"Coffee, please."

The steward set the steaming cup on the table next to the plate.

"Hasif." Adam looked at his steward. "Where are you from originally?"

Hasif set two dirty plates on the wardroom counter and turned back to Adam. "I was born in Kandovan, Iran, and lived there until my parents received approval to emigrate to the United States. I was almost six years old at that time. We moved to Virginia Beach, and that's where I grew up."

Adam lowered his head and pursed his lips. "That's it? That's the shortest biography I've ever heard."

Hasif smiled and shrugged. Adam wondered if Hasif was very secretive or if there really wasn't any more to tell.

"Do you still have family in Iran?"

Hasif grabbed a dishcloth and wiped down the counter. "My grandparents died when I was very young. I believe that my father has a sister still living in Iran, but we have lost contact with her."

Adam took a sip of his coffee. "Do you speak Persian?" Adam asked.

"Oh yes," Hasif answered. "I am fluent in Persian, Arabic, Turkish, and, of course, English."

Adam nodded and considered this new piece of information.

"If we ever needed it, would you feel comfortable helping me as a translator or communicator?"

"Captain," replied Hasif, "I would be proud to help you in any capacity."

Adam finished his coffee, refilled the cup, and headed up to the bridge. Vic had the deck.

"Is that warship still tailing us?" he asked the navigator.

Vic was leaning over the chart table and studying the ship's position. He stood, placed his hands on his hips, and arched his back. "Ugh," Vic groaned. "I'm stiff as a board."

He walked to the port bridgewing and looked at the horizon.

"Yep, she's still with us."

Adam squinted out of the port window until he saw the ship's silhouette.

"Wonder what they want?"

Vic lowered the binoculars. "Probably just curious." He turned his head toward his captain. "I'm guessing that they're wondering the same thing."

Adam walked aft, rounded the superstructure, and climbed up the ladder to the signal bridge. He pushed his forehead against the head guard of the ship's binoculars and stared into the optics. The "Big Eyes" was a very powerful set of large binoculars mounted to the ship's railing.

He swiveled the eyepieces until he found the cruiser. Adam heard footsteps on the deck grating behind him, and he turned to see Scott looking in the direction of the other warship.

Adam turned back and scanned the ship through the Big Eyes. "It's a cruiser all right." He adjusted the focus and the image became much clearer. "Might be the *Cowpens* or maybe the *Port Royal*. Can't tell from this distance." Adam pulled away and furrowed his brow. "Wonder why she's following us?"

Scott shrugged. "Not sure. You weren't exactly hospitable to our friend in Homeland Security. Maybe she contacted a few of her connections to have us tailed."

"Don't think so." Adam walked closer to Scott. "Agent Wilson told me that she was directed to avoid pursuing us." He paused. "She seems pretty straitlaced. Doesn't appear to be the type to blow off orders or directions."

Both Adam and Scott returned to the bridge. Adam asked Vic to call if the cruiser got any closer or if it looked like she was changing course to intercept.

Adam's head ached. He entered his at-sea cabin and looked through his locker for a bottle of Advil. There were bottles of vitamins, some antacid, and even meds for his occasional gout flare-ups, but no headache pain reliever.

He called Doc Kelly in sick bay, who told Adam to come on down.

Adam knocked before entering. He scrunched his nose and squinted at the strong odor of cleaning alcohol and ammonia. Doc Kelly was reading an article on his computer about the Zika virus. The doc pushed his glasses to his forehead, rubbed his eyes, and greeted Adam.

"What can I do for you, Captain?"

"Can you spare a couple of aspirin?" Adam asked. "I need to take the edge off this headache."

Doc Kelly opened his pharmaceutical locker and retrieved a large bottle of pills. He popped off the lid and measured out a dose of Tylenol while Adam casually inspected the medical space.

"Got things looking good," Adam remarked as he pulled down and examined a blood pressure cuff.

The doctor gave Adam a once-over. "Having trouble with your blood pressure?"

Adam apologized for touching the equipment and quickly returned the cuff to its original location. He sat on the medical bed and let out a sigh.

"Something on your mind?" Doc Kelly filled a small pill bottle with twenty capsules of the pain reliever. "You know," the doctor said as he counted, "physicians and bartenders are the best people to listen to your troubles."

Adam chuckled, "Oh, you know, Doc, the same old story. Boy wants a boat. Boy buys a boat. Boy becomes responsible for a boat that's heading into a hostile fire zone."

Adam looked at his shoes, flicked off a piece of dirt, and sighed again. He raised his head and looked at the doctor. Doc Kelly was quietly watching him.

He continued, "I always wanted to command a ship. Never thought that I'd ever captain a fully functional warship. Especially one headed into the Arabian Gulf." He shook his head. "I sure hope that I'm ready for this."

Doc Kelly handed the bottle of pills to Adam. He sat at his desk and leaned back.

"I'm the first to admit that I'm no maritime expert. Before I showed up, I actually purchased three books on ships and sailing just so I'd be a little familiar with the sailor's vocabulary." Doc Kelly smiled and Adam mustered a small laugh. "But I do know a leader when I see one. This is one fine ship, Adam. You and your friends have taken a shell and turned it into a viable wartime platform."

Adam remained silent.

Doc Kelly leaned forward. "I have to be honest, when I first met you I was on the fence whether I believed that you could captain this ship. But I was sold after watching you expertly maneuver the ship during the refueling at sea."

Adam returned the smile. "Scott had the deck during that evolution. He deserves the credit for the maneuvering."

Doc Kelly nodded and pulled his glasses back to the bridge

of his nose. "Scott was definitely driving the ship, but you were in command. You had presence. You directed. You led. You were in charge! And you never flinched." Doc Kelly tilted his head to the side and maintained eye contact with Adam. "You, sir, in my humble opinion, are a natural ship's captain."

"You are gracious and way too kind." Adam was grateful to hear this—even from a non-sailor.

Doc Kelly raised his eyebrows. "Am I? I'm very critical with my observations. I appreciate the fact that you question your abilities and, honestly, I applaud that. Any man who believes that he is all knowing is full of crap and most likely a very insecure individual. On the other hand, a man who questions his abilities is a man who is willing to listen to others and never settle for the status quo."

Doc Kelly stood and went back to his pharmaceutical locker, pulling out a bottle of Ron Zacapa XO rum.

He smiled at Adam. "I wouldn't be on board if I didn't believe in you. Trust me on that." He broke the seal on the bottle. "Now, let's have a drink." He turned and looked at Adam, then the bottle, and back to Adam. "For medicinal purposes, of course."

Scott, Paula, George, Lonnie, and Vic gathered at the wardroom table as Hasif set the table for the evening meal.

George and Scott were telling Lonnie about all of the horrible and disgusting tasks and tests that he would endure during the crossing-the-equator ceremony in two days.

Scott smiled. "I'm looking forward to seeing this young lad meet the royal baby."

George locked eyes with Lonnie and growled, "I'm looking forward to seeing you go through the trough."

Lonnie faked a whimper and then began laughing. "Don't you two idiots remember? I crossed the line back when I was on the *Boxer*. With you! I'm already a shellback."

Lonnie opened his wallet, pulled out his shellback card, and flashed it at Scott and George.

"In your face!" Lonnie shouted.

Scott looked stunned and embarrassed.

George laughed, "OK then. If I can't get you, then I get the doc as my wog dog."

Adam opened the door to the wardroom. He caught the savory aroma of chicken in the oven. He stopped, closed his eyes, and inhaled deeply.

He asked Hasif, "Baked chicken tonight?"

Hasif nodded. "We also have au gratin potatoes and green beans." Hasif placed his index finger on his chin. "And I believe our chef has prepared apple pie for dessert."

Adam smiled and took a seat at the table. "What's up?" he asked the group.

Lonnie turned to Adam. "Just listening to these two geezers and their memory problems," he said, pointing to Scott and George.

Before Adam could respond, Scott began, "Hey, just got a call from Danny. Looks like our friend, the cruiser, has peeled off and is no longer trailing us."

"Interesting," Adam said as Hasif set a bowl of soup in front of him. "Looks like it's going to be a nice dinner."

Later than evening, Adam and Paula took a walk through the main deck spaces. They stopped on the mess decks and watched a group of older sailors discussing preparations for the equator ceremony.

Adam leaned toward Paula. "It's funny," he whispered. "They're so excited. They act like they're still in their twenties."

Paula raised her head slightly and sniffed. "Something's burning." She and Adam walked toward the galley. A thin layer of black smoke hung over the oven. The ship's baker explained that one of the apple pies had flowed over, and some of the filling was covering the oven floor and burning. He told Paula that he would thoroughly clean it once he finished baking bread for the night.

Adam waved to Paula and left the galley. The older sailors were gone. Adam noticed two sailors watching a movie on the mess-deck television, and another two were playing cribbage on the opposite side of the space.

Aside from the humming of the ship's engine and the noise coming from the television, the ship was relatively quiet.

Adam smiled. He always enjoyed evenings at sea. Everyone was tired from the day's work, and unless you were standing a watch, you found some way to relax. Some crewmembers enjoyed reading, some watched movies, and others worked out in the small gym. Everyone had some method of decompressing.

He uttered a small laugh as he remembered a group of sailors on his first ship who would get together each night and play Dungeons and Dragons. *Even sailors can be nerdy*, he thought.

He walked past the door to the chief's mess and knocked. A few seconds passed and the door opened a crack. Alvin Flageolle, the Weapons Department supervisor, poked his head into the passageway.

"Evening, Captain." Alvin grinned. "Fancy seeing you in our neck of the woods."

Alvin opened the door wide and invited Adam inside. Bobby Hardesty and Frank Johnston were playing cards at the mess table. They saw Adam and stood to greet him.

Adam said hello, and gestured both men to sit.

"Cup of coffee?" Bobby asked as he poured a cup.

"I've never turned down a cup of coffee in my life," Adam said as he accepted the cup.

He scanned the mess. The space was tidy and had several comforts from home. He saw a library of DVD movies, a small stereo, and an espresso machine.

Bobby sipped his coffee. "What brings you down here, Captain?"

"Just slumming," Adam answered.

Bobby gave a short laugh.

Adam and the chiefs chatted about the crew, ship operations, and future events. They talked about anticipated challenges and Adam's expectations.

When the discussion came to a close, Adam asked if the chiefs were looking forward to the equator-crossing ceremony. Bobby indicated that there were twelve members of the crew who were still slimy pollywogs. He opened his notebook and showed Adam the recommended schedule of events. Adam reviewed the schedule and saw that Bobby had a day of fun planned.

"I see that you will be playing King Neptune," Adam remarked.

"Yes sir," Bobby answered. "Alvin here is playing Davy Jones." Bobby looked at Frank. "And young Frank is still a slimy pollywog. Because of that he will be my personal wog dog."

Bobby turned to Adam. "I only mention this because someone much more senior than me has already claimed our esteemed crew supervisor, and only soldier, as his own personal wog dog."

Adam laughed. "Guilty as charged." He raised his arms in mock surrender. "Having a soldier, and one of my former bosses, as a personal pollywog is a once-in-a-lifetime opportunity that I just couldn't pass up. Do you blame me?"

Bobby laughed hard. "Since you put it that way, nope. Not one bit."

Adam thanked the chiefs for the time and the coffee, then walked to his cabin to retire for the evening.

A CIC watch stander called the bridge at 0130 the next morning as Danny stood watch as the bridge officer.

"Bridge, this is Combat," the watch stander announced. "We have a surface contact bearing one-nine-zero degrees at approximately nine thousand yards, and cruising at twenty-nine knots." The CIC watch stander paused and then added, "Believe it to be the same warship that was following us a few days ago."

Danny opened the port-side bridgewing door and stepped into the cool air, pulling his binoculars up to scan the horizon. It didn't take long to spot the running lights of the ship trailing them. He watched the ship for a few seconds and reentered the bridge, picking up the phone to dial Adam.

After morning tag-up, Adam sat in the port-side captain's chair and studied the ship, which Terry had identified as the USS *Cowpens* (CG 63). The San Diego–based Ticonderoga-class guided-missile cruiser had a similar propulsion system to the *Kraken*, but, as Adam knew, that was where the similarities ended.

The *Cowpens* was a major weapons platform that carried Tomahawk missiles. There was good reason to be concerned. Adam called Scott, who was standing watch as the bridge officer.

"Has the *Cowpens* tried to make contact with us?"

Scott shook his head. "No. Do you want us to initiate contact?"

"Not right now," Adam answered.

Later that morning Leroy entered the bridge and approached Adam.

"Hey, boss," Leroy began, "I know that I'm new at this sailor thing, but the crew seems to be a little out of focus today. They're all talking about this equator ceremony tomorrow. Should I be doing something to realign them?"

Adam couldn't help but smile. "No. They've worked their butts off. They deserve a little fun. Besides . . ." Adam pushed out his chest as he raised his chin. He took on the look of a very serious and somber man. "The transformation of a sailor from a slimy pollywog to a trusty shellback is a time-honored tradition that dates back to the days when the Spanish and Portuguese controlled the seas. It is our privilege—nay, it is our duty—as veteran travelers through Neptune's realm to cleanse this ship from the diseases associated with pollywogs and other vermin."

Leroy tilted his head and squinted. "Are you screwing with me?"

Adam looked Leroy up and down. He then narrowed his eyes to mere slits and leaned close to the soldier. "Maybe a little. Don't worry about it, Leroy," Adam continued. "You're going to remember tomorrow for the rest of your life."

Paula entered the bridge and smiled at Leroy as they passed each other through the door.

She grabbed Scott and pulled him to where Adam sat.

"Tomorrow after the crossing-the-equator ceremony," she began, "I'd like to schedule a steel beach barbecue on the fantail. I'm going to have the cooks set up a couple barbecue pits so that we can cook up hot dogs and hamburgers. We'll also have potato salad, chips, and some kind of dessert. What do you think?"

"That's a great idea," Adam replied.

"Great." Paula was writing notes. "I think that it would be a good idea for the command leadership team to actually do the barbecuing. This will give our cooks a break."

Adam raised one eyebrow and turned to Scott. "Have you ever tasted my cooking?" he asked his XO. Scott placed his hand over his mouth and pretended to retch.

Adam turned back to Paula. "OK," he agreed, "all senior leaders who are not on watch will cook at the steel beach."

He turned in his chair to face forward, then quickly spun back to Paula. Adam extended his arm and pointed an exaggerated and accusatory finger at Paula. "But I will not be held responsible for any food poisoning."

George, Paula, Scott, and Terry were finishing dinner in the wardroom. Scott smiled at Terry, who was unusually chatty as he described the first time he had crossed the equator.

"I'll never forget that date," Terry said, holding his cup of coffee with both hands. "It was January 29, 1983. I was on the USS *Hoel*." Terry looked at each of the other officers. "Back then it wasn't like it is today. There was no political correctness, no sensitivity and none of that 'I'm feeling stressed' wimpy attitude that is viral in today's Navy. Tell them, George!"

Terry quickly glanced at the engineer, who remained silent.

Terry continued unabated. "Our uniforms were completely destroyed after the ceremony. We literally had to throw them over the side of the ship."

He sat back in his chair and smiled. No one else commented.

Just then the bridge boatswain's mate keyed the 1MC intercom and rang the ship's bell six times to signify the arrival of a senior dignitary.

"Davy Jones arriving," the boatswain announced.

A few seconds later another voice blared from the intercom.

"Good evening, *Kraken*," the voice announced. "This is the bridge officer. We have just boarded a distinguished visitor to the ship. The honorable Davy Jones has arrived from his undersea domain and is now standing directly next to me on the bridge. Davy Jones has requested to speak to each member of the crew."

The mic changed hands, and the crew heard a new speaker.

"Good evening, crew of *Kraken*. This is Davy Jones. I am pleased to have been invited aboard such a fine sailing vessel. I am equally pleased by this ship and the performance of most of your crew, though I have been informed of several unclean members who have never before crossed the equatorial line of our planet. As such, these members have never been cleansed by the traditional ceremonies enacted by King Neptune. I am here to herald the arrival of King Neptune and his royal court, who will arrive tomorrow morning at 0700."

Davy Jones's voice became harsh. "At that time, each slimy pollywog will be escorted through the royal gauntlet and ultimately presented to his majesty, King Neptune. His royal majesty will then be apprised of the pollywog's crimes, and as he is a benevolent and just ruler, he will then pass judgment. A warning to all—punishment will be swift. Captain Decker?" Davy Jones continued. "You and your fellow trusty shellbacks are expected to assist King Neptune in cleansing your ship of these unclean pollywogs."

Adam's voice was heard acknowledging the order.

Davy Jones then finished, "Captain, I thank you for your hospitality. I must now take my leave and return to my locker on the sea bed."

The bridge boatswain piped reveille at 0400 the next morning. The shellbacks dressed in traditional piratical outfits and began pulling the pollywogs out of their racks.

The pollywogs were not allowed to walk upright. Instead they were forced to crawl on their hands and knees to every location on the ship. The shellbacks led the pollywogs to the foc'sle where they were hosed down with firefighting salt water and told to sing songs of the sea. Occasionally a pollywog was ushered forward and directed to stick his or her head out through the bullnose to look for the equator.

Breakfast was served at 0500 when shellback cooks brought pink pancakes, green eggs, and blue spaghetti to the foc'sle. Paper plates were set on the ship's deck, and the pollywogs were required to eat their breakfast without using their hands. Rogue shellbacks also fed the pollywogs a variety of foodstuffs that included patis (the Filipino fish sauce) and Australian Vegemite.

At 0600 the shellbacks held a beauty contest. The pollywogs were escorted in front of a panel of shellback judges and forced to offer their most suggestive pose. The winner was told that he or she would be selected as King Neptune's queen for the day.

Larry Gable, a twenty-seven-year-old from Huntsville, Alabama, won after singing his best version of Marilyn Monroe's "Happy Birthday, Mr. President" song.

The Jolly Roger skull-and-crossbones flag was hoisted up the flag mast at 0630, followed by the bridge boatswain ringing eight bells at 0700 as he announced the arrival of King Neptune and his royal court.

Bobby Hardesty was completely decked out in a King Neptune costume. He wore the long white beard, a tall gold crown, and a long green toga while holding a six-foot trident in his right hand. In the most regal fashion, Bobby strode to a chair set up on the foc'sle where he turned, faced the crowd, and sat. The royal court, consisting of a royal dentist, royal barber, and a royal baby, gathered around him. King Neptune pointed to locations on the deck where each of the royals were to set up shop.

Adam was cheered by the shellback crew when he appeared on the foc'sle. His trousers were shredded at the leg bottoms, and he bore a fake scar on his left cheek and a pirate hat that had been purchased at Disneyland. Adam waved to the shellbacks and took a chair next to King Neptune. He enjoyed the festivities but occasionally glanced at the cruiser *Cowpens*, which continued to mirror *Kraken*'s path.

As the pollywogs made it to the foc'sle, Adam located Leroy crawling on his hands and knees—buried in the mix of the pollywogs.

Adam claimed ownership of Leroy as his personal wog dog and attached a collar and leash to Leroy's neck. Adam then led Leroy to the royal barber, who packed engine grease behind the former soldier's ears. Afterward, Leroy was directed to the royal doctor where he was forced to drink a truth serum concoction of hot sauce, milk, and grape Kool-Aid. Leroy gagged as he drank, but he refused to let the shellbacks see that it affected him.

He was then ushered to the duck pond, which was actually an inflatable children's pool filled with salt water. Leroy was told to waddle around the pool and quack like a duck. He did as he was told without complaining.

He was taken to Charles Biggs next, who played the royal baby. Charles stood five feet seven inches tall and weighed 260 pounds. He was dressed only in a huge diaper. Charles had smeared peanut butter on his bare belly and stuck an olive inside his exposed navel. Leroy looked confused as he peered up at Adam.

Adam smiled down at Leroy. "Suck out the olive, wog."

Leroy stared at the fat man's belly and turned back to Adam. "You've got to be kidding."

Adam laughed, "Get on with it, wog."

Leroy gingerly approached the baby and slowly pushed his face toward the hairy belly.

Before he could bite the olive, Charles grabbed Leroy's head with both hands and forced the soldier's face into his peanut butter–filled belly. Leroy felt like he was smothering. As flab surrounded his head, he struggled to free himself of the royal baby's grip.

Finally, Leroy was released. He looked up to Adam to show that he had the olive between his teeth. He then breeched shellback protocol by standing up, raising his arms in victory, and sucking down the olive. The entire crew cheered, and Adam bent over laughing. He had tears in his eyes when he told Leroy to resume the pollywog position on his knees. Leroy obeyed and was escorted to King Neptune.

The royal scribe read off a list of charges that included spending thirty years in the United States Army. King Neptune sat back in his chair and considered the case. The king finally leaned forward and pointed at Leroy.

"Guilty!" was the King's verdict.

King Neptune rose from his chair and tilted the trident toward Leroy.

"Send him to the trough," the King ordered.

Adam led Leroy to the fifteen-by-three-foot, one-foot-deep pool of sludge, the result of three days of garbage from the crew's mess decks, watered down and turned into a soupy mess.

Leroy leaned over the lip of the pool and gagged. It smelled like a combination of rotting food, old socks, and dirty ass. He took a deep breath and slid in. He half swam and half crawled the entire fifteen feet.

He tried not to look at what he was moving through, and finally reached the end of the pool, sliding over the edge onto the dry deck.

Adam stood there waiting for Leroy. He reached down and pulled Leroy up to his feet.

"Congratulations"—Adam slapped Leroy's back—"fellow shellback."

Once each pollywog had suffered the same, the ceremony ended, King Neptune departed the ship, and the exhausted new shellbacks trudged down to their berthing spaces for hot showers. Bobby and the Deck Department removed the ceremonial props and hosed down the foc'sle. No matter how much water was used, the foc'sle decks continued to smell like rotting food and fish sauce.

Paula's team immediately set up the barbecue pits and began lighting the charcoal. Adam, Scott, and the department heads spent the next two hours cooking hotdogs and hamburgers for their crew. Someone set up a couple speakers and played classic rock music.

Once the entire crew was fed, Adam and his fellow cooks joined in on the feast. The *Kraken* crew sat back, relished the warmth of the equatorial sun, relaxed, and enjoyed the day.

Meanwhile, the *Cowpens* continued to match their track.

Paula met with George, Scott, and Adam the next morning after tag-up. They discussed their next port call in Papua, New Guinea, and the need for supplies and fuel.

"I've made contact with the port representative that was provided by Oliver," she told the group. "I've communicated the need for food, fuel, and other consumables and was told that everything we've requested will be ready and on the pier in Port Moresby when we arrive. I'm also happy to report that the *Kraken* crew is approved for shore leave during our twenty-four-hour layover."

Vic plotted the course for Port Moresby and briefed Adam that the ship would arrive at 1000 the next morning.

CIC contacted the bridge at 1745 that evening to report that the *Cowpens* had, again, broken off from trailing the *Kraken*. Adam had a feeling they would see them again soon.

Paula stood the bridge-officer watch the next morning. As she announced the sea and anchor evolution at 0800, all hands moved quickly to their stations to prepare the ship for arrival.

A tug boat pulled up next to the starboard side and delivered the pilot who would guide the ship into port. The pilot, an expert in these waters, navigated the ship to the fueling pier in Port Moresby. Once all mooring lines tied the ship to the pier and the brow was properly secured, boxes of supplies were carried from the pier to the ship.

It was hot, about eighty degrees, and extremely muggy. Adam's clothes stuck to him as he sat on the bridge.

"Care to join me for dinner tonight?" Adam invited Scott, Leroy, and the department heads. "The National Hotel in town has a restaurant that I hear is pretty good, and I'm going to take full advantage of it."

Leroy was the only individual who politely declined the invitation. He had already been invited to join the chiefs for dinner.

Adam relaxed for an hour in his cabin before showering and dressing for the evening. He met Scott and Paula on the quarterdeck at 1600.

"When is the van coming to pick us up?" Adam asked Paula.

Paula looked at her wristwatch. "He should be here in about ten minutes. Our driver's name is Benny."

The three friends left the ship and waited on the pier for the driver. George, Doc Kelly, and Vic arrived a few minutes later.

"Where's Terry?" Adam asked Scott.

"He's got the duty today," Scott replied. "It'll just be us."

The driver arrived in a rickety and rusty van, and the group of officers piled in. They rode for fifteen minutes, and when they pulled up in front of the hotel, Benny quickly opened the doors for his passengers and notified them that he would wait in the parking lot for their return.

The hotel lobby was large and luxurious but smelled musty and old. Paula and the others wanted to look around before heading into the restaurant. Adam declined and indicated that he just wanted to have a drink before dinner. "Go ahead and look around." Adam waved them off. "I'll meet you in the bar when you're finished."

The bar area had that same musty smell but was well lit and clean. The only two people in there were an older bartender cleaning drinking glasses and a man drinking a beer in the corner.

Adam sat on a stool at the bar and ordered a Bacardi and Coke. The bartender mixed the drink, set it in front of Adam, stepped out from behind the bar, and began wiping down tables that surrounded the small dance floor.

Adam was scanning the liquor selection when he heard "American?" He turned to see the man at the table looking at him.

"Excuse me?" Adam asked.

"Are you American?" the patron asked again.

"Yes, I am." Adam was a little guarded.

The patron rose from his chair, grabbed his beer, and moved to the bar. He sat down next to Adam and offered his hand.

"Me too," he said. "I'm Zach Taggert."

Adam shook the stranger's hand. "Adam Decker."

Zach Taggert had a very firm handshake, and was a pretty good-sized guy too. Adam guessed that he was about six foot three, and 220 pounds. *And fit! This guy must work out a lot,* Adam thought.

"Where you from?" Zach asked.

"Denver," Adam responded a little too curtly. "You?"

"Oh, I'm from all over." Zach took a drink from his beer. "Originally from DC, though." He quickly looked Adam over. "You wouldn't be off of that ship that pulled in this morning, would you?"

The hairs on the back of Adam's neck rose. "Actually, I am." Adam tilted his head to one side. "I'm the ship's captain."

Zach's eyes widened and he smiled. "Are you? Well, it's a pleasure to meet you, Adam."

Zach raised his glass. Adam raised his glass and took a swig.

Adam eyed Zach and asked, "And what do you do, Zach?"

Zach's smile widened. "I'm the commanding officer of the USS *Cowpens.* Really glad to finally meet you."

Adam's stomach sank but he refused to show it. He smiled back at Zach.

"I was wondering if we were going to meet." Adam forced himself to take a drink. "You have a good-looking ship."

"Thank you." Zach was polite, but Adam could tell that he was being sized up.

Zach was quiet for a moment and then began, "I like your ship too. I served on an Oliver Hazard Perry–class frigate when I was much younger. I did my division-officer tour back then." He leaned back slightly. "I hate to be nosy, Adam, but what are you doing with a fully functional Navy warship? I mean, I believe that it's functional with the electronic signature that you've been throwing around."

Adam thought for a moment and then nodded as casually as he could. "Yeah. She is a functional frigate. We're heading east to the gulf to help out a friend who's been having trouble with one of their neighbors."

Zach nodded. "Never heard of a mercenary warship before."

It was Adam's turn to smile. "We're not mercenaries. We're registered in the United States as a merchant vessel, and, as you have seen, we are flying the US flag. We've been asked to perform this one task, and then we're getting back to normal operations in the merchant fleet."

Zach smiled warmly. "Gotcha." He paused. "You seem like a good guy, Adam," he began, "and from the way that you talk, I'm guessing that you're retired US Navy. I truly wish you safe travels and success in whatever business you need to attend."

Zach frowned slightly. "There is one other thing, though. I do need to warn you, Adam. I'm tasked with protecting global sea lanes. I take that responsibility very seriously. Please don't put your ship or your crew into a position where your mission conflicts with my mission."

Zach took another sip and faced Adam. "I promise you, if needed, I will defend my ship and, more importantly, the reputation of the United States. A frigate is a formidable weapon. But we both know that it can't compete with a guided-missile cruiser."

Adam stared at Zach but said nothing.

The captain of the *Cowpens* finished his beer and paid for both his and Adam's. "I hate to do this, but I need to get going. I hope we meet again soon, Adam. I'd love to have another beer and hear more about your business."

They again shook hands, and Zach Taggert left the bar.

Scott and the department heads returned a few minutes later. They were laughing and discussing the various decorations and people in the hotel. Adam stood in the doorway of the bar and waited on his friends. Scott could see that Adam was troubled.

"What's the matter?" Scott asked.

Adam smiled thinly and motioned toward the restaurant.

"Let's go eat. I'll talk with you later in private."

CHAPTER 13

Back aboard the ship, Adam, Scott, George, and Paula sat in the captain's in-port cabin, drinking coffee. Adam replayed the scene with Zach Taggert while his friends listened intently.

"He actually threatened us?" Scott asked. His face had paled.

"I don't believe that he threatened us," Adam responded. "But the warning was clearly delivered."

"I never thought that we would be in the crosshairs of the US Navy," George sighed.

"Again," Adam stated, "I don't believe that we are in any trouble with them. We're OK as long as we don't do anything that would be in conflict with their mission."

Adam stood and forced a smile. "As far as I know, we aren't doing anything illegal or unethical. And we certainly aren't doing anything that could be construed as anti-American or against national interests. As I mentioned to Captain Taggert, we are merely helping a friend get rid of some bullies."

"For monetary gain," added George.

Adam scowled at his friend. "We're not mercenaries."

The room was quiet.

Scott finally broke the silence. "Have you given any thought to which flag we're going to fly when we get to Kuwait?"

Adam, still standing, reached for the coffee pot and refilled his cup. "I actually have given this some thought. We can't allow any foreign power to believe that the United States is involved in this issue, or any aggression will be construed as an act of war. However, while saying that, I believe that we'll have better luck transiting the Strait of Hormuz under the US flag."

He looked around to each of his friends. "Seriously, who would want to cross swords with a warship from the United States?" Adam paused and chewed on his lower lip. "This probably makes me a hypocrite, but I want to be blanketed by the security of the US flag, but I don't want to be identified as a US combatant."

Adam sighed. "We're going to be walking, or rather sailing, on a very thin line, but I don't see any other choice."

Adam considered his last words, then raised his chin in confidence and announced, "We will fly the US flag until we cross into Kuwaiti territory. At that point we'll lower our flag and raise the Kuwaiti national ensign and patrol their sea lanes as if we were from Kuwait."

It was Paula's turn for a question. "Have we coordinated this with the Kuwaiti government?"

"Oliver has assured me that this has already been worked out," Adam replied.

"Oliver?" George harrumphed. "I still don't trust him, Adam. I know that I've said this repeatedly, but those spooks have their own agenda." George stood and went to the door, then turned and pointed at Adam. "We need better assurances before we cross that territorial line, Adam. This may sound like a conspiracy theory, but what if we're being set up?"

Adam looked to Scott and then Paula, but their attention was glued to George.

George continued, "What if we show up and throw around our weight? What if we push these small boats back to their home port? Then, what if Kuwait calls Iran and claims that some warship has just moved into international waters and is harassing ships moving in and out of their sea lanes? Now both Iran and Kuwait don't need to fight each other; they can focus on a common enemy—us!"

George raised his arms, his large hands wide open.

"Iran shows up and eliminates the threat. Kuwait lauds their big brother for the help, and then they continue working together as one big happy family. All previous conflicts and troubles are forgotten."

George dropped his hands. "The only losers in that scenario are the poor crew of the *Kraken*. No loss there. They were just a mercenary ship on a self-serving mission to make money."

He waited for a response.

Adam smiled softly. "I appreciate the fact that you are concerned about this operation. I'm not sure that I completely trust Oliver either, only because everything seems to be moving too quickly and much too smoothly. But I honestly believe that Oliver's organization wants us to succeed. They've invested a lot of money and time in this operation. Why would they do that just to have us defeated?

"I know that political agendas change and that we could be deemed expendable if the interests of our sponsors have also changed, but we, the officers and crew of *Kraken*, are honorable and loyal."

Adam took a step back and addressed his friends. "We will continue our path forward, and we will complete our mission to the best of our abilities." He peered at George and forced a laugh. "That, sir, was an impressive theory. You have quite the imagination. How the hell did you come up with that?"

George's cheeks glowed red, but privately Adam worried George might be right.

The *Kraken* set sail the next morning, and with the exception of a few hangovers, the crew was sharp and ready for sea operations.

Adam held a tag-up as soon as they traveled to open ocean.

"We need to prepare for our time in the gulf," he announced. "Let's start conducting general-quarters battle station drills tomorrow.

I'd like to see some weapons drills as well as damage control and firefighting training."

Adam gestured toward George. "Have Gail work up some situations that involve multiple weapon attacks and hits. I'd like to see the damage-control team fight fires, flooding, broken steam pipes, and collapsing decks."

Adam looked to each individual. "Let's train like we fight. Make the drills as realistic as possible."

The meeting ended, and Adam walked out to the starboard bridgewing, leaned on the railing, and stared at the ocean. He squinted as the sun beamed full blast through the cloudless sky.

For a moment, he was completely relaxed. Adam had always loved the smell of the ocean. The salt air dried his skin, but he just felt so healthy when he was at sea. He lowered his gaze to the water directly below him. The sea rushed past as the ship steamed forward. It always amazed him just how blue the water was in the middle of the ocean; the only color contrast were the whitecaps that topped each wave.

Watching and listening to the small waves crash against the ship was hypnotic. He had to physically pull himself away from the rail.

He walked back into the bridge and asked Vic to set a course for Olongapo City, Philippines.

"Any contacts out there?" Adam asked Paula, who was standing the bridge-officer watch.

Paula shook her head as she stared through the bridge window. "Negative. Looks like we're all alone."

Adam asked Paula to call him if that changed. He walked down to see Gail in Damage Control Central and spent the next hour with her discussing drills.

While Adam and Gail worked the drill set, George napped in Main Control; Frank researched the current threats in the Straits of Hormuz; Doc Johnson worked in sick bay to lance a boil on a sailor's butt; Lonnie sat in the supply office and listened to Pink Floyd's *Dark Side of the Moon*; Cy talked with Terry in CIC about weapons-firing procedures; Scott devoured a sandwich in the wardroom while watching the eighties film *Better Off Dead*; Leroy, Danny, and Bobby smoked Cuban cigars on the signal bridge; and on the bridge Paula told an off-color joke to Vic, who refused to show an ounce of emotion.

Meanwhile, Hasif was on the fantail talking on his cell phone. Reception kept cutting in and out, so the steward attempted to find a better signal by moving around the deck.

Frustrated, he finally gave up and ended the call with "I'll try again tomorrow. Yes, same time."

On the other end of the line Oliver Pratt frowned as the call disconnected.

Low gray clouds hung over the seas the next morning. Sheets of rain battered against the *Kraken*, causing her to rock, roll, and bounce between the six-foot waves. Occasional streaks of lightning reflected off the crests.

Vic reported that the ship would arrive in Olongapo City in just over three days if they maintained speed.

"However," Vic added, "the weather could slow us down a bit, so I'm anticipating four days."

Paula shared that she had already communicated the fuel and food supplies request with Oliver's contact. She had not received confirmation of their request but promised to contact everyone when it had been approved.

George was unusually quiet and left the tag-up without providing input. As George exited the bridge, Adam looked at Paula, who just shrugged.

Just before lunch, Adam stopped by Main Control to check in with George. Gail was discussing the upcoming drills with two machinists, and she stood and greeted Adam.

"Where's George?" he asked.

"He's not feeling his best and is lying down in his stateroom."

Gail provided an update on the drills. He quickly reviewed the drill set and departed.

After a quick walk to officer country, Adam knocked on George's door.

"Yeah" he heard from inside the stateroom. Adam cracked open the door and saw George lying in his rack and reading a book. He sat at the desk.

"You doing OK, old man?"

George removed his glasses and scowled. "You're no spring chicken either, my friend."

Adam smiled. "Heard you were feeling a little under the weather. Everything OK?"

George lowered his book and sat up in the rack. He rubbed his eyes and then slid his hand to his neck where he squeezed out some stiffness.

"Just caught a bit of a bug. I'll be alright. Doc Johnson gave me some meds and told me to get some rest. Thought I'd take him up on that."

Adam nodded. "What are you reading?"

George handed the book to Adam.

"Are you kidding me?" Adam laughed as he read the author's name. "Nora Roberts?"

George raised his nose in the air. "A man, a real man, is not afraid to show his sensitive side."

Adam tossed the book back to George. "OK, real man," he said, "hope you feel better. Give me a call if you're up to it, and we'll meet for dinner."

Adam's smile slipped as he watched George lie back down in his rack and reopen the book.

In the chief's mess, Bobby entered and noticed Leroy lying flat on the couch with a box of saltines on his chest.

"Thought you were finally getting your sea legs," Bobby mused.

Leroy opened one eye. "Thought I was too." He rolled his head toward Bobby. "What's the weather forecast?"

Bobby lifted the box from Leroy's chest and pulled out a sleeve of crackers.

"We'll probably be out of this storm by tomorrow morning." He placed the box back on Leroy's chest. "Go stand on the signal bridge and get some air."

"Maybe later," Leroy moaned.

The *Kraken's* general alarm sounded at 0800 the next morning. Five minutes later, all stations reported manned and ready.

Terry keyed the mic to the ship's 1MC intercom and reported an incoming missile. The imaginary projectile hit the ship's hull just above the waterline on the starboard side. Damage-control parties were sent out and within minutes reported an explosion and fires amidships on the first deck. The firefighting teams battled the imaginary flames until they were under control and then completely out. Then procedures to shore up a buckled bulkhead with wooden timbers were superbly executed.

Adam listened to each report delivered to the bridge. He was pleased with the timeliness and professionalism displayed by the old sailors that made up his crew. These drills were necessary, but he hoped they would never be needed.

General-quarters drills continued for the next two days until the ship reached the territorial waters of the Republic of the Philippines. George was back at work but lacked his usual energy. Adam mentioned this to Doc Kelly, who promised to keep an eye on the old engineer.

The tug pulled alongside, and the pilot was brought on board.

Paula stood with Adam on the starboard bridgewing and watched as the ship closed in on their mooring destination. She was scheduled to meet her logistics contact on the pier as soon as the ship was moored. Scanning the pier from the bridgewing, she hoped to pick him from the crowd of workers who prepared for the ship's arrival.

As the ship inched toward the pier, she noticed a tall, thin man in a black suit and a black fedora hat waving to the ship. Paula squinted.

"Is that . . ." She paused. "Oliver?"

Adam turned to look.

"Oliver! Where?" he asked. Paula pointed, and Adam looked puzzled. "What's he doing here?"

Paula shook her head. "Don't know. I'll bet we find out in a few minutes, though."

Mooring lines were tossed from the ship and placed over the pier bollards while tension was taken at the forward and after capstans. Each capstan turned and coiled the mooring lines, inching the ship closer and closer to its berthing spot until the ship finally touched the pier bumpers.

The brow was then lowered and connected the ship to the pier.

Oliver walked quickly across the brow and was met by Danny, who was on the ship's quarterdeck. The two men shook hands.

"Welcome to the Philippines." Oliver's perpetual smile beamed at Danny. Danny returned the smile and apologized that he couldn't talk at the moment. He pointed Oliver to the bridge and indicated that Adam should still be up there.

Scott and Adam were standing in the corner of the bridge and talking when Oliver entered.

Adam extended a hand. "Oliver! What brings you all the way out here?"

Oliver shook hands. "I have a gift for you."

He reached into a black bag and pulled out a large black, green, red, and white flag.

"This is the national flag of Kuwait. Thought you could use it." He handed the flag to Adam. "Also, since you have superbly executed two-thirds of the voyage, I thought that it would be a good idea to come out and hear about your adventure so far."

"Sure," Adam replied as he turned to Scott. "Can you finish up mooring the ship and meet us in the wardroom?"

Adam led Oliver out of the bridge and down the ladder. Hasif greeted both Adam and Oliver as they entered the wardroom. He poured two steaming cups of coffee and placed them on the table where Adam and Oliver sat.

George opened the wardroom door and stopped in place when he saw Oliver.

"I heard that our friendly spook was paying us a visit," he said with a bit of sarcasm.

Oliver maintained his smile but said nothing.

"Have a seat!" Adam motioned George to a chair at the table. "Oliver would like a brief of our trip."

George poured himself a glass of water and sat at the end of the table.

Adam made small talk, which he hated, and delayed any type of briefing until his entire staff was in the wardroom.

Scott, Danny, Terry, and Cy finally strolled in.

"Where's Paula?" Adam asked the group.

"She's on the pier talking with the local logistics rep," Danny responded. "She'll join us when she's finished."

Adam had the department heads provide an impromptu and positive briefing of their respective departments and the issues that they had faced over the past few weeks.

Oliver listened intently but asked no questions.

Adam wondered why Oliver was here. *Why*, he asked himself, *couldn't I have received that briefing by phone?*

A new thought crossed Adam's mind, which caused him to break the silence. "There's one more thing. We're being followed by a United States cruiser."

Oliver raised an eyebrow.

"The *Cowpens* has been following us off and on since San Diego." Adam sipped his coffee, then continued, "I ran into her commanding officer in Port Moresby, and we had a nice chat at a bar. Not sure what he's looking for, and we haven't seen them since we left New Guinea, but I have a feeling that we'll be running into her again soon."

Oliver flashed his patented smile. "I'll look into that." He cocked his head and scanned the room. "Adam, do you think that we can have a moment alone?"

"Sure," Adam replied. He excused himself from the group, then escorted Oliver to his in-port cabin. Adam sat behind his desk while Oliver pulled up a chair.

"So, what's up?" he asked.

Oliver's smile faded. "We received the medical reports from your crew's physicals. One report came back with some negative and serious findings."

Adam waited patiently.

"George Bannister has been diagnosed with stage-4 small cell carcinoma in his lungs."

Adam's heart stopped. "George has cancer?"

Oliver nodded. "I'm sorry, Adam. Looks like George has known about this for some time. Prognosis is that his life expectancy is about nine to twelve months. Two years at the most."

Adam felt sick.

Oliver stood. "I needed to tell you this news in person. We've got to get him off the ship."

Oliver expressed his sympathy about George's condition and then excused himself from Adam's cabin.

Adam buried his face in his hands.

Eventually, he made his way to George's stateroom. Each step he took felt heavier than the last. He knocked, and George opened the door a few moments later.

"Hey, boss." The big engineer grinned as he held the door open and motioned Adam in.

Adam wouldn't make eye contact, and George sensed that Adam was upset.

"What's the matter?" George asked.

Adam couldn't find the words.

George's grin dropped to a smile. "Found out, did you?"

Adam looked at George and said nothing.

George opened a drawer and began filling it with folded clean laundry. "How'd you find out?"

Adam stared at his friend. "Oliver" was all he said.

George continued smiling and slowly shook his head. "I'm telling you, he's CIA. That guy knows everything."

"George," Adam began, "why didn't you tell me?"

George's smile hardened. "And miss one more deployment? No way. I really wanted this. And I still want this, Adam. I have plenty of time left. From what I understand, this won't get bad for a few months."

Adam's face paled. "How long have you known?"

George placed a pair of folded trousers in the drawer and shut it tight. He sat down and sighed. "Found out right before the ship left Bremerton." George leaned toward Adam. "Please let me finish what we started. I've been mentoring Gail to take over as my assistant so you will have a strong engineer when I'm gone."

Adam was shocked. He blurted out, "Gail knows?!"

George uttered a short laugh. "No. But she knows that I won't be at sea for too many more years, so my mentoring seems natural."

Adam looked at the deck and had trouble maintaining eye contact. "I don't know, George. Nothing good can happen while you're at sea in this condition."

George reached out and placed his hand on Adam's knee. His voice softened. "Adam, you and I have been through a lot together. We are friends and shipmates. I would never compromise our friendship or put our ship in danger." He sat back in his chair. "I promise you that I will be fine during this operation. Besides," he added with a wink, "nothing good will happen if you send me home."

Adam fought back tears as he looked into George's eyes.

George's grin had returned. "I can't spend the last days of my life in bed and relying on others. That would be worse than the dying." He became serious. "Adam, I promise to let you know if I start feeling sick or if I begin experiencing any physical problems."

Adam smiled thinly and nodded. "OK," he said, "but we will keep this information to ourselves. No one else needs to know." Adam rose from the chair, pushed out his chest, and raised his chin. "OK, tough guy." He smiled. "Let's finish what we started."

CHAPTER 14

The port call in Olongapo was short but enjoyed by all of the *Kraken* crew.

Adam invited his staff to join him for a traditional Filipino dinner at a local restaurant. Paula remained on board to take the duty, but Scott, Oliver, and the rest of the department heads walked with Adam.

George was elated to be back in the Philippines. As soon as they crossed the Kalalake River into town, he took in a deep breath. "I'll never forget that smell," he commented. "Smells like barbecue, sweat, and ass."

Terry pulled at his collar and wiped sweat from the back of his neck.

"Disgusting place," he said as he swatted a mosquito from his arm.

The group ended up at Max's restaurant on Magsaysay Boulevard. The feast set before them included chicken adobo, pancit, lumpia, and warm San Miguel beer. George poked fun at Terry and continued to call him a cherry boy—a term used to label sailors who had never been with a Filipino prostitute. Terry became increasingly frustrated with George's jabs until the old engineer bought him a glass of wine and told him to pull the stick out of his ass.

Terry frowned but raised his glass in appreciation.

Meanwhile, just a few hundred yards away, Bobby and Frank were sitting with Leroy and Bobby's nephews, the Rauske boys, at the Brown Fox bar. Timmy and Tom were busy negotiating with a pretty young dancer on the price of a private lap dance while a young and well-developed Filipino woman was spinning around a gold pole on the bar stage.

Bobby, Frank, and Leroy smoked fat Cuban cigars and drank whiskey. Bobby tucked a one-dollar bill into the dancer's G-string and grinned as she seductively gyrated her hips within inches of his face.

Leroy leaned back in his chair and pulled the cigar from his lips. "I should have been a squid!" he laughed as he pulled a single bill from his trouser pocket.

The next morning Adam and Scott watched Oliver grow smaller and smaller as the ship pulled away from the pier. Oliver continued to wave as if he were saying farewell to a family member departing on a cruise liner.

The ship reached open water, and Adam turned to his navigator. "Vic, set a course for Colombo, Sri Lanka. Have that course swing us around Singapore and directly through the Malacca Strait."

Scott's head snapped around. "We're going through the Malacca Strait?"

Adam nodded.

"You do know," Scott whispered as he moved closer to Adam, "that there have been numerous reports of piracy in that region."

Adam nodded and smiled. "I do know that. But this is the quickest way to get to our destination. Plus," he added, "I don't think that we'll have any trouble. The ship is going to be set for battle stations as we sail through the strait."

Adam rose from his chair as Scott secured the ship from sea-and-anchor detail. He asked Scott to assemble the primary staff in the wardroom in fifteen minutes.

Paula, George, and Terry sat silently in the wardroom and waited for the meeting to begin. The door opened and all three turned, expecting to see Adam walk through the door. Cy entered the space and immediately stopped. "What?" he asked.

Adam stepped around Cy, poured a cup of coffee, and sat in his chair. He tossed an oversized magazine facedown on the table. Cy found an empty seat, and Doc Kelly, Vic, and Scott joined them a few minutes later.

"Danny's on the bridge," Scott relayed as he took his seat.

Adam stood and leaned forward, placing both hands on the table.

"We're eight days out from our destination in Kuwaiti waters." Adam looked around the room. "We are currently en route to Sri Lanka for a quick refueling, and then we will set a course for the Strait of Hormuz."

Adam flipped over the large magazine to reveal a world atlas. He quickly turned to the page that showed the Republic of Singapore.

"We're here." He positioned his right index finger just left of the Philippine islands. "And we're heading here." He dragged his finger to Sri Lanka. "The quickest way to get to this location is to sail past Singapore and through the Malacca Strait." Adam traced his finger over the body of water that separated Singapore from the island of Sumatra.

All eyes were glued to Adam's finger as it crossed the map. Each head rose when Adam pulled his hand away to face the team.

"Now, there are reports of pirating activity in the Malaccan Strait. However, I seriously doubt that any of these dubious groups"—he smiled as he stressed the word *dubious*—"would be ambitious enough to challenge a United States warship."

Adam turned to Scott. "We will sound the general alarm just prior to entering the Malaccan Strait and keep the ship at battle stations during our transit."

Scott nodded and Adam continued. "We will secure from general quarters and resume normal at-sea operations once we clear the strait and enter the open waters of the Indian Ocean. Cy and Terry, while we're at GQ I want the fire-control systems lit up and all weapons systems, including our .50-caliber guns, mounted, fully loaded, and manned. I also want our LRAD systems up and running. I want to be prepared for anything."

Cy pulled the key ring from his pocket and stroked the shiny attached bullet. He appeared happy at this news. He raised his hand to ask a question. Adam nodded toward him.

"Will we engage if we are provoked or threatened?"

Adam could see that Cy was interested and even excited at this prospect.

"Yes, Cy. We will protect the ship if we are threatened."

Cy smiled and leaned back in his chair. He gripped the bullet tightly in his left hand.

"Vic?" Adam turned to his navigator. "Please plot the course and prepare a more formal navigation briefing to be held tomorrow evening."

Vic nodded as he wrote notes in a small pad. Adam asked for questions. When none were asked, he ended the meeting.

Adam stopped George before he departed the wardroom. "How are you feeling?"

George offered a small smile. "Not bad. A little tired, but not bad."

Adam frowned. "Tired?"

George winked at Adam. "Yeah, tired. I was in Main Control from 0300 until an hour ago when we started this little tea party get-together. I'm obviously a little tired."

Adam laughed. "You're a dick."

"Yes I am," George said as he turned, and waved goodbye over his shoulder.

Cy and his weapons crew entered the small arms armory and pulled four .50-caliber machine guns from the racks. Each weapon was stripped down, and thoroughly cleaned and oiled. Cy ordered a thousand rounds of ammunition for each weapon and directed his gunners to manually count each bullet. Cy personally inspected the guns, and, once satisfied, he carefully placed each weapon on the armory workbench and covered it with a plastic cover.

He dismissed his team and walked to the small arms rack where he retrieved a brand-new Colt 1911 .45-caliber hand gun. Cy ejected the magazine, then pulled back the slide to reveal an empty chamber.

He glanced back at the door to make sure that it was closed, raised the pistol to his face, and slid it across his cheek. The barrel was cool to the touch. He closed his eyes and inhaled deeply. He smiled as the scent of gun oil wafted through his nostrils.

Cy grabbed the pistol with both hands and extended his arms. He bent his knees and pointed the gun from a standing firing position. He released the slide, aimed the pistol at an imaginary target, and pulled the trigger. The empty pistol clicked.

Cy grinned while he pictured the .45 round tearing through the head of his target. He lowered the pistol and grabbed a holster and belt and a box of Winchester ammunition, placing the pistol, ammo, and holster on the armory workbench next to the larger weapons, then departed the armory and locked the door.

He reached into his pocket and found the .308 bullet.

Adam, Scott, and Danny were in the wardroom finishing a late lunch.

Adam gulped down the last of his water and set the cup on the table. "We've never held a man-overboard drill, have we?" He looked from Danny to Scott.

"No, we haven't," Scott answered. "We can do one today." Scott looked to Danny. "Do we have an Oscar on board?" Scott was referring to the dummy used during man-overboard drills.

International navies had used pennants and flags to communicate important messages since the early sailing days. When raised on the ship's mast at sea, the red-and-yellow pennant "Oscar" indicated that a sailor had fallen overboard. The man-overboard dummy on each ship was also named Oscar since both the pennant and the dummy were used for man-overboard drills.

To initiate a man-overboard drill, Oscar the dummy was tossed over the side of a moving ship, outfitted with an international-orange life jacket and a signal strobe light that was automatically activated when introduced to saltwater.

Lookouts were trained to constantly monitor the ship's wake for signs of a person who had fallen overboard.

Danny nodded. "We do have Oscar, but he's not in the best shape. I can outfit him with a new life jacket and strobe if you want to run a drill."

Adam pushed out his chair. "Let's run a drill this afternoon. In the meantime, Danny, please get Oscar ready to launch."

Oscar was tossed over the side of the ship at 1430.

The lookout stationed on the fantail was daydreaming and failed to notice the orange life jacket or strobe as it floated by the ship's stern.

Danny, who had positioned himself on the fantail, sneaked up behind the incompetent lookout, grabbed his head with both hands, and pointed his nose in the direction of the disappearing man-overboard dummy. Danny screamed, "Aren't you supposed to be looking for these types of things?"

The startled lookout pulled the binoculars up to his eyes and locked in on the flashing light attached to the floating life jacket.

He immediately grabbed his radio and called the bridge: "Bridge, Aft Lookout. We have a man overboard on the starboard side approximately one hundred yards behind us."

The lookout then grabbed a smoke float and threw it in the water as far as he could in Oscar's direction.

On the bridge Adam sat in his starboard chair and watched Paula, who was standing bridge officer. She immediately barked out maneuvering orders.

"All ahead full," Paula commanded. "Right full rudder." The *Kraken* leaned twenty degrees to her starboard side as it turned.

The bridge crew could hear sailors yelling as unsecured items flew across their work spaces. The ship reached the location where

Paula needed to maneuver the ship to the left in order to align their course to the sailor's location. She adjusted the ship's course once and then again to line up the ship.

She realized too late that she had forgotten to slow the ship down, and before she could order "all stop," the ship sailed over the dummy.

Danny leaned over the starboard safety lines and watched as Oscar was pulled through the huge ship's propeller. He ran to the fantail and saw bits and pieces of the dummy shoot into the ship's wake.

He grabbed the lookout's radio. "Bridge, this is Aft Lookout."

The bosun responded, "Bridge."

"This is the deck officer. May I speak with the bridge officer?"

The bosun handed the radio to Paula, who accepted the radio but let it hang by her waist.

With a beet-red face, she turned to face Adam.

Adam stared back at Paula. "Danny is waiting to hear from you."

Paula raised the radio. "Bridge officer here." Danny paused for a moment, then pressed the transmit button on the radio. "Oscar is dead—pulled through the screw."

Paula avoided looking at anyone on the bridge. "Roger. Out."

She handed the radio back to the bosun. Adam rose from his chair and walked over to Paula. He stood close to her and whispered, "You need to work on your maneuvering."

He began to exit the bridge and turned back to face Paula.

"By the way"—he locked eyes with her—"you owe me another Oscar."

Scott met Adam in the passageway just outside of the bridge.

Scott was obviously angry and frustrated. "This was a complete mess," Scott said as he showed Adam the results of the drill. "It took us twenty minutes to complete a full muster, and we never determined the name of the casualty. In fact," Scott continued, "we have five crewmembers who cannot be accounted for. No idea where they are on the ship."

Adam managed a grim smile. "Let's get to work to fix it then." He walked past Scott, entered his at-sea cabin, and closed the door.

Vic meticulously delivered the navigation brief to the senior staff. He hung a large chart of the Strait of Malacca on the wardroom bulkhead and used a laser pointer to show the transit. The 500-nautical-mile distance would mostly be conducted in a straight shot, but Vic identified and pointed out the turning points as well as the documented hazards to navigation.

"To safely navigate the strait, we will need to maintain a standard speed of twelve knots. There will be occasions when we can increase speed to twenty knots, but, of course, that will depend on sea traffic. At this speed we should be able to complete the transit within thirty-five hours."

Adam rose when Vic finished his brief.

"As I mentioned yesterday, there have been reports of piracy at various points throughout the strait. Because of that, I've asked Frank to prepare a brief on current threat activity in the strait."

Adam sat as Frank Johnston stood.

"The Strait of Malacca is a breeding ground for piracy, hijackings, and banditry," he began. "One of the reasons that it's so popular is that there are many places to hide boats and small ships. Another reason is that large ships need to travel at a relatively slow speed due to the shallow waters and high volume of shipping."

Frank turned from the chart and faced the group. "Malaccan pirates are looking for anything valuable. There is no rhyme or reason to the type of ship that they target. Large or small ships, it doesn't matter. Now, after saying that, it's highly unlikely that any group of pirates will be ambitious enough or stupid enough to attack a warship, especially a ship that is obviously manning weapons systems and prepared for combat. However, there may be some terrorist groups in the area who would love to get their hands on this type of a warship."

Frank looked around the room. "My recommendation is that we stay alert and at general quarters during the entire transit."

Adam stood. "I agree with that recommendation." He turned to Scott. "Please prepare to enter the strait at 0600 tomorrow morning. Split the crew into two twelve-hour shifts so that we are fully manned for combat at all hours during the transit. The off-duty crew may rest but will need to be ready to react if necessary."

Adam then pointed at Terry and Cy. "As I mentioned yesterday, ensure that all fire-control systems are online and that all weapons systems are fully manned during the transit."

Adam then looked around the room. "It's going to be a tough two days. Get rested up tonight and be sharp tomorrow morning."

Adam and Scott made their way to the bridge at 0545 the next morning. After Scott relieved Paula as bridge officer, he lifted his binoculars and scanned the horizon for other ships and potential hazards. Once satisfied that their course was clear, he raised his thumb to Adam, who nodded.

Scott directed the bridge boatswain to announce a modified general quarters. Within four minutes all modified general-quarters stations radioed the bridge and indicated that they were manned and ready. All doors and hatches below the waterline were shut and secured to ensure that the ship maintained watertight integrity belowdecks. This procedure was extremely important should the ship suffer a tear in the skin below the waterline. Seawater would enter the ship but would be contained to the spaces protected by closed and secured doors and hatches.

Scott ordered the course and speed to begin the transit.

Adam peered out to the ship's foc'sle and observed two sailors on each side of the deck manning the .50-caliber machine guns. He noticed that both sailors leaned forward on their weapons and were continuously scanning their areas of responsibility.

Adam stepped away from his chair. "Scott," he called. Scott turned and raised his head slightly in acknowledgement. "I'm going to head aft and check on the other weapons watch standers."

On the flight deck, two sailors manned the LRAD systems mounted on each side. Adam recognized the sailor on the port side but couldn't remember his name. He immediately recognized Lonnie on the starboard LRAD. Adam greeted both men and jokingly asked Lonnie if he was qualified to work this equipment. He added that he wasn't sure if he was comfortable with a bean counter working on his ship's weapons.

Lonnie grinned and told Adam that both he and Stan had been working with these systems for over two weeks and that they were excited to finally get a chance to use them.

Adam made a mental note to remember Stan's name.

"What do you think, Stan?" Adam asked the other LRAD operator. "Should I trust this equipment to a supply guy?"

Stan laughed and glanced at Lonnie. "I don't know, Captain," he remarked. "I guess we're just going to have to wait and see."

Lonnie smiled, and the two sailors turned back to scanning the ocean and horizon.

Adam walked back to the flight deck area overlooking the fantail and was glad to see both .50-caliber watch standers leaning on their weapons and diligently scanning the surrounding area. The aft lookout kept watch with the same amount of enthusiasm.

Adam was headed in the direction of the bridge when he heard the lever to the flight-deck watertight door swing upward. Bobby pushed through, carrying a large cup of coffee in his hand.

"Morning, Captain," he said, approaching Adam.

Adam smiled. "How are you doing today, Bobby?"

Bobby pursed his lips and nodded. "Couldn't be better if I were twins," he answered.

Adam smiled and returned the nod. He'd heard that quote before but never quite understood it.

"Are you going to be out on deck all day?" Adam asked.

Again, Bobby nodded. "Yes sir. Why? What's up?"

"Nothing," Adam answered. "Just glad to have some adult supervision back here. Don't want anyone going to sleep."

Bobby sipped his coffee. "No need to worry about that, Captain. I'll make sure that we are alert and ready."

Adam thanked the bosun and walked forward.

On the bridge Vic and Scott timed each turn with Swiss precision. Vic made sure to announce all upcoming maneuvers, and Scott scrupulously executed each turn. Each watch stander was keenly aware of the situation in these precarious waters and maintained high alert as they pushed through the strait.

All was quiet for the first few hours. Paula relieved Scott as bridge officer at 1130 so that he could grab some lunch. A few minutes later, the Inmarsat satellite radio began blaring a distress signal.

A male voice was heard speaking in English: "Mayday mayday mayday. This is the private sailing vessel *Sandy's Dream*. We are being pursued by two fast boats crewed by individuals with guns. We are cruising at twenty-two knots. Request immediate assistance."

"Adam?" Paula asked. "Should I respond? Can we help?"

Adam quickly considered the situation. He stared through the bridge window at the horizon.

"Adam?" Paula repeated.

Adam twisted in his chair to face Paula. "Respond to their distress call. Find out their location."

Paula grabbed the radio mic. "*Sandy's Dream*, this is the warship *Kraken*. What is your status and position?"

A few moments later the same male voice responded, "Warship *Kraken*, this is Robert Kray, captain of the yacht *Sandy's Dream*. I'm not exactly sure of our location. We departed Port Dickson about an hour ago, so I believe we're about twenty-five miles southeast of the port.

"We are being pursued by two fast boats carrying six men in each boat. The men appear to be armed with rifles and pistols and what looks like machetes. We're are cruising at twenty-two knots but I expect to be overtaken within ten to fifteen minutes. Request immediate assistance."

"Vic?" Adam shouted.

"Already on it," Vic yelled as he plotted his best guess of the yacht's location. "Adam." Vic looked up from the chart table. "We can intercept the yacht in seven minutes if we increase speed to thirty knots."

Both Vic and Paula stood facing Adam and waiting for the next order.

"Helmsman," Adam ordered, "increase speed to thirty knots. Boatswain, call away for full general quarters. I want all hands to battle stations." Adam turned to Vic. "Plot a course to intercept!"

The boatswain sounded the general alarm while Vic called out navigation course recommendations and Paula turned the ship to an intercept course. Paula maintained communications with the yacht and assured them that help was on the way.

Adam had trouble sitting in the bridge chair. He wanted to be standing the bridge officer watch and calling out orders. It took every ounce of energy to keep from relieving Paula and taking over. He purposely swung his head around and away from the goings-on of the bridge and watched the two foc'sle .50-caliber machine gunners checking their weapons and preparing for potential action.

A few seconds later Adam noticed a figure walking from the superstructure to the port-side machine gunner. He leaned forward in his chair and squinted to get a better glimpse.

"Is that Cy down there on the foc'sle?" Adam asked Paula.

Paula shifted her focus to the lower deck. "Yes. What's he doing down there?"

Adam slowly shook his head. "Must be checking on the gun crews."

Cy continued talking with the port-side machine gunner and then pointed toward the rear of the ship. The gunner nodded, stepped away from the weapon, and began walking aft. Cy inspected the machine gun and then assumed the position as gunner.

"What the hell is he doing?" Adam asked no one in particular.

Scott reappeared on the bridge, received a quick brief of the situation from Paula, and relieved her as bridge officer. Adam asked her to stay on the bridge and maintain radio communications with the yacht. Paula took the mic and stood between Scott and Adam.

Scott scanned the horizon through his binoculars and within seconds announced, "I have them." Still looking through binoculars, he pointed, and Adam lifted his binoculars in the same direction.

The increased speed caused the ship to bounce violently over the waves. The two forward machine gunners maintained their balance by bending their knees and holding tightly to their weapons. Paula radioed the yacht again and relayed their position. She indicated that the *Kraken* would reach their ship in the next sixty seconds. She requested status of their pursuers.

Captain Kray responded immediately. "Pursuers have fired shots in an effort to get us to stop. Both boats are within seventy feet astern of us."

Paula released the key to the mic and looked at Adam.

Adam calculated distances quickly. "The boats are too close to the yacht for us to use the LRAD. Tell the *Sandy's Dream* to pass by our port side and swing around our fantail. As they pass by the foc'sle, our port-side forward machine gunner will fire over the heads of the pursing boats. Hopefully that will make them disengage their pursuit."

Paula relayed the plan to Captain Kray while Scott grabbed the mic to the sound-powered phone and ran out to the port bridgewing. He called to Cy and shared the plan and the order to fire over the heads of the pursuing boats. Scott then added that deadly force was authorized if individuals in the fast boats returned fire.

Cy acknowledged the order. Scott reentered the bridge and closed the port bridge blast door. The bridge boatswain notified Scott that the gunners on the fantail had also acknowledged the order. The yacht was less than a mile from the *Kraken*.

Adam ran to the port side of the bridge and stared out of the forward window. He could clearly see one of the boats that trailed the yacht. He noticed movement and quickly glanced at the foc'sle to see Cy pulling back the retracting slide handle to load his weapon. The yacht was within 500 yards.

Scott reached above his head and grabbed the ship's whistle lever. He pulled the lever and allowed the whistle to blow for four seconds, hoping that the pursuing boats would see the warship and disengage.

To Scott's disappointment, both boats maintained pursuit.

Sandy's Dream began passing the *Kraken* at approximately thirty yards on the port side. Adam saw six men in the closest boat. Two had rifles pointed toward the yacht, and two had rifles pointed toward the *Kraken*. The second boat was approximately thirty feet behind and to the right of their lead boat.

Adam turned in time to see Cy yank the trigger of the machine gun. He turned back and expected to see tracer rounds flying above the boats but instead saw the machine-gun rounds splashing into the water on a fast track toward the lead boat.

Before Adam could utter a sound, a stream of bullets ripped through the center of the small craft. Two riders in the center of the boat were simultaneously hit by the high-powered rounds. Adam watched in horror as the head of the closest rider exploded. He vaguely heard Paula scream as the bridge team saw brain, blood, skull, and fleshy matter cover the two riders in the rear of the boat.

Scott called all stop, and the ship began to slow.

A sharp piece of bone or boat material must have pierced the eye of the rear starboard rider because he dropped his weapon, jerked his head backward, and covered his left eye with both hands. Blood flowed through his fingers as he leaned over his knees.

Cy continued to fire the weapon. Two more high-powered rounds struck the left arm and shoulder of the middle rider on the starboard side. The rider instinctively lifted his left arm to shield himself from the attack, but the blow from the bullet tore the arm off just under his shoulder. A third round ripped through the rider's throat and separated his spinal column. He was dead within three seconds.

The two riders in the front of the boat tried to scramble over the side and into the water, but Cy swung the gun to their position and fired a new burst. Both men were killed instantly as they took multiple rounds to their backs, necks, and heads. One was thrown overboard while the other fell back into the boat.

The second boat quickly turned and moved at high speed in the direction from which they came.

Cy stopped firing. Though he was breathing heavily, he was completely calm and at peace. He slowly spun the gun toward the rear of the fast boat. The rider on the starboard side was still leaning forward and holding his head, rocking back and forth in obvious pain. The other rider maintained a grip on the rudder lever, though he had released the throttle and allowed the boat to stop. He was obviously in shock as he stared wide-eyed at Cy.

On the *Kraken*, Cy leaned to the right of the gun and inspected the boat. He showed no emotion as he looked over the carnage that he had inflicted. Seawater and blood covered the deck and sloshed back and forth as the waves rocked the boat. Cy squinted, and the corners of his mouth curled upward. His eyes shifted to the two riders in the rear of the boat. He leaned back behind the gun and took aim.

Adam anticipated what was going to happen next and began pounding on the thick bridge window. The boat driver appeared to snap out of his shock and began reaching for his rifle, but before he could lift it from the boat floor, Cy opened fire.

It was over within five seconds. All six boat riders were dead, and the boat was quickly filling with water.

Adam ran out of the bridge while Scott grabbed his radio.

"Danny," Scott called out on the radio, "this is Scott."

"Danny here" was the reply.

Scott keyed the radio. "Where are you?"

Danny responded, "On the fantail. What's up? Why all of the gunfire?"

"I'll explain later," Scott was frantic. "Get to the foc'sle immediately!"

Adam sprinted down the ladder and tore through the watertight door that opened to the foc'sle. He ran across the deck toward Cy, who was still admiring his work.

Adam reached the gun mount and snatched the back of Cy's shirt collar, yanking Cy from the gun and swinging him back toward the superstructure. Cy worked to maintain balance and reached down to his right hip to grab the hand grip to the pistol in his belt holster.

Cy leaned forward from the hip. He held the still-holstered pistol tightly in his grip. From the bridge Cy resembled a cowboy in an old Western getting ready for the big shootout.

Cy bared his teeth and glared at Adam.

"Are you out of your fucking mind?" Adam screamed. "Who authorized you to open fire on that boat? Do you know what you've done?" Adam pointed to Cy's hip. "And why are you carrying that firearm on my ship?"

The two men stared at each other. Neither of them moved.

Danny ran onto the foc'sle and approached Adam and Cy. He saw rage and a wildness in Cy's eyes. Danny traced Cy's arm down to his hip and noticed that Cy was holding a pistol.

"Guys," Danny softly began, "we need to relax."

Neither Adam nor Cy backed down. Both continued to glare at each other.

"Adam," Danny continued, "let's take this to the wardroom. We don't need any confrontation in front of the crew."

Adam relaxed his posture and took a deep breath. Cy removed his hand from the pistol but continued staring at Adam.

Adam turned to Danny and calmly asked, "May I use your radio please?"

Danny handed over his radio. Adam looked up to the bridge window and keyed the radio transmit button.

"Scott, this is Adam. Please contact the captain of *Sandy's Dream* and ask them to tie up to our starboard side fantail. Invite their crew and passengers onboard, and have Doc Kelly meet with them on the mess decks to ensure that everyone on their vessel is OK. Ask George to get with their captain to check out the vessel for damage. Then invite all of them to dinner. Let the cooks know that we'll host the owners and yacht's senior crew in the wardroom. Ask Bobby to host the rest in the chief's mess."

"Will do," Scott replied. "Anything else?"

Adam paused for a moment, then raised the radio and keyed the transmit button. "Yes. Please meet me in the wardroom with Leroy, Bobby, Terry, Danny . . . and you"—Adam pointed at Cy—"in ten minutes."

Adam handed the radio back to Danny. "Please remove Cy's firearm and take his keys to the armory."

Adam spun around and departed the foc'sle.

Danny turned to Cy and held out his hand. "Please, Cy."

Cy paused for a few seconds, pulled the pistol from his holster, ejected the magazine, and cleared the chamber. He then handed the weapon and ammo to Danny, and reached inside his trousers pocket to retrieve a ring with several keys. He removed one key and the attached .308 bullet.

"Stateroom key," he said simply, then handed the rest to Danny.

Before leaving the foc'sle, Cy asked, "Can you please contact Pete Muro? We need him to clean, oil, and man the gun."

"I'll make it happen," Danny agreed and nodded.

George and two of his engineers met Paula and Bobby on the fantail. While they talked, Bobby's nephews arrived and closed around Bobby. Bobby told Timmy and Tom to assist George in tying up the yacht and to help bring the crew and passengers aboard, then left the fantail and headed toward his meeting in the wardroom.

Sandy's Dream maneuvered slowly until she was next to the *Kraken's* starboard fantail. Two crewmembers from the yacht tossed mooring lines to Timmy and Tom, who secured them to the frigate's bollards. A mooring ladder was then lowered over the side of the ship to the yacht.

Paula stood at the top of the ladder and watched as two men, a woman, and a young boy each took turns climbing the ladder to the *Kraken*'s fantail. A tall, well-built man wearing khaki pants and a blue polo shirt approached her.

He extended his hand and smiled. "Hi, I'm Robert Kray. I'm the captain of the *Sandy's Dream*."

Paula grabbed Robert's hand. "I'm Paula Cook. I'm the officer who spoke with you on the radio."

Robert took a small step back and tilted his head, examining Paula with a puzzled look on his face. "Is this an American Navy ship?" he asked. "I don't understand. Why aren't you in uniform?"

Paula laughed. "Let's go inside. Our doctor wants to have a look at you to make sure that you're all good. After that we can sit down and answer all questions."

Captain Kray stepped aside. The second man stepped forward. He was much shorter—Paula guessed about five foot five inches— and chubby. The man had his arm wrapped around the woman from the yacht and appeared to be escorting her forward. The young boy stood directly behind the two.

The man released the woman to walk up to Paula, and grabbed her hand, pumping it up and down.

"Thank you! Thank you." He continued shaking Paula's hand. "I don't know what we would have done without your help. They came out of nowhere and started firing guns. I honestly thought that we were going to be captured . . . or worse."

Paula added her other hand to the handshake, hoping to calm him. "I'm very happy that we were in the area and able to assist you."

The man released Paula. "I'm Kurt Amaya. This is my wife, Lynn, and my son, Christopher."

Lynn Amaya was about six inches taller than her husband, with long blond hair and equally long tan legs. She had to be at least ten years younger than her husband. Though she was obviously shaken from their recent ordeal, Lynn was well dressed and looked like the type of woman who was accustomed to wealth.

Paula nodded at Lynn and smiled. *Trophy wife,* Paula thought. She then smiled at Christopher and said hello. He couldn't have been more than ten, maybe eleven years old. Way too young to be involved in that mess.

Paula gestured toward the ship's superstructure. "Mr. Amaya—"

"Please call me Kurt," he interrupted.

Again, Paula nodded. "Please, Kurt, will you and your family follow me?" She turned back to Captain Kray. "You too, Captain. We're going to make a quick stop at sick bay, and then you're invited to dinner in our wardroom."

Paula escorted the group into the ship.

Adam opened the door to the wardroom and stepped inside. Bobby, Leroy, Terry, Danny, and Cy sat at the table. Adam poured a glass of water and sat in his usual chair. Scanning the individuals sitting on both sides of the table, he turned to Danny.

"Where's Scott?" Adam asked.

"Still on the bridge," Danny answered. "Want me to relieve him?"

"No, I believe we're good." Adam leaned back in his chair. He crossed his arms and calmly turned to Cy. "What gave you the right to fire into that boat?" Adam glared while he spoke.

Cy looked at Danny, then turned back to Adam. "That yacht was under attack," Cy replied evenly. "Those pirates were firing on their ship, and when they were within range, two of them pointed rifles at our ship."

Cy returned Adam's glare. "You gave me the right to fire when you told me that deadly force was authorized if we were threatened."

Adam chewed on his bottom lip. "Why did you relieve the gunner on the foc'sle? And why were you wearing a sidearm?"

Cy raised his head slightly. "We were being put into a position of potential conflict, and I wanted to ensure that the ship's most capable gunners were on station. And I will always wear a sidearm whenever our ship enters a hostile fire zone." Cy looked to each individual at the table. "Actually, my team and I should be armed at all times. The safety and security of our ship is my utmost concern."

Adam paused and absorbed Cy's comments. "You weren't hired to be a gunner. You were hired as our weapons officer." Adam looked at Terry. "Where is the weapons officer stationed during general quarters?"

Terry glanced at Cy and then back to Adam. "The weapons officer is typically in CIC during GQ, at the fire-control station."

Adam nodded. "Interesting." He took a drink from his glass and returned his attention to Cy. "Why then would you jeopardize our ship by absenting yourself from your appointed place of duty?"

Adam stared at Cy, who remained quiet. Cy still showed no emotion. Adam was about to speak again when the wardroom door opened.

Scott walked in, closed the door, and sat next to Adam.

"What's happening?" he asked.

Adam maintained his gaze at Cy and responded, "I'm trying to figure out, one, why our weapons officer left CIC to take over the forward port gun; two, why he disregarded orders to only fire over the pursuers' heads; and three, why he was wearing a loaded firearm on his hip."

Scott turned to Adam. "I may be able to shed some light on the first issue."

Adam twisted in his seat and faced Scott. "OK."

Scott began, "I've just learned that Aaron Bozman, who was the initial gunner on the forward port side, had radioed CIC about ten minutes before we received the distress call. Aaron indicated that he was feeling nauseous and had a blinding headache. I haven't had the opportunity to talk with Cy, but I believe that he needed a forward gunner immediately, so he ran to the post. Cy's only offense here is that he did not turn over his duties to Terry."

Adam twisted his head toward Cy. "Is this true, Cy?"

"Yes," Cy responded dryly.

"Why didn't you tell me this before?" Adam asked.

"When could I do that?" Cy raised his voice and glowered at his captain. "You attacked me on the foc'sle. I didn't know what was going on. I almost shot you."

Adam lifted his chin slightly and narrowed his eyes. "That's a good point. I'm still not sure why you were carrying an unauthorized loaded firearm on my ship."

Cy leaned forward. "I had no idea what was happening out there with the yacht. I've never been in a situation involving piracy on the high seas. As I mentioned earlier, had I thought about it sooner, I would have armed my entire team with handguns, to be prepared for anything."

Adam took a deep breath and paused to think. Cy's logic was valid. They had underestimated the risk in the area and should have been prepared for the unknown.

Adam nodded. "Cy, I agree with your decisions to man the gun and to arm yourself. But you should have informed Scott or me about these decisions. Better communication from you regarding these issues could have negated the need for this inquiry and would have also lessened these negative emotions."

Adam glanced at Danny and back to Cy. "On both sides," Adam added. "But my biggest concern is that you disregarded my order to fire over the pursuers' heads. You took it upon yourself to kill each man in that boat."

It was Cy's turn to take a breath. He looked down to the table and shut his eyes, rubbing the .308 bullet between his fingers.

"Adam, you are correct that my orders were to fire over the heads of the pursuers. You are also correct that my orders were to avoid lethal force unless the pursuers returned fire. Unfortunately, you are not correct in stating that I did not follow those orders."

Cy paused and challenged Adam with another stare.

"Really," Adam responded. "Please then, tell me your side."

Cy sat up. "As the yacht passed by, I saw five men in the boat with rifles and one man steering the boat. Several of the men were pointing rifles at both ships. As the yacht neared our ship, I heard at least two shots fired, though I couldn't determine if they were meant for our ship or the yacht. Based on that information I assumed that we were at risk and being fired upon. At that time, I made the decision to use lethal force.

"I fired a burst at the two men in the middle of the boat and followed up with a burst at the two men in the front. I stopped and turned the gun toward the two men in the rear of the boat. I was hoping that they would surrender, but instead of raising their arms, the man at the rudder reached down and grabbed a rifle positioned at his feet. I then fired a burst to eliminate that threat before he could position himself and take aim. Regrettably, I hit the wounded man who was sitting next to him."

Adam looked into Cy's eyes, then studied Cy's face. Adam saw only cold-blooded satisfaction. He couldn't be sure, but it appeared that Cy was even smiling a bit.

"Adam." Scott pulled him away from his thoughts. "I can confirm Cy's story. The men in the boat were armed and their weapons were pointed at both ships. I can't confirm that shots were fired but only because the blast door prevented me from hearing any external sound."

Adam didn't like Cy's story. Something about it just didn't feel right, but he knew that he couldn't prove malicious intent based on Scott's testimony.

Similarly, Adam did not like what he had to do next. He needed to apologize to Cy for attacking him. His stomach tightened and his head ached. He knew that he was right and didn't want to show remorse for his actions. *Especially to Cy!*

After a few moments, Adam slowly pushed his chair from the table. He stood and faced his weapons officer.

"I'm genuinely sorry for grabbing you on the foc'sle, Cy."

Adam extended his hand. Cy rose from his chair and gripped his hand.

Adam continued, "I assumed the worst and lost my temper. I hope that you can accept my most sincere apology."

Adam released Cy's hand and offered a small smile. Cy pushed both hands into his pockets.

"No need to apologize, Captain. I'm glad that you're happy with my explanation. I will try to improve my communication skills in the future."

Adam was still uneasy with Cy's explanation and lack of remorse.

He nodded and turned to Scott. "Please get Paula and Hasif. We have guests onboard for dinner, and we need get out of the wardroom so that Paula's team may prepare something special."

As everyone piled out, Adam grabbed Scott and Danny. He waited until the door closed.

"Please keep an eye on Cy," Adam whispered. "I'm still not convinced that there isn't more to his story."

Both Scott and Danny agreed to monitor Cy. The three left the wardroom and crossed paths with Hasif, who hurried past them, carrying clean tablecloths.

CHAPTER 15

"A toast." Kurt Amaya raised his glass of iced tea. "To our rescuers and heroes."

The dinner party raised their glasses.

Adam never felt comfortable accepting praise and definitely didn't like being called a hero. He'd heard this for the past few years any time he mentioned that he was a retired military man. "Oh, thank you for your service" or "You're an American hero."

Adam considered a great many men and women who had served with him to be the real, true heroes, but he never included himself in that group.

Adam smiled and thanked Kurt for his kind words. He then pointed around the room at his fellow officers and humbly responded, "There's your heroes."

"American pleasure craft don't usually wander around these parts," Scott noted. "What were you doing in these waters?"

Captain Kray lowered his head and cleared his throat as if he wanted to say something.

Several heads at the table turned toward him but were distracted by Kurt, who began speaking. "That's my fault, actually."

Kurt Amaya indicated that he was an oral maxillofacial surgeon—a specialized dental surgeon who owned his own practice.

He explained that his family had been in Singapore for three weeks and were growing bored.

"For some reason I got the idea in my head to visit Kuala Lumpur. I saw that there were some Asian temples and the Batu Caves, so I asked Captain Kray to take us there."

Kurt glanced quickly at Captain Kray and then back to Adam.

"The captain strongly recommended that we avoid this trip due to high risks and the threat of criminal and pirating activity in the strait. I argued with Captain Kray and finally, against his better judgement, he reluctantly agreed to the trip."

Scott was silent for a moment and then asked, "Did you even get to Kuala Lumpur?"

Kurt's chubby cheeks flushed. "No. We got just north of Port Dickson. That's when those two boats began chasing us and firing their guns."

Scott raised his eyebrows, looked at Adam, and leaned back in his chair. Hasif began clearing dinner plates and pouring coffee and hot tea for the group. It was obvious that Kurt wanted to change the subject.

"So, I have to ask," he began as he inspected the ship's officers, "are you the US Navy?"

Captain Kray choked on the water he had been sipping. Danny clapped him on the back.

Adam leaned back in his chair and smiled. "No. We're not US Navy. In fact, we're not associated with any country."

Kurt twisted his head to Captain Kray, a confused look on his face. Captain Kray raised his eyes and pursed his lips but provided no explanation.

Kurt turned back to Adam. "I don't understand. This is a military warship, but none of the crew are dressed in uniforms. What exactly is this ship?"

Adam maintained a soft smile. He turned slowly to get a look at each of his senior staff members. They were all smiling but silent.

Adam looked back to Kurt. "We're privateers," he said simply.

Kurt's face contorted. "Privateers? You mean mercenaries?"

Adam maintained his smile and calmly replied, "No. We are privateers. We help governments protect and maintain their sea lanes."

Kurt quickly turned to look from one officer to the next until he settled back to Adam. "You're mercenaries! You fight for the highest bidder. You're, well, you're mercenaries! How can you do what you do?"

Adam chuckled. "Kurt, it doesn't matter what you call us. In fact, you didn't seem to care who we were a couple hours ago." He raised his hand to get Hasif's attention. "Hasif, what do we have for dessert?"

The ship's steward turned to the wardroom food bar and grabbed a plate covered with yellow pastries. "We have a very tasty lemon tart. Would you like some, Captain?"

"Please!" Adam replied. "But serve our guests first." He turned back to the table. "Kurt, Lynn, Christopher, and Captain Kray, I'm happy to have you as guests on our ship this evening. I'm equally happy that we were in the area and able to help you."

Captain Kray raised his glass in thanks while Kurt stared at the table.

Adam continued, "The majority of officers and crew on this ship are former US Navy sailors. We grew up in the Navy and loved being at sea. We had the opportunity to procure our own ship and then provide help and assistance at locations throughout the world. We are not guns for hire, and we certainly don't fight for the highest bidder."

Kurt slowly raised his head and peered at Adam, who continued speaking.

"Kurt, we are no threat to you. In fact, you are completely safe while on our ship. Our doctor has assured me that you and the crew are physically okay, and George, our chief engineer, has inspected your craft to ensure that it is seaworthy."

Adam paused for effect. "You may reboard your craft and leave at the time of your choosing. I'd like to believe that we have been courteous and maybe even a little entertaining. I'd also like to also believe that the passengers and crew of the *Sandy's Dream* are now our friends."

Adam stood and held out his hand. Feeling foolish, Kurt stood as well. He'd just insulted the men and women who had saved his family from pirates. He shook Adam's hand and flashed a toothy smile .

"Adam, I apologize. You most certainly have treated my family and me with the utmost kindness. I had no right to be so judgmental. I don't care what you say—you are my heroes and my friends. I'm sorry for my outburst. It's been a long day, and to be quite honest, I wasn't prepared for your answers."

Kurt continued to pump Adam's hand. The up-and-down movement made Kurt's chin jiggle.

"I will leave you my contact information. Let me know if there's ever anything that I can do for you or your crew. I would be happy to help you at any time."

When dinner was over, Adam and Scott escorted their guests to the fantail. Bobby assisted the *Sandy's Dream* passengers and crew back to their vessel and then cast off the mooring lines. Both Adam and Scott waved as the yacht pulled away.

Scott tilted his head toward Adam and grinned. "Think they'll make it back safely?"

A half smile appeared on Adam's face. "As long as Captain Kray doesn't listen to the sage advice of Kurt Amaya." Both men laughed as they made their way to the bridge.

The next twenty-four hours were uneventful and quiet. The *Kraken* passed through the strait and into the Indian Ocean without further interruption.

Adam relaxed the threat condition back to normal steaming operations, and he swore that he could hear the crew breathe a long sigh of relief as they secured from their battle station assignments. Cy's team returned all weapons to the armory for a thorough cleaning and oiling. All major weapons were placed in standby mode.

Adam emailed Oliver and recounted their confrontation with the Malaccan pirates.

They still had roughly 1,200 nautical miles until the next refueling point in Colombo, Sri Lanka, and Adam and Scott planned to spend most of their time training and running drills. Vic anticipated arriving at Colombo in three days.

Oliver replied to Adam and congratulated him and the *Kraken* crew on their performance. He then provided Paula with contact information for the logistics team in Colombo.

Adam leaned back in his starboard bridge chair, kicked his legs up to the window ledge, and stared out at the horizon. His mind rolled over and over the actions of his crew, particularly those of Cy during their confrontation with the pirates. He considered what issues could occur when they came in contact with the Iranian fast boats. Adam couldn't help but think that Cy's overzealous behavior might jeopardize a peaceful solution.

Adam was still deep in thought when Leroy entered the bridge. As he toured the space, Leroy stopped by each watch stander to chat. His interest in ship's operations grew each day, especially those related to positioning and maneuvering. He loved spending time at the helm and hoped to someday qualify as a bridge officer.

He talked with the helmsman and then wandered over to the chart table and spoke briefly with the quartermaster, who was plotting the ship's course.

He made his way to the port bridge windows where Danny was scanning the horizon. Danny heard footsteps behind him and briefly lowered his binoculars to smile at the ship's foreman before resuming his task.

"What brings you up here?" Danny inquired.

Leroy squinted in the direction of Danny's search. The glare of the sun off the water made it difficult to see anything.

"Just thought I'd come up and say hello," Leroy replied. "Anything interesting going on?"

Danny shook his head slightly. "Not really. We did see our old friend the *Cowpens* a little while ago. You know, that cruiser that's been following us."

Leroy nodded and offered a noncommittal grunt of understanding. He ambled to the starboard side where Adam was still staring through the bridge window.

"Hello, Captain!" Leroy cheerfully greeted.

Adam snapped out of his meditation and twisted in his chair.

"Well hello, sir." Adam was happy to be pulled from his thoughts. "And how are you today?"

Leroy raised his chin, narrowed his eyes, and pursed his lips. "Well, you know what they say, any day at sea is better than real work."

Adam cocked his head to one side. "I've never heard that saying before."

Leroy maintained the narrow look but smiled. "I just made it up. Go ahead and quote me."

Leroy paused and did a quick review of his boss. Adam looked tired. Leroy couldn't tell for sure, but it appeared that Adam's hair had turned a bit grayer.

Leroy stepped closer to the captain's chair. "And how are you doing?" he pressed.

Adam took a deep breath. He rubbed his eyes and tried to remove the sting of sleeplessness.

"I'm OK," he yawned while reopening his eyes. "Just tired of dealing with . . ."

Adam caught himself before he completed the sentence. Leroy remained quiet. Adam turned slowly, his eyes darting around the bridge to make sure that no one was within earshot.

"Leroy," Adam whispered, "what do you think about that situation with the pirate attack?"

Leroy curled his bottom lip under his teeth. He knew that Adam was troubled by Cy's actions.

"Well." Leroy glanced down to the deck. "I'm not convinced that the pirate boat was firing at us or even aiming at us."

He raised his head and locked eyes with Adam. "I'm also not convinced that our weapons officer didn't enter that situation with malicious intent."

Both men silently considered the situation.

Adam whispered, "So you believe that Cy had every intention to shoot and kill the pirates?"

Leroy leaned closer to Adam. "I didn't say that." Leroy matched Adam's whisper. "I said that I'm not sure of Cy's intent." He paused. "Adam, I served with a lot of people over my thirty years of active duty. Every now and then we'd get some young kid who had stars in his eyes. Seen one too many war movies and joined the Army just so he could storm that hill like John Wayne and save the platoon from certain disaster."

A smile crept up his face, but he maintained a look of seriousness.

"Those kids were dangerous. Loose cannons. But we always managed to control them with intimidation and fear. Ultimately, they would grow up and lose that hero-fantasy bullshit."

Leroy's smile dropped. "I believe that Cy is a lot like those kids except we can't intimidate or scare him. He's much more dangerous because he is in a position of power and he believes that he is justified in using that power whenever he's put into a position where he has the opportunity to resolve conflict."

A look of bewilderment crossed Adam's face. "When did you become a psychoanalyst?"

Leroy laughed. "Cy is a classic example of someone who wants to be a hero." He dropped his gaze to consider his next words. "Or," Leroy added, "Cy is a complete sociopath who was looking for an opportunity to kill someone."

Adam tilted his head back and closed his eyes. "Leroy, will you do something for me?" Adam met his gaze. "During your many travels through the ship, will you please try to keep tabs on Cy?"

Leroy raised an eyebrow.

"I don't want you to spy on him," Adam continued. "Just keep an eye on him and let me know if you come across anything odd."

The crew drilled hard for the next two days. Though their reaction speed increased and improved, Adam continued to feel uneasy. He was confident in the crew's abilities to handle a nasty situation but had never considered the emotional or psychological state of each individual on the ship. He couldn't afford to have some overzealous hotshot, like Cy, begin firing weapons at a potentially hostile target, especially if there was a chance that a nonviolent solution could be worked out.

No tug or pilot was available for the transit into the port of Colombo, but Adam was convinced of Scott's abilities to moor them without assistance.

Adam sat in his chair and watched Scott expertly maneuver the ship. The *Kraken* glided in just fifteen feet off their pier where Scott used the engines, mooring lines, and capstan to get the ship safely into position. When the bridge bosun announced "moored" on the 1MC intercom, Scott turned to Adam, raised his fist, and pumped it straight down.

"I'm the man!" he shouted.

Adam grinned, glad that Scott could still be cocky. Adam noted that the crew's excitement for pulling into Colombo was not as high as it had been at previous ports. He wondered if maybe they were becoming more and more conscious of the job they were to perform in the next few weeks.

Those thoughts were on his mind as well. He was grateful to see Paula and George enter the bridge and make their way to his chair.

"Howdy, oh Greek god of seamanship," George greeted Scott while delivering a half bow.

Adam laughed, and Paula nudged George in the ribs.

"We're set for refueling and replenishing all stores and ammunition," Paula briefed Adam. "Our contacts and their teams are on the pier and ready to begin."

"Great," Adam replied. He turned to face George. "How's the plant?"

"Good," George answered casually. "Wish I had a system this strong when I was on active duty."

Once the ship had doubled up their mooring lines to the pier, Scott wandered over and joined the group. "Any plans for dinner or drinks ashore tonight?"

Paula opened her notebook. "My contacts here in the port have recommended a couple of restaurants. We're still scheduled to leave port tomorrow at noon, right?"

Adam nodded. "Yeah. Tide is high at noon, so it will be a perfect time to leave. Go ahead and pick whichever restaurant you want. Do we have transportation?"

"Yep," Paula answered. "We have a van that can carry up to eight passengers."

"Nice." Adam paused. "Let's see if Vic, Terry, Doc Kelly, and Danny want to join us. Who has the duty tonight?"

Scott raised his hand.

"It's my turn. You guys go have fun." Scott raised his eyebrows. "Might want to ask Cy to go with you tonight."

Adam grimaced involuntarily and then quickly recovered.

"Good idea. Paula, would you mind inviting everyone to dinner? In the meantime, I'm going to go and catch a quick nap and get ready. Let's leave at 1730, OK?"

Nods all around.

"Hey, Scott?" Adam said before he left. Scott spun around. "Would you please have Vic work up the navigation plan for our next leg to Kuwait?"

"Sure thing, boss. He'll have a draft ready by tomorrow morning."

Adam thanked Scott and left the bridge.

Dinner conversation that evening was awkward at best. Cy refused to engage in any type of discussion and only provided short responses when asked a question. His silence created a tension at the table that could not be broken by any type of levity. The only sound coming from the table was the occasional clink of forks and knives on dinner plates. Halfway through dinner, Adam glanced at George, who gave a slight shrug.

Paula finally broke the silence and asked Adam how long it would take them to get to Kuwait.

Adam sipped his wine and gazed at the ceiling while he calculated the distance. "We're about twenty-three hundred nautical miles from our destination," he began, "so if we travel at twenty five knots . . . let's see, the time in hours traveled is equal to distance divided by speed, so it would be twenty three hundred divided by twenty five, so . . ."

His face scrunched as he figured out the math equation.

"Just about four days," Paula finished, glancing at Adam in a patronizing fashion. She smiled. "See what happens when you decide on a degree in history."

Adam twisted his head to look at George, and both men burst out laughing. Even Terry laughed at the joke.

"I am proud of my degree in the humanities," Adam stated. "It helps me when I'm watching *Jeopardy* on TV. Besides, math is a four-letter word that I don't normally say in polite conversations."

Terry responded in his usual condescending tone, "I don't know. I consider math to be extremely important if you're to spend a career at sea."

Adam and George glanced at each other again and smiled.

Danny sipped his wine and added, "Yep, the best part of math is multiplying."

Each of his friends had a puzzled expression as they tried to figure out Danny's remark.

He placed his wineglass on the table and scanned the group. "After all"—he grinned—"I do have four children."

The entire table roared with laughter.

Terry wiped a tear from his eyes. "I get it," he said. "He has multiplied with children. That's rich." The group laughed harder at Terry's remark.

"You are such a geek." George shook his head at Terry.

Only Cy was quiet. He smiled so that he would appear to be enjoying the evening, but in truth he was still pissed off. His key ring sat in his lap, hidden from the rest of the group. His thumb and finger slid over the smooth casing of the .308 bullet.

The group returned to the ship two hours later. Adam avoided talking with anyone and walked straight to his cabin. His head was pounding. He knew that he shouldn't drink wine. It never agreed with him.

Opening the mirrored cabinet above the sink in his personal bathroom, he found the bottle of aspirin, and tossed three into his mouth, dry-swallowing the pills. He plopped down on his rack without taking off his clothes and turned off the lamp. The steady thump in his head eventually lessened to a dull roar, and he finally and gratefully found sleep.

Three doors down from Adam's cabin, Cy sat in the metal chair next to his desk. He leaned forward, his elbows braced on his knees. Though he twisted the bullet between both hands, he did not see it. His mind focused on his rage.

How dare he question my motives? Cy thought, gritting his teeth. *He's too soft. You can't command a crew of warriors by being soft.* He closed his eyes and visualized the pirate boat in the Malaccan Strait. He saw the risk that those men posed and knew that they needed to be eradicated. *Adam had no idea how to deal with threats like that.* He clenched both fists and squeezed the bullet in his left hand.

Adam opened his eyes and looked at his wristwatch. It was 0546. His lips and throat were both dry. He must have been snoring—loudly.

He smiled as he remembered Chrissy complaining about his snoring.

He ran his dry tongue across chapped lips and thought, *This must be how a cat's tongue feels.* He sat up and winced. His back ached, but at least his head felt better. A nice hot shower would help him feel like normal.

Paula ate a bowl of cereal in the wardroom while Hasif stored newly received food and supplies in the galley. Terry walked in and nodded at Paula before continuing to the food counter. He grabbed an empty cup and poured coffee from the dented metal pot. Raising the cup just under his nose, he inhaled deeply.

"Ahhhh," he sighed as he glanced at Paula. "Nectar of the gods."

Paula swallowed and eyed Terry. He was uncommonly cheerful this morning.

"What are you up to?" she asked.

Terry tried his best "I'm innocent" look, but it only made him look more dubious.

"I'm sure that I don't know what you mean," he replied.

The door to the wardroom opened, and George entered holding two pairs of work trousers, one in each hand. He inspected one pair and then shifted his focus to the other.

"Paula," he asked without looking up, "are you having any trouble with the laundry?"

Paula squinted, and her eyes darted from George, to Terry, and back to George. She suspected foul play.

"Why?" she asked. "What's wrong?"

George continued to gaze at the trousers in his left hand. "It's weird," he began. "My pants seem to have shrunk in the wash."

Paula turned in her seat. Terry was staring at his coffee cup and doing his best not to acknowledge George's presence, but an ear-to-ear smile rose on Terry's thin face.

George stared at the Ops officer for a few seconds and noticed the devious smile. The old engineer returned his attention to the pants and grinned.

"Nice," George said. "That was a good one."

George set the trousers down on the table and poured a cup of coffee.

"How did you get my pants from the laundry?"

Terry wrapped his hands around the coffee cup and shrugged. "Not sure what you're talking about."

George sipped his coffee. He maintained his smile and nodded. "I am impressed. I honestly didn't think you had it in you."

Vic entered the wardroom carrying several documents. "Anyone seen Adam yet?"

Paula and Terry shook their heads in unison. "Not yet."

George replied, "Anything wrong?"

"No," Vic said. He sat next to George. "I've worked up the navigation plan to Kuwait and I just wanted to share it with him."

"I'm guessing four days' travel. Is that correct?" Paula asked.

Vic nodded. "Yeah, I calculated four days if we steam between twenty-five and thirty knots. Hoping that we catch the tide at noon."

George stood and picked up his trousers. "Need to get cracking if we're planning a noon departure." He turned to Paula. "If you see him, please let Adam know that I'm in Main Control."

As George left the wardroom, Paula turned to Terry. "That was a pretty good one, Terry. Nice job."

Terry merely smiled.

CHAPTER 16

At 1215 all mooring lines were pulled in, and the ship was underway.

From the bridge Adam watched the crew on the foc'sle stow the lines and prepare the deck for sea as Scott expertly navigated the ship away from the pier and pushed her to open water.

Aside from a short rain squall, the skies were bright and sunny. It was hot and muggy in the bridge, so all bridgewing doors and windows were open to catch the breeze. Adam sank into his chair and kicked his feet up on the window ledge. His thoughts drifted to Chrissy. He missed her. He wondered what she would think of this venture.

She probably wouldn't have allowed me to even consider such a move, he thought.

Adam had jokingly talked about becoming a mercenary when he retired from active duty. Chrissy humored him for about six seconds before she put her foot down. "You've spent the last three decades traveling the world," she reminded him. "Now you belong to me and will stay home. Get used to it."

"Yes ma'am" was all that he could muster. Adam smiled at the memory.

He tried to keep busy so that his mind and thoughts were focused on more positive things. The only times he felt sad and alone were when he remembered how good his life had once been.

Paula and Lonnie were touring and inspecting their spaces. As Paula pointed out excess dirt buildup in a passageway corner, Lonnie raised his head and cocked it to one side. He appeared to be listening to a distant sound.

Paula looked up. "What's the matter?" she asked.

Lonnie squinted and frowned. "It's really quiet."

Paula stared off. Aside from the sound of ventilation and the hum of the engineering plant, there was no other noise to be heard. No talking. No laughing. No sound of hard-soled shoes moving across the metal decks.

"You're right," she said, turning her head from one side to the other. "That's really odd."

They walked to the mess decks where they saw several sailors cleaning the space and performing maintenance. None were speaking—just going through the motions of their work.

"We're heading into the gulf soon," Lonnie said. "I'm sure that's what's on everyone's minds."

Adam ate his dinner on the bridge. The cook had prepared a simple meal of two BLTs and potato soup. Danny had the deck and was scanning the horizon through the port-side windows. The temperature inside the bridge was pushing ninety degrees, and each sailor sweltered and stood their watches in sweat-soaked shirts.

Adam wiped the sweat off his forehead with his dinner napkin. He hated the heat.

Rising from his chair, he placed his dinner plate on the window ledge and turned to Danny.

"I'm going to take a walk on deck," he announced.

Adam casually inspected the passageways as he headed aft through the ship's interior. He looked up at the electrical cables and steam lines crisscrossing the ship's ceiling areas and checked the cleanliness of the angle irons that held together the skin of the ship. Opening the watertight door that exited the ship's superstructure, he stepped onto the flight deck.

The sun was just beginning to set, turning the ocean a deep orange as it touched the horizon. Adam walked slowly to the edge of the deck and grabbed the lifeline safety cables with both hands. He lifted his chin and closed his eyes.

The warm ocean breeze helped cool him down a bit. He opened his eyes and looked over the side to stare at the whitecaps made by the ship as it knifed through the deep blue water. He smiled. A feeling of calm and peacefulness swept over him as he gazed at the ship's wake.

Adam was so mesmerized that he didn't notice the watertight door open behind him.

A shadowy figure stepped through the door and onto the flight deck. Closing the door, the figure slowly moved toward the ship's captain, closing within ten feet.

Adam's deep concentration was interrupted at the sound of a handgun slide being pulled back and released. He jerked around and was surprised to see Cy standing directly behind him.

Adam was more surprised to see Leroy holding a handgun to the back of Cy's head.

Adam switched his gaze from Leroy to Cy and then back to Leroy.

"What the hell is going on?" Adam demanded as he pressed his body against the lifelines.

Without taking his eyes off the weapons officer, Leroy explained that he had seen Cy wearing a holstered pistol and walking quickly past the crew's mess. Leroy ran to his stateroom to grab his personal handgun and began searching for Cy. Out of pure luck he wandered out to the flight deck, where he saw Cy sneaking up behind Adam.

"He wasn't holding his pistol and didn't have his hand on the holster," Leroy continued. "But I just didn't want to assume any intentions."

Adam's eyes narrowed and quickly shifted to Cy.

"What are your intentions, Cy?"

Cy no longer looked surprised. In fact, Adam thought that he looked frustrated and even a little angry. Without moving his body,

Cy turned his head slightly toward Leroy.

"Would you please take that gun away from my head?"

Leroy looked over Cy's shoulder at Adam, who nodded. Leroy reengaged the slide, opened the pistol's chamber, and lowered the weapon.

Cy turned back to Adam. "I was looking for you. I'm still not happy about what happened the other day and I wanted to sit down and bury the hatchet."

"Bury the hatchet in Adam's head you mean," Leroy accused.

Cy ignored the comment. "And I was under the impression that I was approved to carry my pistol. At least that's what I took away from our last talk."

Adam relaxed. He gestured toward the superstructure. "Let's go to my in-port cabin and talk."

Adam led, Cy followed, and Leroy stayed close behind as the three men made their way to Adam's cabin. Adam closed the door, then sat behind his desk.

"Sit down, guys."

Leroy and Cy sat next to each other. Leroy crossed his arms but kept the pistol visible in his right hand.

Cy glanced at Leroy and then focused on Adam. "I really was looking for you to talk. I want to discuss what I believe my responsibilities are during combat operations." Cy leaned forward. "Adam, I feel like I'm being hampered. I need to react as I see fit in order to fight the battle."

Adam sat back in his chair to consider Cy's words. "Cy, you're right. You're our weapons officer, and as such, you must be allowed to defend the ship as you deem fit."

Adam allowed that to sink in before he continued.

"From this moment forward, you may arm yourself at all times. In fact, you are authorized to arm any crewmember to ensure the safety of our ship."

Leroy's eyes widened.

"All I ask"—Adam pointed toward Leroy—"is that you work with Leroy to determine who is on that list."

Cy's face contorted. His eyes shifted from Adam to Leroy, and back to Adam.

"Why do I need to work this through him?"

Adam shook his head slightly. "You don't need to work through Leroy. I just want him to know who is armed. He will also be authorized to carry a gun and train with your team. After all, Leroy has probably received the best training in handguns of anyone else on this ship."

"OK, Adam," Cy finally said, "I can do that."

"Also," Adam continued, "if you feel that your presence is needed outside of CIC during times of combat, then by all means, go do what is necessary."

Cy smiled slightly.

"Just please communicate your plans and actions with Terry."

Adam noticed Cy's smile drop.

"I just need to ensure that Terry understands that he is in charge of fire control in CIC if you're not there."

Cy chewed his lower lip. "Agreed," he finally answered. "Thank you, Adam."

Adam offered his hand, and both men shook.

"Thanks for bringing this up. I'm looking forward to seeing you and your boys in action when we get to our ultimate destination."

Cy nodded, glanced quickly at Leroy, and left the stateroom.

Leroy glared at Adam in disbelief. "I certainly hope that you know what you're doing."

Adam offered a small smile. "Did you ever see the movie *The Godfather*?"

Leroy nodded. "Sure."

"Well," Adam continued, "I always liked the quote 'Keep your friends close but keep your enemies closer.'"

Leroy leaned slightly forward. "I get it. But is Cy your enemy?"

"I sure hope not," Adam replied. His eyes narrowed and his smile widened. "Leroy, why in the world do you have a gun on board my ship?"

Leroy lifted the pistol and held it in front of his face. He slowly inspected it. "Nobody told me I couldn't bring a gun with me." He placed the gun in his lap and leaned back in his chair. "Besides, aren't you kind of glad that I did?"

"Yes sir," Adam laughed. "I am very happy you did." He pointed toward his cabin door. "Please continue to keep an eye on our weapons officer. I need to be sure that he has no other agenda."

Leroy stood, snapped a quick salute, and left the stateroom.

Adam held tag-up on the bridge the next morning. Cy had the deck and purposely stood on the opposite side of the bridge during the meeting. George, Terry, and Danny listened to the navigation status. Vic expected to enter the Strait of Hormuz in two days. It would take another day to get to Kuwaiti territorial waters.

Paula seemed preoccupied and wasn't as attentive as usual. Bobby stood next to Leroy, who occasionally glanced at Cy.

Adam looked over the group. "Where's Scotty?"

"Haven't seen him this morning," Danny replied.

Adam looked at Paula. "Have you seen him?" Paula shook her head. Adam turned to George, who just shrugged. Adam grabbed his phone and dialed Scott's stateroom. After three rings, a groggy-sounding voice answered.

"Scott, you sound awful." Adam was concerned.

"Terrible toothache," Scott mumbled.

Adam left the bridge and jogged to Scott's stateroom. He knocked and entered after he heard something that sounded like "Come in."

Scott was lying down and clutching his right cheek. He lifted his head, and Adam could clearly see that Scott's cheek was red and swollen.

Adam grabbed his radio. "Bridge, this is the captain."

Seconds later Cy responded, "Bridge here."

"Cy, please have Doc Kelly report to Scott's stateroom."

"Roger."

Several minutes later there was a soft knock on Scott's door, and Adam allowed Doc Kelly in.

"Not sure what's wrong with Scott. Please help him."

After a brief examination the doctor indicated that Scott appeared to be suffering from an abscessed tooth, and that he could provide Scott with meds to take the edge off the pain, but there was nothing that he could do short of pulling the tooth.

An idea struck Adam and he quickly called Paula. "Can you try to contact *Sandy's Dream* and find out where they are currently located? Then get ahold of Oliver and get him to schedule a helicopter to transport Kurt Amaya to us."

"Transport him to us at sea?" she asked.

Adam replied, "Where else?"

Sandy's Dream had returned to Singapore. Kurt was more than happy to break away from his dull life of luxury and to assist his friends on the *Kraken*. Within sixteen hours Doctor Kurt Amaya was back on board. Adam and Danny met Kurt on the flight deck and quickly ushered him down to sick bay where Scott was now located.

Kurt lugged four bags with him, and Danny asked Kurt if he was moving aboard. Kurt, clueless that he was being teased, began opening bags and removing dental instruments.

"Never know what you're going to need," he answered.

Adam watched Kurt place a number of instruments on the sick-bay table that reminded Adam of torture devices from an old horror movie. Doc Kelly stood next to Kurt, interested and even excited to speak to another medical professional.

"Where did you go to school?" he asked to break the ice. Without turning and without emotion Kurt answered, "University of Illinois." Kurt quickly glanced at Doc Kelly. "The same school where you went."

Adam glanced at Doc Kelly's face, which grew visibly pale.

Kraken's doctor inched back toward the rear of the space. "We'll need to get together a little later and talk," he muttered before he opened the sick-bay door and quickly slipped outside.

"What was that about?" Adam asked Kurt.

Kurt continued to work. "We can talk later. I need to take care of our patient first."

He finished prepping the table, then walked over to Scott, who was lying on the sick-bay bed.

"Open your mouth," he directed.

Scott winced and groaned as he slowly obliged. Kurt examined Scott, then told him to close and asked Scott how long he had been in pain. Scott mumbled that he'd had a root canal a couple months previously and that the same tooth was now bothering him.

Kurt nodded. "You have a cracked tooth. It's split in two. I can see that without an X-ray." He then turned to Adam and Danny. "Time for you two gentlemen to leave me to my work."

Adam asked, "How long is this going to take?"

Kurt faced Adam. "A minute shorter than it will take me to come out, raise my hands in victory and shout, 'I win.'"

Adam shut the door as he left the space.

"Can you fix the tooth or am I going to lose it?" Scott asked.

Kurt smiled. "Yes," he replied.

Forty-five minutes later Kurt opened the door to sick bay. Adam and Danny were waiting outside.

Kurt raised his arms and shouted, "I win."

Danny leaned toward Adam and whispered, "He's kind of a smart-ass."

Adam smiled. "I know. I like him."

Scott joined the trio. His cheek was still red, but the swelling was considerably lower than it had been.

"How ya feelin'?" Danny asked, grabbing Scott's shoulder.

Scott tried to smile but could only raise one side of his mouth. "Still numb," he mumbled as a stream of drool trickled down his chin.

He wiped his mouth with the back of his hand and tried to laugh. "I'm going to my stateroom to lie down."

Kurt tapped Adam on the arm. "Mind if we go somewhere to talk for a few minutes?"

"Sure," Adam replied. "Let's go have lunch in my stateroom."

Hasif collected the plates after the meal ended.

"Got something on your mind, Doc?" Adam asked as Hasif departed the space.

"Actually, I do," answered Kurt. "When you first brought us on board, I thought that I recognized your ship's doc from somewhere."

He paused.

Adam was getting agitated. "What's the problem, Doc?"

"When I got back to the yacht it dawned on me where I knew him from. Mark Kelly was in pre-med at the University of Illinois at the same time I was there. A recruiter from the Central Intelligence Agency visited the school. Mark became enamored with joining, and he tried hard to get several of my fellow classmates to go and talk to the recruiter with him."

Kurt placed his hands in his lap and leaned forward. His voice dropped to just above a whisper. "I'm sure that you already know this, but Mark probably still works for the CIA."

Adam was silent.

Kurt looked embarrassed. "When you told me that you worked for other countries, it kind of made sense that some of your crewmembers were employed by the CIA. I just didn't know if you knew."

Adam didn't show any shock. He smiled and thanked Kurt for the information. After a bit of small talk, Adam escorted Kurt back to the flight deck where the helicopter pilot was working through the preflight checks.

"Kurt, I can't begin to thank you for taking care of Scott."

Kurt grinned. "It's nice to have big friends on the high seas." He reached over and hugged Adam, then took his seat.

As the helicopter lifted away from the flight deck, Adam stepped into the superstructure and peered at his watch. It was 1330. He keyed his radio. "Bridge, this is the captain. I'll be in my cabin if anyone needs me."

The next morning Adam called the bridge and rescheduled the tag-up for 0900. He dressed, ate a quick breakfast in the wardroom, and began his rounds.

His first stop was to Scott's stateroom. The swelling in the XO's cheek was gone, and he appeared to be feeling much better.

"Hey, Scotty." Adam grabbed Scott's chin with his thumb and forefinger, then turned his head. "Looking good. How do you feel?"

"Great." Scott rubbed his cheek. "That was one monster toothache."

Adam nodded and smiled lightly. "Good. See you on the bridge at nine."

Adam walked down to Main Control. There was no reason. He just wanted to shoot the breeze with George. He spent the next hour listening to George complain and gripe about the heat outside. Adam just nodded and enjoyed spending time with his friend.

At 0850 he began his trek toward the bridge, climbed to his bridge chair, and sat.

At the conclusion of the tag-up, Adam asked Terry to have Frank prepare an updated brief on the Kuwait/Iran issue and discuss any noteworthy activity inside the gulf.

As the senior leaders exited the bridge, Adam called out to Doc Kelly.

"Hey, Doc." Adam put his hand on the doctor's shoulder. "Got a minute?"

He guided the doctor to his at-sea cabin where both men sat. Doc Kelly's face drained of color.

"Are you all right?" Adam asked.

The doctor raised his hand to his mouth and appeared to burp. "Just a little heartburn, Adam. What can I do for you?"

Adam thought he saw the doc's hand tremble a bit. He wasn't sure, but the medical professional did seem uncomfortable.

"Pretty cool seeing a college buddy so long after graduation, isn't it?" Adam tried to keep the conversation as light as possible.

"Huh? Oh yeah, you mean Amaya. Yeah, it's been quite a few years." His eyes shifted to the right.

Adam leaned back in his chair. He was tired of beating around the bush. "I know that you're working for the CIA, Doc."

Doc Kelly stiffened.

"It's OK, Doc. Relax. I laughed at George when he tried to convince me that Oliver was CIA. Apparently, that wasn't such a far-fetched idea."

Adam glanced away from the doctor. "I've given this a lot of thought over the past twenty-four hours, and it makes sense. The company that Oliver works for is the Central Intelligence Agency, not Worldwide Services, Inc. The CIA is behind this scheme to help rid Kuwait of the Iranian threat. I mean, why wouldn't the CIA have its own special ship-building island and the resources to fund this mission?"

Adam turned back to the doctor. "It only makes sense that the CIA would also place its own people on my ship. People who could provide status reports back to the home office."

No longer pale, Doc Kelly's face flushed at this.

Adam continued, "There are only two members on this ship who were not former US Navy sailors or referrals from our crew. Those two are you and Hasif."

Doc Kelly shook his head. "Now, Adam—" he began, but Adam held up his hand.

"Please, Doc, I know it's true. Again, it's OK. I don't have a problem with you and Hasif being on board. I don't even have a problem with you and Hasif sending reports to Oliver."

Adam lowered his hand and leaned over his desk. "All I want to know is if you are loyal to this ship and our crew."

The doctor continued shaking his head. "Adam, I'm not sure where you're getting your information."

Adam leaned back and rubbed his eyes. "Doc, you're going to give me a headache. I know that you and Hasif are associated with the CIA. For the last time, I'm OK with this. I'm not going to throw you off the ship." Adam let out a deep breath and locked eyes with the doctor. "Unless you lie to me."

Doc Kelly sighed. "Both Hasif and I were assigned to provide situational updates for our director."

"You mean Oliver," Adam interjected.

Doc nodded slightly. "Yes, Oliver. But"—he narrowed his eyes— "we are to perform our duties as ship's personnel to the utmost of our abilities. Adam, I'm part of this crew and a member of your wardroom. I'm loyal to our mission."

"Good," Adam said quickly. "Doc, I like and respect both you and Hasif. I really don't have a problem with you on board. In fact, once we start our cruise line, I was thinking of asking if you'd be interested in staying on. But that's a conversation for a later date. And I truly do appreciate your honesty."

After the meeting, and once the doctor was gone, Adam called the wardroom.

"Hello, Hasif." Adam smiled. "Do you have a few minutes?"

CHAPTER 17

T
he senior leaders gathered in the wardroom for the intel brief the following day.

A giant chart of the Arabian Gulf hung from the wardroom bulkhead. Frank began with an update on the declining relationship between Iran and Kuwait and discussed the political climate in each country. This was followed by Iran's military strengths, especially concerning their maritime capabilities.

"What ship threats should we be concerned with?" Adam asked.

Frank provided recent updates on Iranian ships and their last known operating conditions. He then pointed out the high-risk areas inside the gulf and focused on the passage within the Strait of Hormuz and the area surrounding Kuwaiti territorial waters.

Adam rose to stand next to Frank.

"I plan on flying the US flag through the strait and all the way to Kuwaiti territorial waters," Adam announced. "Once at our destination, we will raise the Kuwaiti flag and perform our duties as a representative of that country."

Frank nodded. "That would be wise. We shouldn't have problems getting to our destination as long as we are seen as a US weapon."

George raised his hand. "What about getting out?"

Frank asked, "What do you mean?"

George stood and looked around the room. "We're going to bully a group of Iranian ships from their ordered position. Don't you think that we'll have a little trouble getting out of the gulf? Do you honestly believe that the Iranians, who, by the way, are in our path out of the gulf, will roll out the red carpet and allow us to leave without challenging us?"

Every head in the room turned toward Adam. It was a great question, and one that had been on Adam's mind.

"Once we complete our mission, we will again raise the US flag and attempt to leave peacefully."

George only smirked. Adam reached toward the map and drew an imaginary line from Kuwait to the strait. "Look, I'm sure that we will be challenged on our way out." He looked back at George. "Nobody likes to be pushed around." Adam scanned the room. "We will be armed and at battle stations until we clear the strait and are back in the Gulf of Oman."

He raised his shoulders, puffed out his chest, and smiled. "We are going to look big and bad." Shifting his eyes again to George, he said, "I'm hoping that we will be able to leave peacefully. But we're going to be ready for anything."

Adam turned to Vic. "We're about thirty-six hours away from entering the Hormuz Strait. Let's schedule the navigation brief tomorrow at 1400."

George and Terry remained in the wardroom after all others had left. They drank coffee and enjoyed the quiet of each other's company, a rarity.

Finally, George spoke. "I'm not so sure that getting in and out is going to be as easy as Adam is hoping."

Terry considered George's statement. He sipped his coffee and set the cup on the table. "I'm not too worried about the Iranian patrol boats. The question that keeps popping up in my mind is what if we run into something that's more formidable than us?"

Both men sat and silently ruminated on that question.

The senior staff spent the rest of the day holding inspections and testing their equipment. Cy's team oiled down each weapon and ran various tests on the LRAD systems. George, Gail, and Paula walked through each repair locker to inspect the firefighting and damage-control equipment. And Terry sat in Combat Information Control and quizzed his team on strategies and tactics with a variety of scenarios.

Adam was pleased to see each team focus on their responsibilities. He wasn't sure if the crew's dedicated efforts were a result of teamwork or just for the purpose of self-preservation. *Probably both*, he thought. Either way, Adam was happy to see each crewmember hard at work and performing preventative maintenance, lubricating and cleaning the equipment.

He passed sick bay and watched Doc Kelly stocking his shelves and kits with meds and medical materials. When Adam poked his head inside, he winced at the strong odor of alcohol and ammonia. He greeted the doctor, who was kneeling on the deck and filling an emergency medical kit. Doc Kelly turned his head, smiled, and waved before returning to his work. Adam continued on his walk.

That evening, Paula, George, Scott, Terry, and Adam were seated in the wardroom for dinner. Nobody spoke. The only sound was the dishwasher in the wardroom galley. Adam took a final gulp from his water glass, pushed his seat away from the table, and excused himself. He thanked Hasif as he exited the wardroom.

Scott sat back and wiped his mouth with a dinner napkin. He felt tired. He scanned the others in the room, but no one returned eye contact. Everyone kept to themselves. All thoughts revolved around the upcoming mission and unsettling possibilities. The normally upbeat Scott was no different.

The sun rose the next morning to a beautiful sky. There was no hint of a breeze, which kept the whitecaps down and made the ocean look like a solid plate of blue glass.

Adam sat at his favorite spot—the starboard bridge chair. He marveled at the calm, clear blue water and would have considered stopping the ship and allowing the crew to hold swim call in the ocean if they weren't pressed for time.

Maybe we can do that on the way out, he mused. A small bead of sweat trickled down behind his ear to his neck. He instinctively grabbed the back of his neck and collected the stream of salty water, then wiped his hand on the front of his shirt.

His mind shifted to the brightness of the sun. *Gonna be hot again today,* he thought.

"Captain," the bridge officer called, snapping him out of his daydream.

Adam raised his eyes to see Paula standing at his side.

"We have a contact bearing 165 degrees relative . . . about six nautical miles behind us. Believe it's that cruiser—the *Cowpens*. It's got the same electronic signature."

Adam walked to the starboard bridgewing and stared at the horizon. He shaded his eyes, but the glare of the sun made it impossible to see anything.

"How long have they been following us?" he asked.

"Probably ten minutes or so," Paula answered.

Adam continued to scan the seas behind the ship. "Do they seem like they're trying to intercept?"

Paula slowly shook her head. "Nope. Just shadowing us."

Adam sat back in his chair. He grabbed his ball cap from the angle iron and pulled it over his eyes, then slid down into the seat and propped his feet on the bridge window ledge.

"Let 'em follow us," he said before he drifted into a nap.

The navigation brief was held at 1400, and Vic's course was expertly plotted and discussed. Adam stood in front of the group and relayed Frank's updated intelligence reports.

"At 0900 tomorrow morning we will set the sea-and-anchor detail and man battle stations. At 0915 we will begin the transit into the Strait of Hormuz."

He turned to Paula. "It's going to be hot. Please make sure that we have plenty of water for our sailors who are working outside the skin of the ship."

He shifted his gaze to Cy. "Cy, please make sure that our small-arms teams have plenty of ammo."

Cy nodded. "Already done."

Adam scanned the room and found Terry. "Is that cruiser still following us?"

Terry nodded. "It is. Still around six to seven miles behind."

Adam pondered this information. "We're about to get to the meat of our mission. I know that most of our crew has spent time in this part of the world, so we all know the risks."

He looked at each individual in the room. "Our presence inside the gulf may be challenged, but I don't believe that anyone will want a fight. I think that we may see some fast boats zip close and harass us a bit."

Adam zeroed in on Cy. "But I don't want us to overreact and do anything that could escalate the situation. We will use the LRAD systems on any craft that comes within five hundred yards of us. If a craft gets close to one hundred yards, we will sound the ship's whistle in an effort to warn them off. If anyone gets within one hundred yards, I will make the decision on whether or not to engage." Adam locked eyes with Cy. "Do not fire on any craft until approval from me has been granted."

Cy nodded and jotted down some notes.

Adam informed the group that the US flag would be flown until the ship arrived at Kuwaiti territorial waters.

"What happens then?" Terry asked.

Adam pulled out the flag that Oliver had given him, holding it in front of him. A smile appeared on his face. "Then we become part of the Kuwaiti navy." Adam folded the flag and placed in on the wardroom table. "Any questions?"

No hands were raised.

"OK. Paula and her team have prepared a nice meal for us tonight." He twisted his head toward Paula. "Steak and lobster, I believe."

A half smile rose on Paula's face. "And ice cream for dessert."

"Great," Adam said. "Let's all get a good night's sleep. I need everyone mentally and physically rested for tomorrow's evolution."

Very few members of the crew slept well that night. George sat in Main Control and performed system checks. He was happy. It didn't matter if he was sailing into hostile territory or through the warm waters of the Caribbean. He just loved being on ships and steaming at sea.

I could do this for the rest of my life, he mused.

Scott stared at the photos of his wife and kids. He was confident in the abilities of the ship and crew, and he had no doubt about his skills and talents as a ship driver, but there were always unknown variables when engaging an enemy. The only fear that crept into his mind was that he would not see his family again.

Terry tried reading a novel that he'd been working on for a week. He realized that he'd had the same page open for the past twenty minutes but had not read a single word.

As he lay in his rack with the curtains closed, Danny recited a prayer. A penitent Catholic, he quickly rolled out of his bed and knelt on the deck. "Lord," he began, "please take care of my family while I'm gone. Please keep this ship and crew safe, and please grant me wisdom for the days to come." Danny prayed for the next forty minutes.

Leroy leaned back in his chair in the chief's mess. Some action film was playing on the TV, but the sound was muted. His thoughts were a million miles away. He smiled to himself and wondered, *How does a career soldier with several campaigns under his belt end up as a squid?* He never thought much of sailors, and now he had become one.

Adam paced the deck in his cabin. He tried to consider all of the possibilities and challenges that lay ahead of them. He finally sat at his desk and leaned against the bulkhead. He was exhausted and his mind was fried. He knew that he needed sleep. *Need to be sharp for tomorrow,* he told himself. He stripped down to his skivvies and climbed into his rack.

As he flipped off the lamp on his nightstand, his mind immediately flashed to Chrissy. *I hope that I've made you proud,* he thought.

Memories of his wife ran through his mind until he finally and gratefully slipped into sleep.

Paula sat at her desk in the supply office. Inventory sheets were spread in front of her, but her head was in her hands and eyes were closed. The memory of her man-overboard maneuvering debacle kept running through her mind.

Attention to detail, she repeated to herself. *Top of my game.*

Cy slept like a baby.

Scott and Vic were both on the bridge at 0800. They meticulously ran through the course-transition checklist.

Scott grabbed his binoculars and walked out to the port bridgewing. It was going to be another scorcher. The temperature outside was already eighty degrees. He scanned the horizon but couldn't see another contact. Even the cruiser was nowhere to be found.

Adam arrived on the bridge at 0845. He wore a blue button-down short-sleeve shirt sporting a faded Señor Frogs logo above his left breast pocket. His favorite University of Oklahoma ball cap sat on his head, pulled down low to his sunglasses. It had a white salt-and-sweat ring where the brim met the soft top of the cap.

Adam set a large cup of coffee on the bridge window ledge as he climbed into his starboard-side chair and asked Scott for a status update on ship's systems and current location.

After a quick brief, Scott ended with, "We are deep into the Gulf of Oman—approximately sixty miles northwest of Muscat, Oman."

Vic chimed in that they would begin the ninety-degree turn into the Strait of Hormuz in approximately seventy miles. After that turn, the ship would travel another 550 miles to their destination. "At twenty-five knots we can be in Kuwaiti territorial waters in about twenty-seven hours.

Adam turned to Vic. "How about at thirty knots?"

Scott raised his eyebrows.

Vic traced out the equation with his finger in the air. "Just over twenty hours."

Adam turned to Scott. "Thirty knots at the turn, please."

Scott acknowledged and then turned back to Adam. "Almost forgot," he said. "Our friends on the cruiser have disappeared and are nowhere to be seen."

Adam nodded and took a sip of his coffee. He stuck his tongue out and grimaced. "Ugh. This pot must have been brewing all night."

Scott smiled and had the bridge bosun call Hasif to brew a fresh pot. Adam scanned the horizon and saw nothing but open ocean. He looked at his watch—0902. He turned to Scott and grinned. "Let's go to general quarters, Scottie."

Scott flipped a casual salute and then called to the bosun, "Sound the general alarm."

The bosun affirmed the order with an "aye-aye" and flipped the switch. The steady gong of the general alarm sounded throughout the ship. After fifteen seconds the bosun flipped the alarm off and keyed the microphone to the 1MC ship's intercom.

"General quarters. All hands, man your battle stations. Set material condition zebra throughout the ship. Send manned-and-ready reports to the bridge."

The bosun turned to Scott, who flashed a thumbs-up.

Footsteps pounded over the metal decks of the ship as the crew moved quickly to their battle stations. Adam watched the two gunners on the foc'sle pull the covers off the .50-caliber guns. Ammo canisters were opened, and belts of bullets were fed into the weapons.

A few minutes later Scott reported that all battle stations were manned and ready. Adam again looked at his watch. Vic stepped up next to Scott. Both men waited for the next order.

Adam looked up. "Let's get to it. Set the sea-and-anchor detail and start the transit."

Vic turned and hovered above the navigation chart. Scott looked from right to left and verified that sailors were standing on the bridgewings and preparing to take bearing readings.

"All ahead full. Bring us to thirty knots," Scott commanded.

Adam felt oddly relaxed as he watched the sea lanes tighten between the two landmasses of the United Arab Emirates and Iran. He knew that the ship was being watched, but thankfully he hadn't received any reports from Terry that indicated electronic targeting. The two gunners on the foc'sle continued a vigilant watch and never seemed to tire. They only broke away from their duties for an occasional water break. Adam assumed that the other sailors manning the ship's weapons were also devoted to their watch-standing responsibilities.

After the initial two-hour transit, the ship reached the ninety-degree turning point approximately ten miles south of the strait. The bearing takers on the bridgewings called out distances and bearings as they identified and tracked their marked targets.

Vic compiled all of the information and timed the transit turns down to the second. He called out, "Next turn is in ninety seconds. Recommend turn left to two-six-five degrees."

Scott repeated the navigation recommendation to ensure that he correctly heard the next turn. At the precise moment Vic replied, Scott called out to the helmsman, "Helmsman, turn left to course two-six-five degrees." The ship quickly responded and turned to the exact plotted course.

Adam grabbed his bridge telephone and dialed CIC. Terry answered.

"How are we looking?" Adam asked.

"Nothing yet, Adam," Terry responded. "We do see a Russian TU-95 Bear bomber just southeast of us, but it seems to be heading away from our position."

Adam thanked Terry and returned the phone to the cradle. Several merchant ships carrying oil and materials were traveling back and forth through the sea lanes. He was happy to see so much traffic and hoped that the other ships would help mask the fact that the *Kraken* was not an actual US Navy warship. At least to this point, they hadn't been discovered.

The ship completed the turn, and Vic told Scott that they would maintain course until the ship passed Dubai. Adam felt the tension on the bridge subside a bit as they moved through the strait.

He leaped from his chair. "Scott, I'm going to take a walk and check on the LRAD teams. Be back in about fifteen minutes." Scott nodded and returned to scanning the sea lanes.

Adam walked back to the flight deck and talked with the sailors manning the LRAD devices. He continued aft and spoke with Cy's two .50 cal gunners. He was correct—each weaponeer was performing his duties professionally and diligently. He made sure that they had plenty of water.

As he started up the ladder to the flight deck, he saw movement to his right. The usually subdued Bobby was chewing out the aft watch lookout. The bosun jabbed his finger at the lookout's chest and then waved it from right to left, pointing out various spots in the ship's path. The lookout hung his head and nodded.

Bobby stepped away from the spot and walked to Adam.

"Everything OK?" Adam asked.

Bobby twisted his neck to glare at the lookout and then turned back.

"Yeah," he grumbled. "Just a little training on attention to detail."

Adam clapped Bobby on the back. "It's all good," he said.

The next fifteen hours saw the ship turning at Dubai, passing Qatar and then Bahrain. Paula's team made box meals, which were passed out to the crew. Bottles of water were continuously distributed throughout the day. Doc Kelly conducted routine walks on the main decks to ensure that the watch standers and deck workers weren't suffering from heat exhaustion.

Adam found it necessary to order Cy to relieve all gun teams for a short rest. The ship needed the "A team" to be sharp when they hit the Kuwaiti territorial waters.

Terry's team monitored electronic signals and external radio communications, but nothing indicated that the ship was being targeted.

Bursts of adrenaline pumped through each sailor when Adam announced the 100-mile mark on the ship's 1MC intercom system. Adam asked every crew member to stay sharp and ready for anything.

He returned the mic to the bosun. "How are we doing on fuel?"

Scott called Engineering Main Control on the bitch box—the intercom directly connected to the engineering spaces and CIC. George's familiar gruff voice indicated that the ship had just less than a half tank of gas. Adam smiled and shook his head at the informality of that response.

"Let's raise the Kuwaiti colors," Adam directed Scott.

Scott pointed to the bosun, who grabbed the folded flag from under the chart table.

Adam walked out to the starboard bridgewing and watched the US ensign being lowered and replaced by the Kuwaiti national flag on the main mast. His stomach tightened; he didn't like seeing another country's flag flying over his ship. He understood why this needed to be done but couldn't help wondering if it was bad luck.

Adam stepped back inside the bridge. "Scott," he called. "Please call Danny and ask him to add one more lookout on both the forward and aft stations." Adam wanted extra eyes on deck to scan the seas for the Iranian fast boats.

Scott called Danny, then Cy in CIC.

"Energize the LRAD systems," he ordered.

Adam called Hasif and asked him to report to the bridge.

CHAPTER 18

The ship was now five miles from the southern point of the Kuwaiti territorial line. Hasif entered the bridge and was told to stand near the Inmarsat bridge-to-bridge radio. Terry contacted the bridge and indicated that there was still no sign of electronic signals or radio chatter.

The temperature on the bridge neared ninety degrees, but no one noticed. The crew focused on their responsibilities and the surrounding seas.

The *Kraken* finally reached the southernmost point of the Kuwaiti territorial waters where Scott slowed the speed to ten knots. All hands on deck and in the bridge scanned the horizon, but no boats or any other craft were in sight. Vic recommended a course that paralleled the territorial line, and Scott ordered the course change.

Three hours later a call was received on the Inmarsat radio, channel 16, the emergency channel. The voice on the radio spoke with an English accent.

"This is radio call sign UKMZZ, merchant vessel *Annapolis Royal*, a cargo freighter en route to the port of Shuwaikh in Kuwait. We are currently at coordinates 29.111471 and 48.945081 traveling at fifteen knots. Two hostile medium-size seacraft have appeared from the north and northeast. These craft are fast and maneuverable.

"They are armed with small-caliber automatic weapons mounted on their forward exterior decks. Both craft are continuously cutting into our path while firing their weapons into the water. Though the weapon fire is not directed at us, I am concerned that may change if we do not alter our course. We have attempted to contact these craft and explain that we are operating in international waters, but they are either unable or unwilling to respond. Again, we are being harassed by two hostile seacraft. They are attempting to force us to alter course. Request assistance."

"This is it!" Adam shouted to Scott. "Contact the merchant vessel and offer assistance. Have them switch to channel 25." He spun in his chair to face the chart table. "Vic, plot a course to intercept." He turned back and peered out of the forward window. "Let's crank it up to thirty knots."

Vic lifted his head from the chart table. "The freighter is twelve nautical miles from our position. Bearing zero-one-four. Should take us about fifteen minutes."

Adam looked to Scott. "Please pass that information as well."

Scott communicated assistance to the freighter, then grabbed the mic to the 1MC intercom.

"*Kraken*, this is the XO. We've received a distress call from a merchant vessel approximately ten nautical miles away and in international waters. Two hostile craft are firing weapons in an effort to forcibly change the merchant vessel's course. It appears that this is the scenario we have been training for. We are on course to pursue and engage. Expect arrival in fifteen minutes. XO out."

Adam called CIC and confirmed with Cy that the LRAD systems were fired up and ready to go. Cy informed Adam that he was going to take position on the fantail and assist his gunners. Adam concurred but directed Cy to stop by the bridge first.

"Roger" was the reply.

The ship bounced up and down in the water as it sped toward the targets. Adam pulled his sunglasses off and wrapped them around his ball cap just above the brim. His adrenaline was pumping, and he found it hard to sit. He spun around in his chair as he heard the door to the bridge open.

Cy walked through, and Adam waved the weapons officer over to him and called Scott to join them. Adam spread his hands apart. His eyes narrowed and darted back and forth between the two men.

"OK, here's the deal." Adam was focused. "Those boats are very fast and carry rockets. Our LRADs have an effective range of about five hundred feet. Scott, I need you to try to split those boats up so that we have one on each side of us. Cy, tell your men to keep the LRAD trained on the bridge and gunners of each boat. I want that volume cranked up high. I'm hoping that the LRAD will force those boats to think about something other than firing at us."

Cy interjected, "And what if the forward gunner decides to open fire?"

"Cy." Adam pointed at his weapons officer. "You are not—let me repeat—not authorized to use lethal force unless we are fired upon." Adam paused. "If they do fire at us, then you have permission to light them up. Are we clear?"

Cy's expression certainly made it clear that he didn't like being directed. "Clear," he repeated.

Adam nodded. "OK, go!"

Cy bolted through the starboard bridge door.

"Bosun," Adam shouted. The bridge bosun jumped. "Why are the blast doors wide open? C'mon, let's get the bridge buttoned up."

The bosun ran to each side of the bridge and slammed the doors closed.

"I've got him," Scott shouted as he stared through binoculars out of the forward bridge window. "Looks like they're about five miles or so." Scott squinted. "Can't see the two . . . Wait, there they are." Scott pointed toward the boats with his free hand.

Adam keyed his radio. "Cy, can you get up to the flight deck? I need you to help those guys on the LRADs."

The radio clicked and buzzed. "Will do," Cy responded.

Adam lowered his radio and turned back to Scott. "XO, we've got to get the freighter to appear as if she's altering course." Adam thought for a moment. "Contact the freighter and ask them to maneuver their ship to the east."

Scott keyed the radio. "Merchant vessel *Annapolis Royal*, this is warship *Kraken*. We expect to reach your location within five minutes. Our intention is to engage with the hostile craft. Request you turn hard to port and increase speed to twenty knots."

The quick crackle of radio static was interrupted by the English accent: "Acknowledged."

Adam grabbed Hasif by the arm and led him to the Inmarsat radio.

"I need you to speak to the attack boats. I'm assuming that they're speaking Persian, so please use that language." Adam handed the mic to Hasif. "Repeat what I say to them." Adam cleared his throat. "Attention sea vessels that are pursuing the freighter *Annapolis Royal*—this is Kuwaiti warship *Kraken*. You are in international waters and attacking a cargo ship destined for the country of Kuwait."

Adam paused while Hasif repeated the message.

"You are ordered to cease and desist your hostile actions and depart the area. Failure to adhere to this order may result in hostilities."

Hasif released the mic key.

"Good. Now, repeat what you just said, but this time in Arabic." While Hasif repeated the message, Adam climbed back into his chair.

Scott continued to scan the horizon. "Adam, the freighter has turned and is now steaming eastward. The two boats are running alongside the freighter's starboard side. We are approximately two miles away. Should be there within two minutes."

Adam squinted through the bridge window. He could clearly see the freighter, and after shielding his eyes from the sun, he managed to locate the two boats at the freighter's waterline.

"Adam!" Scott shouted. "The boats are turning toward us."

"Yeah, I see that." Adam keyed his radio. "Cy, hit 'em now with the LRADs!"

"Roger," Cy responded.

"Scott, let's bring the speed down to about fifteen knots. Start maneuvering to get between them."

Scott ordered the decrease in speed and began instinctively calling out course changes.

As the boats closed to 500 feet, they began showing signs of distress. Instead of approaching the *Kraken* in a tight formation, they moved away from each other. Scott maneuvered the ship to drive a wedge right between the two boats. He then backed the engines down to ten knots.

The boat approaching the port side veered in toward the *Kraken* and then back out again. Their speed dropped significantly. The boat on the starboard side stopped completely.

Cy's starboard LRAD team targeted the forward gunner on the starboard side, who clapped his hands around his ears and fell to the deck. The boat on the port side turned north and fled the area at high speed. The *Kraken* slowed to a stop next to the starboard-side boat. The gunner lay on the deck in the fetal position and had vomited on the boat's deck. Adam directed his team to cease LRAD operations.

He grabbed the bullhorn and took Hasif out to the bridgewing. An Iranian officer staggered out of his boat's bridge and craned his head upward. As he scanned the deck, he observed the machine gunner who was training his weapon directly at the boat's bridge.

The officer looked up to the *Kraken*'s starboard bridgewing. Adam handed the bullhorn to Hasif and whispered, "Repeat after me in Persian and use your most commanding voice."

Hasif nodded.

Adam began, "Iranian gunboat, we have no desire to board your craft or do you harm. You are directed to return to your home port and to never harass Kuwaiti shipping vessels again. Nod if you understand."

Both Adam and Hasif watched as the Iranian officer hung his

head for a moment, then looked up and nodded.

Hasif continued to interpret, "Be warned that further hostile incidents on Kuwaiti shipping vessels by you or any other craft will be met with aggression. There are now ships of war in this area that are standing by to assist in eradicating any threat. Thank you."

A quizzical look crossed Hasif's face. Adam just smiled and shrugged. The fast boat's officer returned inside his vessel, and Adam and Hasif stepped back into the bridge.

"Let's get out of here, Scott."

Adam hooked his arm over Hasif's shoulder and turned to Vic. "Navigator, plot a course for Bahrain. Hasif and I need a drink."

CHAPTER 19

Vic charted the course to Bahrain. The trek was about 250 nautical miles, and they would be in port in about twelve hours. The ship battle condition was relaxed, and all crew not on watch were allowed to rest for the remainder of the day.

Adam called Oliver and shared the good news about the confrontation with the fast boats. Oliver congratulated Adam and the crew for a job well done and asked if he expected the boats to return.

"Not sure," answered Adam. "We're going to spend a couple of days in Bahrain and then swing back to patrol the area to see if our Iranian friends have returned. If they haven't, then we're going to head back home."

Oliver agreed with the plan and then congratulated Adam again. "I'd like to sit down with you and your senior staff when you return. After, of course, a nice period of rest."

Adam placed the phone in its cradle and went to take a nice long nap.

Paula also contacted Oliver, to coordinate a ship's visit in Bahrain. She asked for points of contact so that she could request fuel, food, and other supplies. Meanwhile, Cy ordered his team to cover the weapons and place the ammunition in storage containers near the guns. He didn't want to relax the battle condition. This was still, in fact, the Arabian Gulf. The threat remained high, and he needed his team to be ready to react to any hostility.

That evening, Danny brought the ship into port. He glided the ship pier-side as if he were driving a luxury sedan. His movements were smooth and deliberate. The ship gently bounced off the pier bumpers, and Bobby's team tossed mooring lines to workers on the pier.

Once the ship was tied up, Adam jumped out of his chair. "I'm heading down to the wardroom," he announced. He was about to leave the bridge but turned back. "There's a great Irish bar in town called JJ's. Want to go tonight, Danny?"

Danny was storing the bridge-officer binoculars.

"Irish bar? In Bahrain?"

Adam nodded once. "It was one of my favorite watering holes when I was on active duty. Wanna come?"

Danny winked. "Absolutely. Just let me get cleaned up."

Adam invited all of the department heads and senior leaders to join him for drinks at the bar that evening. Only Paula, Scott, Danny, and George were interested in attending. The group left the ship at 1730, negotiated a taxi, and rode to the bar together. As the others seated themselves at a table, Adam remained standing in the doorway. He surveyed the bar as a flood of memories coursed through him.

The last time he was in this establishment was when he helped host his wetting-down party following his promotion to lieutenant commander. Traditionally, when a US Navy officer was promoted, the respective officer contributed funds to a party for his wardroom.

Adam ordered a Guinness at the bar. He always appreciated Irish and English pubs. The bars always seemed to be made in heavy oak, and the walls were always lined with the most nostalgic whiskey and beer mirrors and decorations.

Adam's focus was interrupted as he spied a familiar face. Alone at a corner table sat Zach Taggert, captain of the cruiser *Cowpens*. Adam eyed the captain, who reclined in a wooden chair, one hand gripping a pint of ale. Zach raised his glass in a toast and then tipped it for a drink before reaching over, grabbing another chair, and pulling it to his table, waving at Adam to join him. The bartender finished filling the Guinness and handed it to Adam, who joined his fellow captain.

Adam half smiled. "Why is it that I always seem to find you drinking in bars?"

Zach returned the smile. "There are definitely worse circumstances and places where we could meet."

Adam nodded. "Amen!" he said and raised his glass in response to Zach's toast.

"Gotta tell you, Adam," Zach began, "I saw what you guys did with those two boats off the coast of Kuwait." Zach paused and Adam said nothing. "Impressive. Really nice work. You guys definitely helped out that freighter."

Adam remained silent. Zach's smile dropped a bit. He narrowed his eyes and pointed an accusatory finger at Adam. "I knew that you were a ship of mercenaries."

Adam closed his eyes and slowly shook his head. He calmly replied, "Zach, I told you before, we're not mercenaries."

"Really?" Zach cocked his head slightly. "Then why would you be flying the flag of Kuwait on your mast? And why were you so intent on helping clear the sea lanes of vessels that were hostile to Kuwaiti merchant craft?"

Adam scratched the back of his head and looked at the floor. "It's a long story. We really aren't mercenaries, but we are helping clean up the Kuwaiti merchant sea lanes." Adam regained eye contact with Zach. "We're more like privateers. You know, like Jean Lafitte and his sailors helping out Andrew Jackson during the Battle of New Orleans in the War of 1812."

Zach's smile returned. "Lafitte was a pirate. Are you pirates?"

"Sometimes it feels like we are," Adam chuckled. "As you've seen, we are in the middle of doing someone a favor. In a couple days we're going to swing back and check to see if the seas around Kuwait are still clear. Once that's done, we're going to head home—never to be seen in this part of the world again."

Zach's smile faded. "A favor, huh?" He finished his beer and set the empty glass on the table, then stood. "OK, Adam. I believe you. Just be careful. There are too many bad guys in this neighborhood, and I'm sure that a few of them have noticed your handiwork."

He offered his hand to Adam. "And like I cautioned you before, please don't put me in a position where I need to consider you a threat. I like you, Adam. I'd like to remain friends."

Adam stood and grabbed Zach's hand. "I appreciate the advice, Zach. Hope we get a chance to have another beer together in the future. I'd like to tell you the whole story."

"Sounds like a good plan."

Adam breathed a heavy sigh and walked over to his friends at their table.

"Who was that?" George asked.

"That, my fellow adventurers"—Adam sat—"was Zach Taggert, the commanding officer of the *Cowpens*."

Scott frowned. "What'd he want?"

"Well, he congratulated us on getting rid of the Iranian boats, and then he told me to be careful. Apparently, there are some very bad people in this part of the world."

"There are some very bad people sitting at this table!" Scott raised his glass. "The worst, actually. George's indigestion is kicking up again. Very powerful gasses!"

George frowned while the rest of the group broke up in laughter.

"Let's get drunk." Adam raised his glass to the cheers of his fellow shipmates.

Vic held a navigation brief at 1400 the next day. All of the senior staff attended, though some of them looked and smelled as if they had been out drinking all night. Vic used a laser pointer to show the track that the ship would take to reach the southernmost point of Kuwaiti territorial waters. When he finished, Adam stood in front of the chart.

"We're going to get underway tomorrow morning at 0500. Once we reach this point"—Adam pointed to an area approximately ten miles east of the Saudi Arabian/Kuwaiti border—"we will travel around the Kuwaiti territorial boundary to make sure that our Iranian friends have not returned. Let's plan to steam at twenty knots."

He turned back to address the group. "Following that, and assuming that we don't run into any Iranian challenges, we will turn east and begin our trek back through the strait."

Adam spotted Terry sitting on the wardroom couch. "Ops, have your guys heard any chatter on the radio about our presence or recent actions?"

Terry shook his head. "Nothing. We've been checking all of our sources but haven't heard a thing."

Adam gave a quick nod. "Great. Any questions?"

The room was silent. Adam offered a quick thanks and dismissed the group.

Most of the officers and crew remained aboard the ship for the evening, though a few did leave for dinner and drinks. Everyone was just happy to have successfully finished the mission and ready to go home. It was nice to relax for a change.

Adam and George played a game of cribbage and drank coffee at the wardroom dining table. Paula wrapped herself up in a blanket and was engulfed in a horror book that she'd been aching to read. Terry and Scott sat on the wardroom couch and watched Terry's favorite war film: *Kelly's Heroes*.

Bobby took Leroy, Frank, and Lonnie out to town for dinner. Danny spent a fortune on a three-hour phone call to his wife and children. Vic shut down every light in his stateroom, and slept heavily under three layers of blankets. Doc Kelly opened a bottle of brandy that he kept in sick bay. He poured a glass and took a sip. He would, of course, argue that this drink was for medicinal purposes.

Cy locked himself in the weapons locker. He sat at the workbench and field-stripped a .45-caliber pistol. When he was finished, he instinctively grabbed his key chain and stroked the .308 bullet on the ring. He closed his eyes and smiled. The images of killing the pirates in the Malacca Strait were crystal clear in Cy's mind. He prayed that another opportunity like that would come soon.

The *Kraken* pulled away from port at 0459 the next morning. The sun was just cracking the horizon. As was typical, Scott expertly guided the ship into the open sea. Adam noticed that the mood of the crew was dramatically different from when they first entered the gulf. Sailors were chatty and upbeat.

He smiled. It was good to have a happy crew again.

Tag-up was held on the bridge at the usual 0730 time. Adam reminded his officers that they were still in hostile waters and to be ready for anything. Because of that, he was going to set the ship at general quarters at 1530—an hour before arriving at Kuwaiti territorial waters.

CHAPTER 20

Paula's team was busy cleaning the galley after lunch. The deep aroma of beef barbecue ribs lingered throughout the ship.

Scott had turned over the bridge to Danny, who leaned against a port-side bridge bulkhead and scanned the horizon. Vic and the helmsman were in the middle of a friendly argument over whose professional football team was going to be more successful in the coming year. Adam sat in his starboard-side chair and daydreamed. His focus was a million miles away as his thoughts flashed between the chat he had with Zach Taggert two nights ago and how he would reorganize the ship's crew when they ultimately set up the cruise-line business.

In sick bay, George discussed his condition with Doc Kelly, and how to obtain some meds that would take the edge off his anxiety.

Adam's phone startled him out of his reverie. He lurched forward and cracked his knee on the angle iron.

"Son of a—" Adam grabbed the phone. Terry was on the other end.

"Adam, need you in CIC please."

"Be right there."

Adam entered CIC and paused for a moment to adjust to the lack of light. The lighting in Combat was kept dim so that the radar operators could monitor their systems without the distraction of glare from ambient lighting.

Once his eyes adjusted, Adam found Terry and Frank huddled around one of the analysts, who was sitting at a console and wearing a large set of radio headphones.

"What's going on?" Adam asked as he approached.

Terry held his hand up for silence, and Adam felt slightly annoyed. The analyst raised his head and nodded to Terry. Terry turned to Adam. "We're hearing some chatter on the radio about possible retaliation against a Kuwaiti warship that recently ran off two Iranian patrol boats."

Terry glanced at Frank. "The signal is pretty weak, and we can't determine the origin of the transmission. We believe that it's coming from somewhere near the southern coast of Iran but can't quite pinpoint an area."

Adam chewed on his lower lip. "Do we have any specifics on what they're planning?"

Terry shook his head. "Not yet. We'll continue to monitor all channels. I'll keep you updated on anything we hear. In the meantime, I'd recommend sounding the general alarm and getting the ship ready for action." Terry offered a weak smile. "Just in case."

Adam called the senior leaders to the wardroom for a quick briefing. Once they were all seated, Terry briefed them of the situation.

Adam stood and gestured Terry to take his seat. "I'm not sure what this means or if anything is being planned," Adam began, "but we're not going to take any chances. I've asked Danny to sound the general alarm in a few minutes. We expect to arrive at the southern tip of Kuwaiti waters in about ninety minutes. We're going to steam a course that parallels the territorial boundary for five hours."

Adam involuntarily shifted his gaze to Cy. "If we don't run into any problems, we will begin a course toward the Strait of Hormuz at around 2030."

Adam's eyes bounced from one person to the next. "Ladies and gents, it's going to be an all-nighter. Navigating through the strait is more challenging and dangerous at night, but there are also advantages to sailing under the cover of darkness."

Adam lowered his chin and narrowed his eyes. "Stay sharp and keep your people and systems ready." He scanned the room one last time. "Any questions?"

There were no responses until George raised his hand.

Adam pointed at his engineer. "George."

"So much for the optimism of no confrontation," George muttered.

The general alarm sounded a few minutes later, and the crew scrambled to their battle stations. Scott relieved Danny as bridge officer. Once their turnover was complete, Scott ambled over to Adam's chair.

"All stations manned and ready," he reported.

Adam nodded. "Have someone call Paula and ask her to make sure that all external gunnery and watch standers are provided with water and coffee throughout the night."

Scott acknowledged the order and started to turn back toward the port side.

"Oh, and Scott?"

Scott did his best military about-face.

Adam had to smile. "Let me know if you need a break throughout the night."

Scott gave a smart Roman salute from his chest, then another about-face. Adam shook his head.

At 1525 the ship reached the southern tip of Kuwait. Adam called CIC for a report, but, to Adam's frustration, no other radio transmissions had been intercepted. He ordered the course change, and Scott maneuvered the ship north, paralleling the Kuwaiti territorial waters at twenty-five knots. It was unusually quiet.

All individuals with binoculars, including Adam, scanned the horizon in search of any type of hostile contact.

At 1558 the ship had traveled thirty miles into their tour when the bitch box rang out.

"Bridge, this is CIC. We have a surface contact bearing one-three-five degrees at ten miles out. She's traveling toward us at approximately thirty knots. It's a warship."

Scott keyed the transmit button on the box. "Why didn't we pick this up earlier?"

Terry answered, "These guys were quiet. Appears they were just sitting out in the water and not transmitting anything electronic. May have been waiting for us and using passive listening tactics. About sixty seconds ago they lit up our boards and began steaming hard in our direction."

Adam looked at Scott. "We don't have time to get away. Turn us around so we're facing them when they arrive. Make sure to position the ship so that we're still in international waters but can back into Kuwaiti territory if we need to."

Scott barked out maneuvering orders. The ship turned quickly and within two minutes was facing the approaching contact.

"Any idea who these guys are?" Adam keyed the box.

"They're Iranian" was the answer. "Maybe a Corvette."

Adam flipped the transmit key. "Get Frank to find out what they have on board. Need to know their armament."

"Stand by."

Moments later, Frank's voice came on the box. "Adam, based on their electronic signatures I believe that this is the Iranian warship *Bayandor*. It's a Corvette—their equivalent to a frigate. If this is accurate, then they can pack a pretty healthy punch if engaged. They typically carry four anti-ship missiles, looks like a 76 mm naval cannon, torpedoes, and two mounted machine guns."

Terry jumped on the line. "It's those missiles that are the biggest concern, Adam."

Adam flipped the transmit key. "Roger."

Scott ordered the bosun to get Hasif back on the bridge, then moved next to Adam.

Adam twisted in his seat to address him. "Get all weapons

systems online and ready to fire. Get CIC to begin plotting firing solutions for the torpedoes."

Adam was grateful that Cy had modified the torpedoes for anti-ship warfare.

Scott repeated Adam's order to CIC and continued scanning the horizon.

"I see 'em," Adam announced.

Scott turned his binoculars. "Got him," Scott acknowledged. He let the binoculars hang from the strap around his neck as he ran over to the 1MC intercom. Hasif entered through the bridge door.

Grabbing the mic, Scott keyed the transmit button. "Attention, *Kraken* crew, this is the XO. We have a possible hostile surface contact approaching us. Stay sharp at your stations."

He replaced the mic and stepped to the Inmarsat radio, making sure that channel 16 was set before he grabbed the mic. Scott motioned Hasif over to the radio and handed it to him. "Please translate in Persian."

Hasif began speaking. "Iranian warship." Scott's nerves were on edge, and he hoped that Hasif's voice sounded calm. "This is Kuwaiti warship *Kraken*. We are monitoring your presence and rapid transit toward our position. Please acknowledge your intentions. Over."

No response.

Scott had Hasif repeat the message, but, again, there was no reply from the approaching vessel. Frank quickly opened the bridge door and ran to the forward window, raising his binoculars to carefully inspect the ship.

"Yep, that's the *Bayandor*," he said.

Adam again keyed the box to CIC. "Terry, what's the distance of the Iranian ship?"

"Three miles and closing. They're moving at thirty knots."

"She'll be here in the next two minutes," Adam said under his breath. "Scott, are we ready for action?"

"Yes sir," Scott answered. "And we have a torpedo firing solution."

Adam said nothing. His heart was pounding so hard it felt as if it would burst through his chest. He turned back to Scott. "Anything on the radio?"

Scott continued to stare through his binoculars but shook his head. "Not yet."

The *Bayandor* finally slowed and stopped a quarter mile in front of *Kraken*. Still no radio transmissions or obvious intent toward hostile action. Both ships seemed to be sizing each other up.

Adam rose from his seat and joined Scott and Hasif. He placed his hand on Hasif's shoulder.

"Need you to translate, please."

Before Adam could begin his message, the radio crackled. A Middle Eastern voice began speaking angrily. When the voice finished, Hasif turned to Adam. "It is the captain of the Iranian ship. He is ordering you to lower all weapon systems. He intends to send a boat over and orders you to prepare to be boarded."

Adam looked at Scott, then back to Hasif.

"Translate another message. Captain of the *Bayandor*, this is the captain of the *Kraken*, a Kuwaiti warship. Greetings and my compliments on your fine ship. You have requested my ship to lower our defenses and to prepare for your team to board us. As you can see, we are in international waters. I request to understand the nature of your demands."

The Middle Eastern voice replied, sounding much angrier and louder.

Scott looked at Adam. "He sounds pissed."

Hasif translated, "Captain of the *Kraken*. You will lower your defenses and prepare for boarding. Two days ago, you attacked two patrol boats of the Iranian navy in international waters. You and your crew must now be held accountable for your crimes."

Adam keyed the bitch box. "Cy, this is Adam. Do you have the LRAD warmed up?"

Terry's voice crackled over the speaker. "Adam, Cy went back to the fantail to check on his team. The LRAD is charged and ready."

"Cy's on the fantail?" Adam looked at Scott.

Scott shared a look of mock surprise.

"Hasif," Adam began, "another message, please. Captain of the *Bayandor*, you are correct that we chased away two Iranian patrol boats two days ago. Those boats were firing weapons and harassing Kuwaiti shipping vessels in international waters. As you are aware, only nonlethal deterrents were used at that time. I will not lower our defenses. However, to show good faith I invite you and two of your officers to visit my ship and discuss our situation."

Hasif relayed the message.

"Do you really think that they'll accept that invitation?" Scott asked with one eyebrow raised.

Adam shrugged. "Dunno. Let's see what they say."

The radio crackled and the Iranian captain responded.

Hasif translated, "Your invitation is accepted. I will send my first officer and security officer. Prepare your port-side fantail for their arrival."

Adam called Danny on the radio and explained the situation. He asked to have Bobby and two sailors bring the boat alongside and to assist the officers and crew in boarding the ship.

Adam continued, "Once they are aboard, would you please escort the officers to the wardroom?"

Danny took a moment to comprehend what was being asked.

"We have Iranian naval officers coming aboard, and you want me to escort them to the wardroom? Seriously?"

Adam smiled to himself. He'd never heard Danny question an order. "We're trying to work out a diplomatic solution with this one."

"Understood" was the quick reply.

Bobby, Tim, and Tom were already on the fantail when Danny arrived. One of Cy's gunners manned the .50-caliber gun on the port side. Danny was surprised to see Cy manning the starboard-side gun.

Danny quickly explained the situation to Bobby.

"Once the boat arrives, Tim or Tom will tie up the boat, then help the Iranians up the ladder. You"—Danny pointed at Bobby—"will position yourself about ten feet away and, when the Iranians are onboard, approach and greet them. I will then escort the officers to the wardroom. Please coordinate water and a snack for their boat crew and keep them on the fantail until we return."

Bobby smiled. "I can have our galley whip them up a ham sandwich?"

Danny wanted to smile but didn't. "You're a true diplomat."

Adam and Scott watched the boat travel from the Iranian ship toward their position. They counted six in the boat. The two individuals in the middle of the boat had nicer and cleaner-looking uniforms. Adam assumed that they must be the officers.

Danny leaned over the port-side fantail lifelines and watched as the Iranian boat glided up to the ship. A sailor sitting at the bow of the boat tossed a mooring line to Tim, who pulled the mooring line under the ship's safety lines and tied it off to one of the port-side deck cleats.

One of the officers hauled himself to the ladder. He climbed to the fantail deck, and Tim helped the man climb aboard. Danny noticed that the officer wore a holstered pistol at his hip. The second officer stood in the boat, and grabbed the ladder. Just as he began hauling himself up, water movement pulled the boat slightly away from the ship. The Iranian officer lost his footing and swung from the boat, his legs entering the water. He maintained his grip on the bottom rung of the ladder but was helpless as his legs dangled.

The boat swung back toward the ship, and the Iranian sailors helped the officer regain his footing and resume his climb up the ladder. Tim reached a hand down to help, but the officer ignored the offer. As the Iranian reached the deck, Tim squatted down and grabbed his upper arm to stabilize his movement.

The officer quickly scrambled up to the deck, grabbed Tim's hand, and threw it to the side. He hissed something in Persian and thrust both of his fists into Tim's chest, knocking the young sailor back and to the deck. In protective mode, Tom grabbed the angry officer and forcefully pushed him away from his brother.

As the Iranian staggered and fell forward, the other officer pulled the pistol from his holster and quickly fired two rounds into Tom's chest. The blast knocked the young man back two feet before he collapsed to the deck.

Everyone on the fantail froze except for the Iranian with the pistol . . . and Cy.

The Iranian swung the pistol toward Tim and was about to pull the trigger when Cy unloaded two .45-caliber rounds that penetrated the officer's right ear.

The officer on the deck had begun to rise but now only stared at Cy. Before Danny or Bobby could stop him, Cy emptied the rest of the magazine into the second officer's chest. Blood from the five bullet wounds rapidly seeped through and stained the officer's white uniform blouse.

Cy ran to the port side to view the four remaining Iranian sailors frantically trying to untie the boat's mooring lines. He placed his hand on the .50 cal gunner's shoulder and, without taking his eyes off the Iranian boat crew, calmly ordered, "Take them out."

The gunner pulled back and released the slide to the weapon. He lowered the gun barrel and sighted in on the boat. Danny felt like everything was happening in slow motion. He tried to move, but it was as if his feet were frozen to the deck.

Cy's gunner opened fire. The loud chatter from the machine gun was only outdone by Cy's laughter. The short range to the targets greatly intensified the violence and the carnage inflicted by the high-powered weapon. Heads, torsos, and limbs exploded as the gunner targeted each victim. Seawater rushed into the craft through newly punched holes and tears in the boat's hull. It sank within seconds.

Cy wiped tears from his eyes. "Well done," he said, patting the gunner on the back.

At the sound of the automatic gunfire, Adam ran to the furthest point aft of the port bridgewing. He leaned over the railing and craned his neck to see what was happening.

He keyed his radio. "Danny!" he called. "Danny, are you there?"

After a pause, Danny responded, "I'm here. They're dead." Danny sounded disjointed.

"Danny, who's dead?"

A few seconds later Cy radioed, "Adam, this is Cy."

Adam was shocked. He keyed the radio and shouted, "Cy? Where's Danny? Is he OK?"

"Adam!" Scott screamed from the bridge.

Adam snapped his head around in time to see the flame of a freshly launched missile as it left the decks of the Iranian ship.

He watched the white, smoky path stream up to the sky. Adam vaguely heard Scott yelling on the 1MC intercom, "Incoming missile! Brace for shock!!!" The missile took three and a half seconds to find its target.

Arcing down, it turned left, and flew five feet above the waterline until it struck the *Kraken* at the starboard-side amidships. The missile pierced the skin of the ship and penetrated two bulkheads before it finally came to rest in the crew's galley.

Adam felt the ship shudder at the missile's impact but was surprised that there was no explosion.

Must be a dud, he thought.

"Scott!" he screamed as he ran back into the bridge. "Back us into Kuwaiti waters."

Scott shouted maneuvering orders, and the ship began to move. He ordered the bridge bosun to contact Damage Control and determine the damage. Paula darted from her locker to assess the situation. She was about to enter the ship's dining area when she ran into George.

"Hey, kid." George stopped Paula before she could open the watertight door to the dining area. "Go on back to the damage-control locker. I'll check this one. I'll call if we need your team."

Paula took a step back. *Does he look older? Sadder?* Paula shook off these thoughts. "Are you sure?" she asked.

"Yeah." George waved her off. "Go on back. Git goin'!"

Paula ran back to the locker.

George opened the watertight door and entered the dining area, immediately smelling the fuel from the Iranian missile. The lights were flashing on and off, and electrical cables snapped and crackled. He walked to the center of the dining area but saw no damage.

The galley area was dark, with the occasional flicker of lights. He peered through the serving window but still couldn't see anything. George pulled his flashlight from his coveralls and felt the galley door with the back of his hand. *No heat*, he thought. *If there's no heat, then there's no fire.*

He opened the door. Pots, pans, and other galley equipment were scattered on the deck. The lights continued to flicker, which made it difficult to focus. He rounded the corner to the supervising cook's office and found what he was looking for. What appeared to be a fifteen-foot-long missile had penetrated the starboard-side bulkhead to the galley.

The missile was pretty beat up and looked like someone had mounted it on the bulkhead, with half of it protruding. Squatting to the deck, he slid his hand on its surface and rubbed his fingers past his nose. *Rocket fuel*, he thought. *This thing's leaking.* George stood and grabbed his radio. "Adam, this is George."

Adam had made it back to his chair on the bridge. "Go ahead." Adam released the radio key.

The flashlight's beam bounced all over the missile. "I'm in the galley. This is one ugly critter. We were lucky. It hit about four or five feet above the waterline." George flashed his light around the space. "I can't see where the missile entered, but I do know that it had to pass through the starboard-side passageway to get here."

Adam radioed, "George, maybe you should get out of there. How can you be sure that thing's not going to explode?"

George smiled. "Adam, the only risk that I have right now is slipping on rocket fuel. I'm sure that it's harmless. In fact—"

The missile exploded.

Massive heat and force shot through the galley at incredible speed, vaporizing the engineer.

The solid boundary of the bulkheads and freezers in the galley luckily forced the impact back into the passageway and out through the missile's entry point on the skin of the ship. The power of the explosion rolled the ship five degrees to port. Rocket fuel ignited and fueled a fireball that completely engulfed the galley.

"Holy shit!" Scott shouted.

Adam snapped his head around to Scott. "George is in the galley!"

The blood drained from Scott's face. "Oh God."

Adam grabbed the radio and screamed George's name. He prayed that George would respond, but all he received was the crackle of radio silence.

Adam dropped the radio to his lap.

His initial instinct was to mourn his friend, but had 119 other sailors who needed his leadership, so he snapped himself back to the reality of the situation.

"Why hasn't he fired again?" Adam asked no one in particular as he stared at the Iranian ship.

"Maybe it's because we're in Kuwaiti territory?" Vic answered.

"Are we?" Adam spun in the chair to face his navigator. Vic nodded.

"Yeah. About a half mile in."

Scott had the bosun calling all departments for a damage report.

Adam keyed the bitch box. "Terry, what's our weapon status?"

Terry answered, "We're pretty shaken up. All radars are operational, but we've lost the 76 mm gun and the LRAD."

Adam frowned. "How about the torpedoes?"

There was a slight pause. "Looks OK. Thought we lost fire control, but it appears to be online."

Adam thanked Terry and told him to keep working to get the LRAD and forward gun back online.

Adam's bridge phone rang. Paula was frantic. "Adam, we're about to start fighting the fire in the galley but I can't find George. Have you heard from him?"

Adam felt a huge tug on his heart. "Paula . . ." He hesitated. He didn't want to break this news on the phone. Adam's voice was strong and confident. "I need you to focus on the fire right now. Get your team ready and keep them safe."

Paula took a deep breath. "You're right." She sounded a little better. "I'll call with an update when we enter the space."

Adam leaned forward in his chair and peered out of the forward bridge window. He saw the silhouette of the Iranian ship moving on the horizon from right to left.

"Adam," Scott called. He sounded worried. *What now?* "Need you on the Inmarsat radio, please."

Adam stepped away from his chair and took the mic.

He keyed the transmit button. "This is commanding officer of warship *Kraken.*"

The radio squelched. "Commanding officer of warship *Kraken.* This is Commander Mohammed Al-Ahmad, Kuwait naval base. Your vessel has illegally entered Kuwaiti territorial waters. Overhead surveillance indicates that you are sailing under the guise of the Kuwaiti national flag. You are directed to lower the national flag of Kuwait and leave Kuwaiti territory. Failure to adhere to these demands will result in military action against your vessel. You have fifteen minutes to comply."

Adam returned the mic to its cradle. He leaned forward on the bridge window ledge and stared at the sky. He felt sick.

"What the hell is that about?" Scott questioned. "Don't they know that we're here to help them?"

Adam offered a quick nod. A small, cynical smile crossed his face. "Actually, Scott," he began, "it's brilliant."

Adam turned and leaned back against the window ledge. Scott looked confused.

"Think about it, Scott. Why isn't the Kuwaiti navy hot on our tail right now? Why do you suppose they give us a fifteen-minute grace period? I'll tell you why. They're repaying the favor."

Adam paused but continued to smile. "Now the Kuwaitis need to show the Iranians that there isn't any type of relationship between their country and us."

Adam paused again and chuckled. "We were contracted to sail out to the Arabian Gulf and remove boats that were harassing the Kuwaiti merchant fleet. After that it became a matter of luck for us. Maybe we sail away and go home, or maybe the Iranians send out a ship to sink us. Either way, the government of Kuwait doesn't care. Either way, they win!"

Scott was still baffled.

Adam was patient. "OK, let me ask you—what happens if we clear out all of the patrol boats and then leave? Will the Iranian patrol boats return?"

Scott shrugged and answered, "Yeah, probably."

Adam smiled. "Of course they will. But once the international media gets wind that a rogue warship is in the Arabian Gulf pushing around helpless patrol craft, well, the United States government has to get involved. The United States can't afford vigilante maritime tactics in the gulf. That could ruin the already sensitive relationships in this area and, more importantly, affect oil flow back to the States.

"So, the United States would have no choice but to add more ships and increase warship patrols in the gulf. With more US warships actively patrolling the gulf waters, the Iranians will find it extremely difficult to continue harassing Kuwaiti merchant ships. So, like I said, it's a win-win for the Kuwaitis."

Scott gave a short and sad laugh. "Those bastards used us as patsies."

Adam's smile faded. "No. We're not patsies. We've been used exactly how we should have been used. I've been denying it all along, but it's true. They treated us like the mercenaries we are."

Adam narrowed his eyes. His jaw clenched. Now he was pissed. "Let's figure a way out of this mess."

He pointed to Scott. "Pull the ship up to the territorial border. We need to keep the Kuwaiti government and the Iranian ship guessing on whether we're in international waters or not. We only need about fifteen minutes in that position anyway."

Adam tilted his head in thought. He had just come up with an idea.

"Hey, Scott, do we still have that skull-and-crossbones flag that we used when we crossed the equator?"

"Sure," Scott replied. "Why?"

A sly smile formed under Adam's narrowed eyes. "Have a sailor go to the signal bridge right now and lower the Kuwaiti flag. Have him take the skull and crossbones with him. Tell him to stay on station, and when I give the order, he needs to raise that flag high on the mast."

Adam called Terry to join him and Scott on the bridge. Scott and Vic quickly worked out a course and speed solution to get the ship to the Kuwaiti territorial line, and Scott began maneuvering the ship into position as Terry arrived on the bridge.

Adam stood on the bridgewing and looked aft. Thick smoke still poured out of the hole caused by the missile.

Adam began with Terry. "The missile that hit us wasn't a heat-seeker because it didn't hit one of our stacks. It had to be trained on our electronic signals. Can you get one of your electronic-warfare wizards to shift our electronic signature and make it look like it's about one hundred feet behind us?"

Terry cocked his head and looked up, considering. "I believe that we can work up something like that. This should confuse the next missile that they fire." Terry regained eye contact with Adam. "But that will only work once. If they figure out what we did, the next missile would most likely hit us. And don't forget, that won't affect cannons or torpedoes."

Adam remained expressionless. "I'm hoping that they won't get a third opportunity to fire a missile." He used his hands as he talked. "OK, here's the tactic that we're going to use. We're going to change course and head directly at the Iranians. At that point, they should fire a missile at us. That's when we need our electronic countermeasure activated. Again, we want to make the missile think that we're actually one hundred feet behind our actual position.

"As we gain speed and close distance on the Iranians, they will turn to avoid collision. Scott, I need you to be quick on this. When they turn, we will need to turn in the opposite direction. Immediately after that turn, we will be broadside of the Iranian ship; they will be heading one way, and we will be heading in the opposite direction. At that point I will give the order to fire torpedoes. With any luck, we will have more than one strike."

Both Terry and Scott nodded.

Adam continued, "Terry once we begin our high-speed collision course toward their ship, you will need to plot and maintain a torpedo firing solution and be ready to fire when directed."

Terry took a deep breath. "Not a problem."

"Good." Adam felt a little more confident. "Let's get ready."

Adam was about to reenter the bridge when he felt a tug on his arm and Danny pulled him back onto the bridgewing.

"Danny!" Adam grabbed both of Danny's arms. Adam was genuinely happy to see that his friend was OK. *But is he OK?* Danny looked terrible. His head hung low, and his shoulders sagged. This wasn't the deck officer that everyone knew.

"Danny, what happened?"

Danny relayed the story, and Adam angrily asked, "So Cy was the cause of this?"

Danny shook his head. "No, Adam. In fact, if Cy hadn't opened fire then, I believe the Iranian officers would have shot and killed us all."

Adam stared at Danny in silence, then finally asked, "In your opinion, did he need to kill the sailors in the boat?"

Danny looked sick at the memory. "I don't know, Adam. One thing is for sure, though: Cy acted quickly, and Bobby and I believe that he saved our lives."

Adam was still skeptical about Cy and his agenda but didn't reveal it to Danny. Instead he shared the upcoming torpedo plan and asked Danny to take his station. Adam returned to the bridge and sat in his chair. His thoughts about Cy were disrupted by the bridge telephone. It was Paula.

She was happy to report that the fire was under control. She made it a point to recognize the actions of Leroy, who quickly jumped in a firefighting suit when one of the firefighting team members was injured.

Adam beamed. "I knew that Leroy would make a great sailor," he said. "Please pass my thanks to him and the rest of the team."

Paula was about to hang up when Adam called her back. "Paula, please get your team some water and get back to the repair locker. We're about to begin round two. By the way, have you seen Doc Kelly?"

Paula told Adam that the doctor had set up a triage center in the passageway outside of sick bay. There were about four or five wounded on stretchers.

CHAPTER 21

Adam reclined back in his chair. He called to Scott, "Ready, XO?"

"Ready!" he confirmed with a tight grin.

Adam keyed the bitch box. "Ready, Terry?"

Terry's voice echoed in the speaker: "Affirmative."

"All right, Scott, all ahead full."

Adam waited for Scott to finish the maneuvering orders. "OK, haul up the flag!"

Thirty seconds later a large skull-and-crossbones flag was flying over the mercenary ship *Kraken*.

After a second course change, the *Kraken* gained speed, steaming on a collision course toward the *Bayandor*. Adam stared out of the forward bridge window as the ship moved. He caught a glimpse of someone and turned his head to see Cy standing inches away.

Cy faced forward, his hands clasped together at his waist. He was also staring at the Iranian ship. Adam returned his focus to the forward window.

"Busy afternoon on the fantail I hear," he said, his voice soft, calm, and clear.

"Yes, sir, it was," Cy replied.

Silence for the next few seconds.

Adam asked, "Did they suffer?"

Adam and Cy's eyes locked.

"No," Cy answered.

Adam turned back to the window. "Good. Can you get up to the foc'sle and man a .50? We're going to get busy in a couple of minutes."

As the captain of the *Bayandor* prepared to fire an anti-ship missile, a junior officer on his bridge caught sight of the opposing ship's flag. The Iranian dropped his binoculars and rubbed his eyes. He glanced toward his captain but was reluctant to report what he had seen. He wouldn't want to be beaten for telling stories.

The *Kraken* continued to gain momentum. Scott maintained the course. "What's our speed?" he called to the helmsman.

"Twenty-five knots" was the reply.

Scott kept his visual of the Iranian ship. "Maintain twenty-five knots."

Adam stood next to his chair on the starboard side. He keyed his radio. "Cy, this is Adam."

The radio crackled. "Cy here. Go ahead."

Adam rekeyed. "Cy, we're about to turn broadside to the Iranian ship. When we're close enough, I need the forward and aft .50s lighting up the Iranian bridge. Can you turn that place into shredded metal?"

"Will do, boss," Cy quickly responded.

Adam could swear he heard Cy smiling.

Scott pressed the key to the bitch box. "CIC, how fast is the *Bayandor* moving?"

"Ten knots."

"Two-point-five miles to target," announced Vic. "Anticipate collision in fifty-five seconds."

Terry's voice was clear on the box. "Reading incoming missile ignition."

Scott and Adam watched the flame of a missile being launched from the Iranian ship.

Terry announced, "Missile launched. Electronic countermeasures activated."

The missile flew over the *Kraken* and splashed into the water 150 feet behind the ship.

The *Kraken* continued steaming forward.

Adam shouted, "She's turning."

The *Bayandor* began a right full rudder turn to avoid a collision. Scott shouted, "Right full rudder." The *Kraken* turned quickly.

Adam keyed the bitch box. "Terry, prepare to fire torpedoes."

Three seconds later, both ships were side by side but pointed in opposite directions. The *Kraken*'s forward and aft .50 cal machine guns began firing.

Adam watched directional tracer fire move toward the Iranian bridge, and at once the *Bayandor*'s bridge was being peppered by machine-gun rounds. Windows exploded and flashes of bullets ricocheted off the exterior bridge skin.

Again Adam pressed the box transmit button. "Fire torpedoes, Terry."

Two thumps were heard as the port-side torpedoes were launched.

Scott, standing next to his captain, screamed, "Adam!" and tackled his friend to the deck. The *Kraken*'s bridge windows burst inward as a variety of holes were introduced to the bridge windows and port bulkheads.

A machine gunner on the *Bayandor* fantail had returned the compliment and targeted the *Kraken*'s bridge. Machine-gun rounds flashed and bounced inside the space. Twenty or so rounds penetrated the *Kraken*'s bridge before Cy cut down the Iranian gunner.

"Are you all right?" Scott asked, inspecting his captain.

Adam sat up and brushed himself off. He placed his hand on Scott's shoulder. "I'm OK. Thanks to you." Adam stood. "Lucky you saw that gunner."

He turned and surveyed the bridge. Vic and his bosun were not as lucky. Vic had taken two rounds in his back and collapsed on the chart table. Blood covered the chart of the Arabian Gulf and trickled down the side of the table.

The bosun was sprawled in a corner of the bridge. A bullet round had torn through his throat. Adam ran to the port-side blast door and watched the torpedoes speed toward the Iranian ship. Halfway through the transit, one torpedo malfunctioned and sank into the sea. The remaining torpedo closed in on the *Bayandor*.

The Iranian ship turned hard left, and it appeared as if the ship was going to avoid being hit, but the torpedo found its mark and struck the ship just below the waterline near the port-side rudder. The *Bayandor* rocked from the impact. Its rudder slammed to the right and froze in place.

Adam opened the blast door and stepped outside to assess the *Bayandor*'s damage. He heard Terry's voice on the bitch box.

"They're firing another missile."

Adam turned in time to see the flash of the missile being launched.

Terry calmly indicated that electronic countermeasures were initiated and the SRBoc chaff was being fired. The tiny bits of aluminum were a last-ditch effort to confuse the incoming missile. The SRBoc canisters popped, and a cloud of chaff filled the sky. Adam shifted his attention to the missile, which quickly rose and then dove at the ship.

Stan and Lonnie were diligently waiting at their posts on the flight deck when the missile struck the port LRAD. The concussion of the explosion blew Stan over the side of the ship. Unconscious and unable to save himself, he soon drowned in the warm gulf water. Lonnie's neck snapped as he was rocketed into the hangar doors. He died instantly. The explosion, heat, and shrapnel also killed the two fantail gunners and the aft lookout.

The blast slammed the fantail down, and the bow rose out of the water.

Adam was still on the bridgewing. The explosion had forced him to the grating of the external platform. When he picked himself up and looked aft, he saw thick smoke rising from the fantail, and felt intense pain from his legs. His trousers were cut and covered in blood from being scraped across the metal grating. Limping into the bridge, he saw that Scott had been thrown headfirst into the helm stanchion. Blood oozed down Scott's cheek and matted his hair to his head. Lying on the floor, he pressed his hand against the wound in an effort to stop the bleeding.

The bodies of Vic and the bridge bosun had been thrown together and lumped under the chart table. Adam made his way to the bitch box and called Damage Control.

"Gail, this is Adam. Where were we hit? What's the damage?"

There was no immediate reply.

Adam was beginning to worry that DC central had been affected by the missile hits when Gail finally responded, "Adam, we were hit somewhere on the fantail. Not sure, but I believe that the missile flew straight down and impacted on our deck. We don't have communication with the aft lookout, so I can't determine the damage."

Scott crawled to the base of the helm stanchion and lifted himself to the ship's wheel.

Adam could see that he was in pain and a little groggy. He hoped Scott hadn't suffered a concussion.

Adam pressed the Main Control button on the bitch box.

"Main Control, this is the captain."

The response was immediate: "Main here."

"What's the status of the plant? Any damage?"

The Main Control watch stander indicated that there was no apparent damage and that the plant was in full operation.

Adam was relieved.

He keyed CIC on the box and asked Terry to come up to the bridge.

"I think that we have one more trick to play," Adam told Scott.

The door to the bridge was jammed shut, and Terry had to kick it open. The devastation of the bridge was clearly evident in the shocked look on his face. His shoulders and face dropped as he located Vic's body on the deck.

"Good lord," he uttered.

Terry spun around and saw Adam leaning against the bridge windows, his trousers covered with blood. Scott, half lying on the helm, looked like he'd been in a car accident, and Adam looked like he'd been dragged over a cheese grater.

Terry rushed over to Adam. "Are you OK? Is there anything I can do to help? Want me to call Doc Kelly?"

Adam shook his head. Terry turned to Scott, who also waved off medical assistance.

"Terry," Adam began, "we still have two good torpedoes, right?"

Terry nodded, still staring at Adam's legs.

Adam continued, "Is fire control still operational?"

"Yes." Terry raised his head and made eye contact with Adam. "But I'm not sure of the condition of the torpedo tubes."

Adam explained his plan to finally eradicate the threat of this Iranian ship. Both Scott and Terry looked grim.

One hour later the two ships maintained a one-mile distance between them. Neither ship appeared anxious to take the next action. The *Bayandor* was stopped in the water while the *Kraken* steamed in an arc around the Iranian ship at a slow five-knot speed.

Paula's team had extinguished the fantail fire, but the damage was irreparable. Scott maneuvered the ship and expertly kept the starboard side hidden from the Iranians.

Adam spied workers on the *Bayandor* working feverishly to repair their rudder.

Why haven't they fired another missile at us? he wondered. *We may have inflicted more damage than we thought.* He glanced over his left shoulder. "I don't believe we have much time left."

Scott stepped to the 1MC intercom, keyed the mic, and addressed the crew. He began by directing Doc Kelly, the wounded, and all individuals not assigned to a fighting battle station to muster on the starboard fantail and to prepare to abandon ship. All other crewmembers were to stay on station but prepare to abandon ship at a moment's notice.

Fifteen minutes later, Danny radioed Adam when the first group had been loaded in the rafts and pushed away from the ship.

Adam keyed the 1MC intercom. "*Kraken* crew, prepare for a high-speed run."

Scott keyed the bitch box. "Main, this is the bridge. All ahead full."

The two LM2500 gas turbine engines kicked in. The powerful engines turned the shaft and screw faster and faster, launching the *Kraken* forward.

As the *Kraken* steamed to the position where the *Bayandor* was pointed in the opposite direction, Adam shouted, "Now, Scott!"

Scott spun the helm wheel counterclockwise which caused the ship to turn and lean hard to the left. Adam called CIC and ordered Terry to fire the torpedoes. Terry acknowledged the order. A second later Terry reported that only one torpedo fired but appeared to be on course and traveling at eighteen knots.

Scott turned the wheel clockwise and ordered, "All engines full speed." The *Kraken* was now aimed directly at the Iranian ship, speeding toward the enemy at twelve knots and climbing.

Adam grabbed the 1MC mic and directed the remaining crew except those in Main Control to abandon ship and jump as far away from the side of the ship as possible, then swim hard to avoid being pulled into the ship's screw.

The ship was now a half mile from the *Bayandor*—the torpedo leading the way. Their speed had reached sixteen knots.

The captain of the Iranian vessel realized what Adam was doing and started advancing his ship. The torpedo continued to speed forward and on target. The *Bayandor* was directly in the path of the *Kraken*. Scott keyed the mic. "All engines flank speed!" The *Kraken* was on a full-speed collision course.

Adam called Main Control and ordered them to abandon ship. Scott and Adam saw a flash of a missile launch on the deck of the *Bayandor*.

Adam heard Scott scream, "This just sucks!"

The *Kraken* closed the distance to 1,200 feet, speeding at twenty-one knots and closing in on their torpedo.

Adam limped to the starboard-side blast door and yanked it open. "C'mon, Scott," he yelled.

He moved out to the bridgewing and looked over the side, staring at the speed of the water rushing past the ship. *This is definitely not going to end well*, he thought.

Scott sprinted toward Adam as the Iranian missile struck the *Kraken*'s superstructure just above the foc'sle. Adam was catapulted off the bridgewing and into the gulf. He flew backward into the wave created by the ship's wake and slammed his head on the surface of the water.

The explosion helped Scott's movement. He was thrown through the blast door and flew like Superman over the bridgewing railing. He managed to tuck his body in midflight, hitting the water feet first and swimming away from the ship as hard and as quickly as he could while keeping his head above water.

He needed to find his captain.

The *Kraken*'s superstructure was engulfed in flame and black smoke. Three seconds later the torpedo found its mark on the Iranian ship. It exploded at the waterline, port-side amidships. The torpedo ripped a hole seventeen feet in diameter between three frames of the ship. Two seconds later, the *Kraken*, traveling at flank speed, collided with the *Bayandor* twenty feet aft of where the torpedo had hit.

The knife edge of the *Kraken*'s bow plowed through the skin of the *Bayandor*. The Iranian ship rolled twenty degrees to its starboard side. The *Kraken*'s powerful engines continued to drive the ship forward. She climbed up and sliced into the Iranian ship.

The *Kraken*'s hull began to weaken and collapse, bending the foc'sle upward. From a distance it appeared as if the ship was folding in on itself.

Gravity finally lent a hand, and the weight of the *Kraken* proved too much for the Iranian ship. The *Kraken* knifed through several decks and finally smashed through the *Bayandor*'s keel. Screams from Iranian sailors could be heard across the waves, only silenced by multiple explosions. The *Bayandor*'s hull twisted around the *Kraken*. The forward half of the Iranian ship rolled to her port side and sank quickly into the sea.

The *Bayandor*'s aft half was still attached to the *Kraken*. Sparks from torn electrical cables arced off the *Bayandor*'s warped decks and bulkheads. Before the high-speed run, Adam had given the order to relax watertight integrity; no doors or hatches in the *Kraken*'s deck were secured tightly, so as the seawater entered the ship, it quickly flowed from one space to the next. Within minutes, the Iranian ship *Bayandor* and the mercenary ship *Kraken* were pulled beneath the waters of the Arabian Gulf.

Only 3 of the 140 sailors on the *Bayandor* survived.

Scott screamed for Adam. He attempted to lift himself above the waves, but physical exhaustion made this exercise extremely difficult. He felt something choking him and found the strap to his binoculars still wrapped around his neck. Pulling the strap from his throat, he tossed the glasses into the water and spun, looking for Adam, but his life jacket restricted his movement. Scott kicked up hard and rose inches above the waterline.

Thirty feet away he spied an orange life jacket. It was Adam.

Scott called his name but heard no reply. He dug down deep and found the energy to swim hard to his friend. For a moment thought he would vomit from all the seawater he was swallowing. He found Adam unconscious but breathing. Attaching his life jacket to Adam's, Scott leaned back to rest, exhausted.

Scott and Adam were pulled out of the water forty-five minutes later. The USS *Cowpens* Guided-Missile Cruiser 63, commanded by

Commander Zach Taggert, United States Navy, just happened to be in the area. The officers and crew of the *Cowpens* were happy to provide rescue services for the crews of both ships.

CHAPTER 22

Three days later Adam regained consciousness. His eyes stung, and the brightness in his room made it difficult to focus. He didn't know where he was and couldn't understand why he was in bed. Adam winced in pain as he lifted his arms toward his head. He rubbed his stinging eyes and then shielded them from the light.

The room came into focus. It was a hospital room. More pain came as Adam turned his neck to view his surroundings. An IV tower next to his bed connected a long, clear tube to his left hand. Adam saw a buzzer attached to the bed railing. He pressed it. A few minutes later a large, bald black man in a hospital smock appeared in his door.

"Well hello, sunshine!" The man smiled at Adam. "Welcome back."

Adam's throat felt like sandpaper, and he asked for water. The man filled a glass from the sink in the adjoining bathroom and handed it to Adam. The water soothed his throat.

"Where am I?" he asked.

The man walked around Adam's bed and inspected the IV. "You, sir, are a guest in the US Navy hospital in Bahrain."

Adam squinted. "Bahrain?"

The man nodded. "Yes sir."

Adam groaned as he tried to sit up. The man came to the right side of the bed. "Now, that wasn't very smart," he said, pulling out a blood-pressure cuff and stethoscope.

Adam tried to focus on the man's face. "My eyes burn."

The man pulled out a small flashlight and peered into each of Adam's eyes. "Probably a combination of flash burns, smoke, and saltwater. They should be OK in a couple of days."

"Who are you?" Adam's voice was weak.

"Well now, that's more like it. A polite question." The man beamed at Adam. "I'm George—your nurse."

Adam closed his eyes. Hearing the name made his heart ache.

Adam reopened his eyes and rubbed the tears from them. "Where is my crew? Where's Scott?"

George took Adam's vitals. "You just relax now, my friend. Get well and strong." He walked out of the room and closed the door.

Adam passed out.

Adam woke that afternoon to find Scott and Paula on chairs next to his bed.

He looked to each of his friends. "How many made it out?" he asked without preamble.

Paula looked at Scott.

Scott answered, "Eighty-five were rescued."

Adam slowly comprehended the number of losses. He pushed his head back into his pillow and shut his eyes, devastated.

"We lost thirty-five of our people? Who?" Adam asked.

Paula reached over and grabbed his hand. "Adam, we can talk about this later."

Adam glared at Paula. "Who?!"

She sat back and solemnly looked away. Scott locked eyes with Adam. "Besides George and Vic, we lost Lonnie, Hasif, and Tom Rauske."

"What happened to Hasif?"

Scott hesitated and then answered, "Apparently he was outside on the main deck when the second missile hit. He was decapitated. Died instantly."

Adam dropped his gaze. "Who else?"

Scott glanced at Paula and then back to Adam. "No one has seen Frank."

"Frank? What do you mean no one has seen him?"

Scott's face showed no emotion. "Nobody saw him leave the ship, and he wasn't accounted for when we were rescued."

Adam said nothing. He just continued to stare at his two friends.

"Well," Scott continued, "some good news is that Bobby, Leroy, and Gail made it out, though Leroy took some shrapnel in the face and may have lost an eye."

Adam slowly shook his head, tears welling in his eyes.

"This was all my fault," he whispered. "Total and complete hubris."

Scott and Paula now were silent. They both knew that nothing they said could help console their friend.

A tear rolled down Adam's cheek. "What did this accomplish? All of this was for nothing."

Adam told Scott and Paula that he was really tired and asked if he could talk with them some other time. His friends stood, flashed strained smiles, and left the room.

Once again, as he had when this adventure began, Adam felt alone. This time, though, he also felt defeated and sick. The realization of losing a command weighed heavily on his mind. *My crew trusted me to keep them safe, and I failed them*, he thought as he wiped away a tear.

He had only felt this level of pain and loss once before—when he lost his best friend and companion.

For the first time since Chrissy's death, Adam cried.

Six months later Adam was back home in Colorado. He was happy to be out of Bahrain and even happier to be out of the hospital. He'd lost 15 pounds during his recovery and was trying to get back to his fighting weight of 185.

As he sat on his couch, he thought about the debriefs and the grilling that he and his senior leaders were subjected to when they were released from the hospital. He had been scheduled to meet with representatives from the FBI and, his favorite, Agent Maria Wilson, from Homeland Security, but for some reason these briefings were miraculously and curiously cancelled. Adam assumed that Oliver had a hand in that.

Now that he was home, Adam made a point to contact each of his friends once a week to see how they were doing.

Briget still refused to speak with Adam, but he didn't care. He was just happy that Scott was okay. Danny was seeing a counselor about PTSD issues. He was having trouble transitioning back to normal life and also suffering from terrible nightmares. Paula had moved to Colorado and was actively seeking a job in finance. Adam asked her why she was so aggressive in looking for a job. After all, Oliver had honored the contracts and paid each crewmember in full. Paula told him that she needed to get back into the swing of things.

"You know me," she said. "I just need to keep busy."

Leroy had indeed lost his left eye. When he was offered a glass eye, he opted for an eye patch.

"After all," he remarked to Adam, "if I'm going to be a pirate, I need to look like one."

Terry went back to his plant nursery. He was still pompous but now seemed to treat Adam with a little more respect; and perhaps his time with George taught him to not take himself so seriously. Bobby and Tim took Tom's body home. Adam heard a rumor that Tom's ashes were buried at sea.

Paula told Adam that Gail had applied for a job with the Merchant Marine and wanted to ask Adam for a referral but wasn't sure how that would look on a job application.

No one had seen Cy since Bahrain. Adam was pretty sure that he'd run into him again.

George had made Adam his beneficiary for the million-dollar life insurance policy Oliver arranged for Adam's crew. After Adam settled with the insurance company, he and Paula called their attorney, Nathaniel, and set up a program in San Diego where each year on Christmas Eve Santa would visit the children's hospitals and deliver gifts to all of the child patients.

They named the program the George Bannister Christmas Foundation.

The television was turned on but muted. Adam sat on the couch and stared at nothing. He was far, far away.

Memories of the *Kraken* cruise flashed in his mind. A small smile appeared when he remembered the good and fun times: the first time they set sail from California, the shellback ceremony, and even saving the yacht from the pirates in the Malaccan Strait.

The smile faded when he thought of the friends he'd lost. He quickly pushed those thoughts aside and rose from his sofa. In the kitchen he began pulling out pots and ingredients from his cupboards. He was going to make one of his favorites—pasta with shrimp.

Adam had just filled the pot with water and was about to place it on the stove when he heard the doorbell. Setting the pot on the kitchen counter, he made his way to the front door.

There in front of him, standing on his front porch, was Oliver Pratt.

Adam's head snapped back and his eyes narrowed. "Hello, Oliver."

Oliver stood quietly at the door and didn't attempt to shake hands or step inside. He wore the same black suit that he wore when Adam first met him in San Diego. Oliver held his fedora at his chest, both sets of fingers clasped around the brim.

"Hello, Adam," he said softly. "May I come in?"

Adam stepped back and swung his arm toward the living room. Oliver walked inside and scanned the place. "You have a very lovely home, Adam."

Adam thanked his guest and led him into the living room. "Please have a seat," he offered.

Oliver placed his hat on Adam's coffee table and sat on the sofa. Adam sat in his favorite recliner on the opposite side of the room.

"Care for something to drink?" Adam asked.

Oliver politely declined. "How are you feeling, Adam?"

Adam offered a small smile. "Pretty good, I guess. How are you?"

Oliver returned the smile and offered a quick nod. His smile dropped. A look of genuine sadness now covered Oliver's face. Adam saw deep lines in his forehead.

Oliver spoke: "I can't tell you how sorry I am for the loss of your friends and shipmates. As you know, I had the opportunity to get to know several of them, and I found each of them to be very good people as well as true professionals."

"Thank you," Adam said softly.

Oliver continued, "Adam, I'm equally sorry that your ship and your future business met with such a horrible ending. I never wanted that."

Adam nodded. He believed Oliver's sincerity.

Oliver was obviously not finished. "I hope that the insurance and pay compensation was conducted quickly and discretely."

Again, Adam nodded. "It was."

Oliver said, "Adam, you and your crew did an amazing job. My organization and the representatives from Kuwait are equally very proud and impressed with your achievements. You were professional and thorough. We couldn't have orchestrated this mission any better. Adam, it is definitely too soon to be discussing this issue, but my organization and I need you and your team."

Adam squinted. He knew what was coming next.

Oliver flashed his patented smile. "You've probably heard that we're having some trouble with pirating off the coast of Somalia. I happen to have a beautiful reconditioned Spruance-class destroyer at our disposal. It can be yours." He cocked his head, eyebrows raised. "Interested?"